FAMILY OF THE DAMNED

"We are here," Meleas said, his voice quiet as always, "to find demons and destroy them."

"There haven't been demons for two hundred years," Jazen said sharply.

"My mother was taken by a demon," Meleas answered, his voice still quiet, still calm. "I watched her die of it. It took almost a year. Twice after she was possessed, she was able to speak to me herself. The first time she told me she loved me. The second time she asked me to kill her."

Jazen could barely breathe. "Did . . . did you?"

"If I had killed her, the demon would have taken me. Instead she died, and the demon moved on to my little sister. Firaloy came then and tried to cast the demon out. But it was too late. My sister died, too . . ."

The Fountains of Mirlacca
The first chapter of the stunning *Demon Wars* trilogy by

Ashley McConnell

Ace Books by Ashley McConnell

The Quantum Leap Series
QUANTUM LEAP: THE NOVEL
TOO CLOSE FOR COMFORT
THE WALL
PRELUDE
RANDOM MEASURES

THE FOUNTAINS OF MIRLACCA

THE FOUNTAINS OF MIRLACCA

ASHLEY McCONNELL

ACE BOOKS, NEW YORK

If you purchased this book without a cover, you should be aware that this book is stolen property. It was reported as "unsold and destroyed" to the publisher, and neither the author nor the publisher has received any payment for this "stripped book."

This book is an Ace original edition,
and has never been previously published.

THE FOUNTAINS OF MIRLACCA

An Ace Book / published by arrangement with
the author

PRINTING HISTORY
Ace edition / July 1995

All rights reserved.
Copyright © 1995 by Ashley McConnell.
Cover art by Peter Peebles.
This book may not be reproduced in whole or in part,
by mimeograph or any other means, without permission.
For information address: The Berkley Publishing Group,
200 Madison Avenue, New York, NY 10016.

ISBN: 0-441-00206-4

ACE®
Ace Books are published by The Berkley Publishing Group,
200 Madison Avenue, New York, NY 10016.
ACE and the "A" design are trademarks
belonging to Charter Communications, Inc.

PRINTED IN THE UNITED STATES OF AMERICA

10 9 8 7 6 5 4 3 2 1

*To Pat Gribben, who wanted to know more,
in hopes that this book will approach
her high standards and expectations*

PART 1

The Journeying

Chapter 1

Jazen wiped a film of sweat off his upper lip with the back of his hand, studying the color of the lumpy, rectangular strip of metal in the flame. It wasn't quite right yet, he judged. The piece of metal looked, to the untutored, like nothing much; to his eye it represented a good beginning to a decent knife.

He pumped the small bellows, and the flames roared, showering sparks high in the air to fall glittering on his skin, his hair, his clothing. He ignored them, even with the evening breeze coaxing them to a moment of fiercer life. The metal should be wine-red by now.

It should be, but it wasn't. An imp, tiny creature made of fire, sat cross-legged on the flat of the blade and giggled at him. He muttered a curse and pumped the bellows harder. The rush of air made the fire roar, and the imp stood and twirled in the blaze.

From across the smithy Belzec looked up and laughed at him. "What's the matter, boy? Got to put some back into it!"

The imp yelped with laughter again and vanished.

Jazen shot Belzec a glare through the roughly chopped tangle of dark hair falling over his forehead and kept on pumping. Belzec looked like the smiths in all the stories—or maybe the smiths in the stories looked like Belzec, all knotted muscles, tall, with huge, rounded shoulders and a network of scars from the burns acquired over a lifetime of working with red-hot metal. Belzec had a deep voice and a hearty laugh and Jazen had hated him ever since he could remember.

"You're lettin' the fire drop, fool." Belzec crossed the

smithy floor in five strides, shifted the large bellows one-handed from the large forge to the smaller one Jazen was working, and pumped it hard. Ashes and cinders flew everywhere, spitting against the dirt-packed floor of the forge, and Jazen flinched back.

"What, you're afraid of a little heat?" Belzec thought this was vastly funny. The flames leaped from the coal bed, and the blade blank slid between two logs and disappeared to the bottom of the firebox.

Jazen watched it go. He'd have to wait, now, until the little forge was cold, to rescue the piece of metal and start over. There was no way to tell when Belzec would give him a chance to work it again for a project of his own. The knife was supposed to be finished by tomorrow. It was a commission, a common household knife; he was sometimes able to pick up a few coppers of his own that way. This customer was one of the few who paid fairly, too, so he had particularly wanted to deliver it as promised.

Belzec knew that, of course.

"Oh, too bad," Belzec said, still laughing. "You'll have to go back to real work, boy." He dropped the bellows and let it hiss open. "We've got ox shoes to make for spring. You do them well, I'll let you sharpen ploughs!"

Jazen knew better than to react. He swung the great bellows out of the way and set the tongs against the wall.

The smith grinned. "Until then, boy, you earn your keep. Go fill the slack tub, and clean out the ashes. I'm going to try something new, I think."

"New" to Belzec meant new today. He wasn't an imaginative man; shown new techniques by visiting smiths, he'd like as not spend more time jeering at them than trying them for himself. He had steel he'd never heated because it meant using a better—and different—grade of charcoal.

Carefully expressionless, Jazen pushed the hair out of his face—he needed to cut it again—and went to get the buckets in silence. They clanked as he swung the yoke over his shoulders, clanked again as he swung cautiously around Belzec and out the open front of the smithy.

He'd heard Belzec talk, once, about a smithy that had its

own spring. The forge boy there never had to walk halfway across the village to the well for water, his master's metal buckets swinging from either end of the yoke. The forge boy there probably had his own tools, too. Jazen had nothing of his own, not even the clothes on his back, much less the buckets he carried.

Belzec used to use leather skins to carry water. They carried more, but sparks burned holes through them, and he had to replace them every few weeks, especially when Jazen was first learning how to work the bellows. The copper buckets were Belzec's most prized, and most valuable, possession. They meant more to the smith than even the anvil, a long-horned, broad block of good steel handed down from his great-grandfather's time.

The sun was beginning to slant golden across the thatched housetops of Smattac, and the late summer air cooled the sweat on his forehead. The road from the smithy was a pair of wide ruts leading alongside Smattac stream, past the mill, up the hill. Between the ruts a few scraggly leaves of grass waved feebly in the evening breeze.

Here, as he entered the village proper, there were a good two dozen houses, thatch and lathe plastered with mud and the whitish cement that kept them from crumbling in the rains. Maybe half a dozen more, belonging to the aleman, the traders, were built of wood and stone, painted white to match their poorer kinsmen, but with the lintels glossed in clan colors to show the difference. Smattac was a prosperous place.

The road flattened out past the inn courtyard, leading to the broad square that held the village well. The square was mostly abandoned at this hour; the goodwives of Smattac would be at home, having already drawn water for the evening meal. Jazen slipped the yoke free and attached the first bucket to the hook, let it down and took the opportunity to stretch, rotating his arms high. Across the dusty square, a six-year-old girl wearing Yellowtree greens chased a sheep through a flock of frantic chickens.

If Eri Weaver's-daughter was already back with the sheep, it meant the farmers would be coming in soon. Jazen pulled up the bucket, replaced it on the hook and lowered its mate, moving faster. He had no desire to meet the farmers. It was bad enough to have to make rough, shapeless shoes for their oxen, scythes and ploughs for their stony fields; he didn't have to listen to them, too. They never spoke to him anyway save to curse him.

The second bucket came back up brimful, and he balanced both buckets on the yoke with care. Grunting, he lifted and settled it back across his shoulders and started back down the path. He had done this at least twice a day every day he could remember. When he was little he could barely walk under the yoke with the buckets empty. Now he barely noticed the weight pressing into the groove across his shoulders.

He could remember seventeen harvest festivals in Smattac. In that time he'd grown from a babe in swaddling, left one night beside the smith's house by some unknown person, to a well-grown youth, almost a man. He wasn't as thick through the chest as he'd one day be, and he would never have the huge, knotted muscles of which Belzec was so proud, but he could handle everything the older man could, and some of it better. It was part of him, the smithy was, even if he wasn't part of it.

It made no difference, of course. He should be grateful for the shelter and the food he was given. So he lost a commission—Belzec could take the coin from him anyway, if he wished, claiming it was made with his metal, tempered in his forge, beaten out on his anvil with his hammer.

He was, after all, a bastard. Jazen sr'Yat, in the Old Words. Not for him the colors of Yellowtree, or Meadowlark, or the families of the Seven Streams; he wore plain undyed cloth for a shirt, dusty grayish-green for leggings, and every day Belzec Smith made sure he knew who he owed for them, and beat him in case he forgot. He might eat of the smith's bread, but never at his table. And nothing would change for him, no matter how many knives he made.

A rock clanged against the side of one of the buckets, and water sloshed over the lip and into the dust. Startled, Jazen looked up to see Eri standing in the alleyway, hefting another stone with a calculating look in her eye.

THE FOUNTAINS OF MIRLACCA

"Hey!" he yelled, helpless with the weight of the loaded yoke across his shoulders.

"Demonspawn!" she yipped. But the stone fell short as he took a step toward her, and she ran backward as if propelled by a sudden wind. She'd tell her brothers, no doubt. Another fight to look forward to.

He swung away, more water sloshing, and stomped back down the road. He'd have to check the bucket now and hope it wasn't dented. It meant another beating, if it was.

The trees along the road were well grown, considering; some of them were taller than he was, even the ironwoods that took more than a man's lifetime to reach the level of his eyes. It spoke well of the farmers of Smattac and their care of the land. They spent their lives coaxing it to live. The fields surrounding the village were extensive, well irrigated, green.

He hated it. He hated the fields, the farmers, even little Eri. He hated the clan youth who mocked him, the women who thought it was only good thrift to pay him half the value of a well-made knife because he had no name to wrap under the hilt. He hated the forge and the slack tub and the quench tank and Belzec.

He *hated*—

Next to him on the path a dried twig burst into sudden flame. Without breaking stride, he swiveled and stomped it to ash and kept going.

That was the sort of thing that didn't get noticed in a smithy. It was the sort of thing that would get *him* burned, if he weren't careful. "Demonspawn," Eri called him. If the good people of Smattac saw flames around him, others besides little girls would be cursing him. And he couldn't prove otherwise. sr'Yat had no family to speak for them. They couldn't even speak for each other. sr'Yat were Sons of Shadow, conceived in secrecy, born in shame, left abandoned behind a forgefire by some desperate mother.

When he was small, small enough to listen to the stories Belzec's wife told her own children and young enough to believe them, he wondered if perhaps he was a lost prince, heir to one of the northern principalities, abandoned by some courtier who would one day come back and reclaim him, restore him to his rightful place. As he grew older he realized that it was more likely that one of the village women who glanced at him sidewise on the street was really his mother, one of Belzec's contemporaries was really his father. He looked, often, but couldn't find anyone who might have bequeathed him straight, dark hair and green eyes; none of the others even looked like him. Certainly none of them would claim him, this late in his life.

The forge was in sight now, glowing against the gathering dusk. There were horses tethered to the great tree, and a blue roan mule standing by the open side. Strange animals, not from Smattac— He picked up his pace. And yes, the village youngsters were gathered to gawk; these were the first visitors Smattac had seen since the river rose in the spring, blocking access to the main trade paths across Miralat. Strangers meant news of the outside world, new people to look at. Even little Eri was there, pushing her way to the front of the cluster of children.

Belzec was bellowing already, as if that would hurry him along, creating more heat than his own forge about the lack of water in the slack tub. Jazen pushed through the half-dozen young men of the village, pretending not to see how they drew back from him, and slid the yoke off. Emptying the buckets, he surreptitiously checked. No dents. That was a blessing, at least

He looked up from his task to find himself staring into the eyes of a middle-aged woman. Gray eyes, smiling, surrounded by wrinkles put there by too much time looking into the sun perhaps, or laughter. Then Belzec said something about shoeing the mule, and she turned away.

Jazen put the buckets and yoke away and went to the back wall to get Belzec a set of roughed-out horseshoes. The smith barely acknowledged him as he set the iron down on the face of the anvil. Jazen took the opportunity to step back behind the smaller forge, busying himself with building up the fire while he studied the strangers, looking for the signs that would tell the world who they were.

There were three men with the woman, all dressed in traveling clothes—long tunics and sturdy shoes, laced leggings and

THE FOUNTAINS OF MIRLACCA

broad leather belts. The mule's pack lay against the stone wall, good oiled cloth covering some kind of boxes as well as the soft rolls one would expect, containing clothing or bedding.

All of them wore sturdy boots, shaped properly to their feet—a sign of wealth in itself. And their clothes were stained with much travel, but he could see no holes; their tunics seemed too heavy for the weather, even though the temperature was dropping quickly as the stars came out. Jazen could see no gold or jewels, not even rings upon their hands, but the woman carried a fat purse at her hip, and the two younger men did likewise.

The third man was several years older than the others, thin and frail, shorter than the rest. He had a wispy beard that shivered in the breeze. He trembled as he stood, and the woman moved over to him and supported him unobtrusively. He didn't appear to notice, but Jazen saw him shift his weight to take advantage of her arm nonetheless.

The other two members of the party were men of about Jazen's years. One blond, one dark, they were clad alike in serviceable, tight-woven travel cloaks, and the dark-haired one sported a bedraggled feather in his cap. They too watched the old man, poised as if to catch him if the woman's arm should fail. They might be his sons or servingmen, though Jazen could see no family sashes or trade marks. The dark-haired one looked up and caught his eyes much as the woman had, half-smiled absent-mindedly, and then forgot him as all their attention sharpened upon the old man, who was staggering now.

He, for his part, seemed to have gotten all the support he wanted; he shook all their concern away, irascible, and dug into a belt pouch, thinner than the others', for copper coins. Belzec tested them, grunted, and nodded.

"You can stay at the aleman's if you want," he said. "It's up the way, the sign of the cup. I'll have my boy take the mule up after we're done."

The old man nodded, betraying gratitude and weakness at once, despite himself. The young blond man went over to the blue roan mule and stroked its nose for a moment, whispered something into the long ear. The observers gave way for him as he hurried to catch up to the others, already started up the road to the aleman's. The children followed after, talking amongst themselves.

Jazen stared after them, a fire iron dangling forgotten in his hand.

"Wake up, boy; y'act like you've never seen a stranger before. Shoe the beast, then take him up. I'm for dinner."

Jazen nodded. Belzec disappeared, and Jazen sighed and went over to the hapless mule. It whuffled companionably at him, looking for food.

At least the beast didn't seem to consider *him* food. Jazen still bore the scars from his first attempt to shoe an animal by himself. This one, though, was mild-tempered, making no objection to being tied as long as the hay net was well filled, obediently picking up its feet on demand.

A second shoe was loose, and all of them were badly worn, though the hooves were in good shape, needing only trimming. The tack was patched in only a few places. The mule didn't flinch from Jazen's hands; these travelers took good care of their animals.

Fitting and replacing the shoe took very little time. Glancing over his shoulder to make sure neither Belzec nor any of his numerous family were watching, Jazen went on to replace the other, worn-down shoes as well. He could make new roughs in the morning; Belzec would never notice some additional hammering, and the mule would be better for the even wear. The travelers might never know the quiet favor—a fact which pleased Jazen even more.

The hay net was nearly empty by the time he was finished and had put his tools away. He untied the animal and led it back up the road to the central square and the sign of the alecup.

Tadeus Aleman hadn't had such custom in months. The travelers' other animals, jammed into the little stable behind the alehouse, whickered greetings to their erstwhile companion. There was, of course, no one there to take the mule. Jazen had to find a place for it and get dusty feed down from the loft himself. He knocked at the door at the back of the alehouse to tell Tadeus what he'd done. When no one answered immediately, he eased it open to look inside.

As he'd hoped, the aleman's eldest, Tiralay, was presiding over the great-kitchen in the back, where the fireplace and ale tuns held pride of place. Three of Tadeus' lesser cousins, sweating in the heat of the fireplace and torch flames, stirred and kneaded and polished and poured under Tiralay's supervision. Jazen paused to watch her moving lightly from the great-table in the middle of the kitchen to the massive kettle, giving the youngest boy a light buffet on the shoulder as she passed. Tiralay was Jazen's age, or a year younger, and had hair the color of the leaves in autumn, and his breath went short as he watched her move.

Her skirts brushed the floor as she turned, drawn to his movement in the doorway.

She blushed at the sight of him. Setting aside the tankard she had been filling, she hurried to the door, practically knocking him over in her haste to shove him back over the threshold and out into the stable alley. "What are you doing here?" she whispered. "Are you completely crazy?"

Jazen shook his head, gave a wary glance to make sure no one was watching, and gave her a quick kiss on the cheek. "Why shouldn't I be here, sweetheart? Is Tadeus afraid I'm going to set fire to the ale?"

Tiralay's full lips thinned. "You *did* once."

Jazen closed his eyes and let go a long breath. "Tira, I did not, and you know it. That was your own clumsiness. Are you trying to get me burned?"

For a moment she seemed inclined to argue, then changed her mind. "What are you doing here?" she asked again, stepping closer, her breasts brushing against his ragged shirt, her hands resting on his upper arms.

He lifted a stray lock of hair away from her cheek, looked deep into her brown eyes, and said soulfully, "My dearest, my heart, how could I stay away? I had no choice: I'm delivering a mule."

Tiralay yelped with laughter and slapped him.

He staggered back, holding his face, laughing as well, despite the pain. Tiralay would one day own her father's alehouse, and she had no fear of unruly customers. "Truly!" he protested. "For the travelers. The mule threw a shoe. Belzec told me to replace it and bring the beast up here."

Glancing back over her shoulder, Tiralay pushed farther out into the passageway between the alehouse and the stable, nearly sending Jazen tumbling backward over a pile of rubbish, and then caught at him. "You couldn't think of another reason?" she whispered, and kissed him fiercely.

He reciprocated with enthusiasm, until a sound from the doorway made them break away from each other as if burned. Behind them, one of the cousins threw a pan of dirty water onto the ground, splashing Jazen's legs.

"They're in the great room now, eating," Tiralay said, too loudly. "They've come from the north, but Da doesn't think they live there. They don't talk like northmen. And they brought their own plates, even."

The cousin pretended not to see them, going back into the kitchen. But the mood was broken, even as Jazen reached for Tiralay's hand and ran his thumb over its back. Besides, he was curious, too, about the visitors. "Where does he think they're from?"

"Oh, far. Farther than Hipsola."

For an instant Jazen glared at her. Two summers ago Tiralay's father had taken her with him to a clan-gather in Hipsola, ten days' journey—an unimaginable distance—from Smattac. She'd returned filled with stories about her new-met kin, about the dangers of the journey through the edge of the Burned Lands, about how Hipsola was different, larger, louder, better than Smattac. Jazen was very, very tired of hearing about it.

"I didn't know there *was* anything farther than Hipsola," he said dryly, but Tiralay wasn't listening.

"They're going to stay two nights," she said. "They want to talk to Neesen, they said."

"Neesen? They know Neesen?" He felt a rush of wariness. Neesen was his friend—gave him salves for his back when he was beaten, small tasks for which she paid him when she could. The knife he was making was for her. What did these strangers want with her?

"Well, no. They said they want to talk to our healer."

THE FOUNTAINS OF MIRLACCA

Tiralay giggled suddenly. "The old ones, anyway. The young ones want to talk to me."

"Or at least you want to talk to them. What clan are they?"

Tiralay paused and looked up at him, startled. "I don't know!"

"Well, what are their colors?" He was becoming exasperated again; how could she overlook anything so basic, especially if she was flirting?

"I don't know their colors," she said after a moment. "I couldn't tell." At his look of disbelief, she defended herself. "Well, I was busy. And you saw them, didn't you? What colors did you see?"

He thought back to the crowd of people at the forge, to the glimpses of a cloak, clothing, a feathered cap. There were colors, dusty under the road dirt, greens and browns and reds and blue—yes, there was blue—but nothing he recognized as clan badge or colors. "Maybe it's a clan we don't have here."

"Maybe," Tiralay said. "They had six new clans in Hipsola."

"Why don't you come in and see for yourself?" she added impulsively. "Come and have an ale. Maybe you can talk to them."

Jazen smiled gently and shook his head. Tiralay was going to have to lose that optimism before she took over the alehouse for herself, he thought. No one was going to talk to *him*.

Still, the temptation was overwhelming, and he had money. Money for the making of a blade he hadn't finished yet, he reminded himself; he'd be up all night to have it done in time.

But how often did travelers come, and from farther away than the fabled Hipsola?

"All right," he said. "But water the ale." If he was dealing with fire later, he'd not want to be drunk. He'd seen enough of Belzec's scars to be wary.

Tiralay grinned. "I, water ale? What sort of alehouse do you think we have?"

"One that makes your father money," Jazen retorted, finally letting go of her hand. He started back up the alley to the front of the building.

"Wipe your feet!" she called after him, not in the least annoyed.

Chapter 2

The alehouse had four long tables reserved for the four major clans represented in Smattac, and five smaller ones scattered about them. The room was lit by torches, brightly enough that Jazen had to let his eyes adjust before he closed the door behind him.

The travelers were seated at one of the long tables, Yellowtree's, with the clan head herself hosting them, Eri Weaver's-daughter's mother. Jazen stepped around the edge of the room, carefully, not drawing attention to himself, until Tiralay met him with a mug of ale near the entry to the kitchen.

Here, under the eyes of the village, she said nothing to him, took his coin and tested it between her teeth as if he were a stranger to her, and turned her back on him. He took the mug back to where he usually sat when he felt daring enough to visit this place openly, one of the seats that folded out from the wall, and sipped at his drink. It was watered, but not as much as it could have been. He looked over the rim of the mug for Tiralay, but she was ignoring him, talking and laughing with one of the travelers, the dark-haired young man with the bright smile and the feather in his cap.

The room was warm from the heat of all the bodies, a different kind of heat than that of the forge. He had been noticed, of course—how not, when he had had to walk past them all?—and one man lifted his lip in a sneer, but no one said anything. He was only Jazen, after all. And he wasn't presuming to sit with any of them.

THE FOUNTAINS OF MIRLACCA

The Yellowtree table was in the middle of the room. Jazen sank back against the wall, rubbing his back against the roughness of a beam, and watched the strangers and the villagers over the rim of his mug. He didn't often have the chance to relax in relative comfort this way; he might as well take advantage of it.

They'd almost finished their bread and stew and were sipping at their own mugs. From the look on the younger men's faces, they'd never tasted Smattac ale before, and they weren't sure they liked it. The woman savored it; the old man might have been drinking water for all the notice he gave. The men and women at the other tables watched and listened and nudged each other.

Then Tadeus, Tiralay's father, came out from the kitchen, wiping his hands on his long sleeves, and stood over the visitors. "You're the first travelers we've seen since the chea harvest," he said by way of greeting. "We're pleased to welcome you to Smattac, pleased to hear whatever news you have. Have you come from far?"

The woman looked up and smiled. "Far enough," she said. "And far enough to go, too. We're glad to find a kindly place to rest in."

Tadeus grinned widely. "A kindly place and a good one, we are. We hope you'll carry our name with you." It was a ritual greeting, but heartfelt for all that.

"We will, surely. We've never been this way before, though, and we'd like some word of the road south."

A murmur, punctuated with a groan, rippled against the walls. The younger men looked around nervously. The old man, oblivious, scraped up a last spoonful of stew and sucked it down. The woman looked around, curious.

"South?" said Tadeus, grinning. He pulled up a short bench and straddled it. "I've been south, all the way to Hipsola. South is the Burned Lands."

The others might have heard the story a dozen times before, but the room became silent. For a moment the only sound was the rattle of the wooden bowl as the old man set it down and looked up. "The Burned Lands?" he asked. His voice was stronger than Jazen expected. "That would be the Wasted Lands, on our maps. Why would you visit the Wasted Lands?"

Tadeus laughed. "To get to the other side, old man, why else? Gods know there's nothing there for anything human. Two summers ago we, eight of us, went to Hipsola on the other side of the Burned Lands for our clan-gather, and the trade."

The visitors looked at each other. "Tell us about the Burned Lands," the woman said. All four of them leaned forward. From his sheltered corner, Jazen leaned forward too. He might be tired of hearing Tiralay brag, but this was a storytelling, and Tadeus was known to be a good storyteller.

The aleman's voice echoed against the rafters.

When we traveled in the Burned Lands, he said, *we carried much water. We had three beasts for nothing but water. You die sooner from lack of water. . . . You know you're there when the ground turns black underfoot and it crunches to ash with every step. The place was cursed ages ago, and hasn't forgotten.*

We saw the memories of demons in the Burned Lands. We dreamed strange dreams of winged men, and cats that spoke and hawks that prophesied. . . . We camped within circles of fire, and we fed our fires with the bones of men taken by demons, their souls eaten while they still lived, trapped in their own bodies while demons moved their hands, spoke from their mouths and ate them alive from the inside out.

These were the lands that burned in the last battles, when heroes fought and died to free us from the bitter rule of the Yaan Maat, two hundred years ago. It stinks to this day of the blood spilled in that battle; the air tastes of ashes, and no living thing moves there. . . .

The fire flickered; dancing shadows against the walls made huge shadows of the listeners. Tadeus' audience was silent, as if holding its collective breath, caught up in the rhythm and the sorrow of the tale.

We found skulls, mataals, broken, crushed. By the well in that place we found gold, crowns . . .

"Books?" the old man interrupted.

Yes, books, torn tattered pages that stuck to the ground even when the wind blew. Glued to the ground by demon's blood, they were. We didn't touch them. Not even to start our fires. Nothing grows in that place. There's a well there; the water is good, but nothing grows. There's no forage.

That's the site of the Great Battle two hundred years ago, where men drove the demons back, where men broke the mataal and found a way to drive demons out. . . .

"How?" the old man interrupted again, a desperate intensity in his eyes. The woman laid a hand lightly on his arm.

Tadeus shrugged. "It was long ago."

It was long ago. It was magic, back when there was such a thing as magic. They say some demons fought with men against their own kind, but in the end men killed those demons too, so they couldn't possess men any more. Because that's how they lived, you know. They'd come from the mataals and take a man's soul and eat it, and you'd look at him and never know it was a demon you spoke to, until one day he would crumble and die before your eyes, and the demon would go and take another, and another, and another. Men killed them all.

It is seven days across the Burned Lands, and three more to Hipsola, and in all that time we never saw a holy thing but ourselves and what we brought with us.

"All men know this is history, and true. But intelligent men"—he cast a glance at Belzec, and the villagers snickered, but softly—"know that the demons were defeated in our grandfathers' grandfathers' time, and those heroes killed them all. There's no such thing as magic these days."

Belzec turned red and knotted his fists. The rest of the audience nodded to each other with an air of confidence. Of course, there was so such thing as magic any more. Of course.

"But there were books. Pages. And there was the well. You did say there was a well, with good water. Did it look like your village well, or was there a fountain?" The old man seemed unaffected by the story; his questions were sharp, impatient, obsessed for detail.

Tadeus was taken aback. Even his fellow townsmen, who had heard it a dozen dozen times, were caught up in the tale, but this listener wasn't impressed.

"Aye," Tadeus said. "There was a fountain, all broken and burned. Even the stones were black. What of it?"

"We are interested in fountains," the woman said, her hand on the old man's arm again, soothing.

"Fountains?" someone echoed. "Why fountains?"

Tadeus frowned. "There aren't any fountains in Hipsola."

"They're like us," one of the shepherds agreed. "We use wells."

"Why go to Hipsola, then?" Tadeus asked, a little displeased that the visitors were not more impressed by his epic journey. On the other hand, the travelers carried good coin. Jazen could see the alekeeper struggling to be gracious.

"We're not going to Hipsola," one of the younger men spoke up. "We're going home."

"Where's home, then?" Belzec roared from across the room. Jazen shrank back against the wall, knowing he'd already been seen. He would hear of it in the morning, no doubt, when Belzec recovered from the night's drinking.

The rest of the audience, meanwhile, sat up. It was a rudeness for anyone but Tadeus to ask such direct questions, but as long as someone was going to be rude, Smattac found no contradiction in listening to the answers.

"Mirlacca," the young man replied.

Silence. The others in the room looked at each other, openmouthed. Jazen nearly lost his grip on his mug.

Mirlacca?

Mirlacca, home of the Emperor? Mirlacca, where all the buildings were made of stone and people ate meat every day, where everyone was rich and rode horses, where the Court danced to the tunes of invisible musicians every hour, day and night, around the great throne? Where nobles and princes schemed, and dukes vied with merchants, and lords laid down great taxes; where poisoners paraded their wares openly in the streets, which all men knew were paved with gold, and the houses were built to the very skies?

"You're from Mirlacca?" Tiralay asked, pushing forward, hands on her hips. "You can't be. Mirlacca is—Mirlacca is too far away. No one comes from Mirlacca."

The dark-haired man laughed, as if genuinely amused.

THE FOUNTAINS OF MIRLACCA

Jazen's eyes narrowed at the tone of it. The woman snapped something at him, but he drank deep of his ale, unabashed. "*We* come from Mirlacca, mistress, by way of the mountains and the north, and thousands more do too. It isn't such a wonderful thing, to come from Mirlacca."

Tadeus got to his feet, not incidentally towering over the dark-haired man. "Aye. But you say that you also wish to go through the Burned Lands, and that you have not done it yet." He looked the visitors in the face, and added, "And may not do it at all." Tadeus did not take kindly to the suggestion that his epic journey might be one that just anyone could duplicate.

The dark-haired man laughed again, but there was uncertainty in it now, and he met the gray eyes of the woman traveler and was still.

"We come from Mirlacca," the old man piped up, "to gather information, to visit the sites of the great battles. We are historians. We seek stories of the old times. Does anyone here have a tale of the old times, and how men finally conquered the people of the mataals? Indeed, have you tales of how men were possessed by the Yaan Maat?"

There was a sudden murmuring.

Even Tadeus stepped back. "It's ill done to tell such tales, ill done to speak the name."

"Did you not just do so?" the old man pointed out reasonably.

"It was a tale of traveling."

There was a rumble of agreement from the audience.

Belzec heaved himself up from the opposite side of the room, drawing all eyes to himself. "This is a good place, is Smattac. We have good families here. Two days hence we have a Welcoming, and you may watch if you like. We're growing. We're winning land back from the twisted forest.

"But we do not forget, not ever, that demons walked once." He shook his ponderous head back and forth. "Maybe in Mirlacca, in the Court, you no longer believe demons ever were. Or mayhap you think it's all history—that the war was won, two hundred years ago. Here, we know better." He glared defiantly at Tadeus. "Though some say otherwise."

He didn't look over at Jazen. No one did. Jazen shrank back

against the wall all the same, feeling their thoughts. There were still demons. Demons took human form, and you could tell them only by their eyes. Their eyes—and the things they did, like starting fires in a fit of temper.

"When we Welcome our young men, then we tell them the tales of the demons, and how they were found in the old times, how they were dealt with then. Are those the tales you wish to hear?"

The old man, the woman, the two younger men, all nodded eagerly, leaned forward.

"Yes," the woman said. She was the calmest of them.

Belzec made a noise that was half-laugh, half-snarl. "Nay. We do not give away our secrets. Not to strangers, even strangers who say they're from Mirlacca."

"Do you get many demons here?" the blond man asked, almost innocently.

This time, Jazen was almost sure, people glanced at him.

"We keep good watch," Belzec said after a long moment. "We know our own. We protect our own. We teach our young men at the Welcoming. That's what makes a man of Smattac. *In* Smattac."

And without it, a boy was not a man in Smattac.

He would never walk in a Welcoming, from outside the village to the central square to be greeted as a man among other men. He had no one to welcome him, and he never would.

And he couldn't even make a knife for the boys who would become men tomorrow. Simple eating-knives for a healer, yes, but Belzec had made the passage-knives for the six candidates; no one would let Jazen touch the symbols of manhood. He too was a stranger, after all. He had lived in the village as long as he could remember, but he would always be a stranger, because no one knew who his family was.

He thought again about the blade blank that had slipped into the charcoal. While making it he had thought of doing another, a man's-knife of his own, even if he'd never have anyone to give it to him. He would never be more than a forge boy, a water-carrier for Belzec the Smith, spending his life doing the filthy tasks that the smith thought appropriate, never able to claim his own work, his fortune limited to the cot in the smithy and the work under Belzec's eye.

He looked at Belzec and realized, suddenly, that when the smith died, he would have no place at all.

He waited, numb, for conversation to pick up again, for people to get up and move around, so that he could get up and walk to the door. All eyes followed him anyway; he could feel their gaze.

Tiralay glanced up as he passed. She showed no recognition either.

He walked back down the path to the forge, thinking about it. More than anything in his life, at this moment, he wanted to do something, but he despaired of knowing what. Something that would make them all pay attention, perhaps, make them admit that he was good at what he did with fire and metal.

He deserved at least that much.

Sparks of flame lighted his path, died as he left them behind.

Chapter 3

In the dawnlight of the next day, in the thatched house of Neesen the healer, Firaloy of Mirlacca sat on a low stool, waving his hands agitatedly, threatening to knock a steaming mug of watered wine into the laps of the two women at the table.

"You can't believe that!" he was saying to Neesen. "All of the records show otherwise. If you'd only come with us—"

"We have a sponsor now," his companion, less excited, interrupted. The old man sat back, grumbling.

"Aye, who?" Neesen asked, with all the uninvolved interest of an inhabitant of a rural town for the complex politics of a city. She was no longer a young woman, almost the age of Firaloy's companion, and she comfortably overflowed the seat of her own stool, resting her arms on the cluttered table they shared. Her hands were busy with a life of their own, plaiting a straw basket identical to the dozens hanging from the rafters of her small hut on the edge of the village. At her feet, a small brown cat rubbed his chin on the box holding the rushes she used.

"Lasvennat. One of the Great Lords of the council. Kin to the Emperor Himself," the woman answered her. She was splitting reeds and stacking them in a loose bundle within their hostess' reach.

Neesen looked up sharply. "You stretch very high, Vettazen. One hears things even here about Lasvennat—Is he really going to do it? Magic's not fashionable. Will they believe enough in Mirlacca to give you a proper Charter?"

Firaloy snorted. "Oh, they're like your aleman, no doubt,

with his great sophistication. But he hangs spiritbane at his doorway.

"Aye, some don't believe at all, but they're quick enough to ask for magical help in their love affairs, or against a rival. Lasvennat will persuade the council if he thinks he'll get something out of it."

"And will he?" Neesen said, still skeptical. Her callused fingers were quick and efficient as she wove the reeds in and out of their frame, tapping them down with an edge of stone to make the growing basket watertight.

"Of course he won't get anything from us—nothing important, anyway. The Heir is sickly, and we're not about to take the risk of getting involved in *that* nest of snakes. They're quick enough to burn the witch when the backspell goes wrong—as in the desert riots," Vettazen added. "Those were put down too late. A guild will protect you, Neesen. It will protect us all, so we can work in peace. And more efficiently, too, with all of us in place. Even Rizard is coming. There's a place for you, you know there is."

Neesen raised her eyebrows high. "What, I and every hedge witch in Miralat? Forgive me for doubting you, but where will you put us all?"

"There's a place, a compound in Mirlacca. With what Lasvennat pays—"

"And what will you owe him? —It doesn't matter what I believe, magisters," Neesen returned quietly, setting the basket aside and letting her hands rest idle in her lap. She drew a deep breath. "It doesn't matter, here, about the Emperor or his court. This village needs me and my knowledge more than you and your guild do, and I'll stay with them." She looked at the other woman. "Vettazen, do you at least understand?"

Vettazen nodded reluctantly. "Aye. The shame of it is, I think we're both right. We'd love to have you join us, Neesen; we need someone with your skills. The only other healer we've found with anything close is Demachee, and you know how *she* is."

Neesen shrugged. "I'm sorry. But no."

Firaloy threw up his hands, exasperated. "When I wrote to

you before, you said you'd consider it. We need the best we can get, if we're to be sponsored—"

"I have considered it, and the answer is no," Neesen repeated, without anger. "Smattac has done wonders, just in the last few years, in reclaiming land. It's growing. And when its children fall ill, when its mothers take to childbed, when its young men hurt themselves, they have no one else to go to but me. I'll not leave them."

"You run the risk of being burned or ignored," Vettazen warned her. "It's happened before, in other places."

Neesen smiled. "I know. That's why I spread my knowledge out, as much as I can, and why I sell baskets too. It makes me just one more woman who knows a bit more of herb lore than most, but who earns honest coin in a way anyone can see.

"Besides, you need someone to watch here, too. Demons don't confine themselves to cities."

"They don't know about your spells, of course?"

She pursed her lips. "They might suspect, some of them. But as we all know, magic is all make-believe—"

"That smith didn't sound like he thought it was make-believe," Firaloy snapped.

"Belzec? He wouldn't. He has more to work with in that area than most, I think, with his poor forge boy. There may be real talent there, by the way; he's the one to feel sorry for. He hasn't any family, either, and that makes it hard for him.

"But so long as I don't make mystic passes and chant in odd languages"—she grinned at Firaloy, who looked affronted—"no one is likely to call me a witch. Or worse, a demon. They don't want to offend my whole clan, after all. I earn good money for Yellowtree as well as for myself."

Firaloy threw up his hands. "Well, will you accept a 'prentice, then?"

Neesen bit her lip, her good nature warring with words that would surely disappoint them. "You'd need to find one from Yellowtree," she said at last. "It would be too hard to bring in someone else. Smattac isn't very friendly to strangers settling here.

"But I'll keep in touch with you gladly, and exchange information, and I can offer a night or two of lodging to one of yours. That's the best I can do just now. Will that help, at least?"

The two visitors shrugged helplessly. It was less than they hoped for, but more than nothing, and they accepted it.

The dawn came for Jazen when Natara, Belzec's third wife, brought him his breakfast, juggling the bowl of overcooked chea with Belzec's youngest, a two-year-old with a nasty temper.

"Where's Belzec?" Jazen mumbled through a mouthful of the mush. It had no flavor; he never expected any. The child screamed, grabbing for the bowl.

"Setting up the arches for the Welcoming," she said. "He wants you to finish sharpening that harrow, and clean out the pit." She looked around the large shed that was Belzec's place of business, with its forge and anvil and grinding wheel, the neat racks of chisels and hammers and peens and tongs, the tanks, the little stack of raw iron ingots and other materials, plain and layered-metal, in the back. "It's almost time to make more charcoal, too."

Jazen's face twisted. He hated making charcoal—it was a messy, smelly process, contaminating the fresh autumn air, and he always had trouble breathing for weeks afterward. It was, however, necessary for burning away the dross of iron ore to make steel, necessary for stoking the forge. Smattac didn't have a charcoal-maker, so the task fell to Jazen, as so many of the less pleasant ones did.

"And Tadeus spoke to me this morning," Natara added abruptly. "You're not to go back to the alehouse. Not to speak to Tiralay either. People saw you last night. He doesn't want rumors starting about his daughter, so leave her alone, understand?"

The mouthful of mush was suddenly too dry to swallow. "You mean, I can't even get a cup of ale—"

"That's exactly what I mean. You don't add enough to his custom to make it worth his while. Stay away from the place, understand? We won't have it said that Ironworkers can't control their bondsmen."

That made him flinch too—there was no "bond" between him and Belzec, never had been; he worked for the smith, and in return the smith fed and clothed him, provided him with a place to sleep. He had thought of himself as an apprentice, learning a trade. From the sidelong look in Natara's eye, she knew it. And she knew a bondsman was something else entirely.

"I have no bond here," Jazen said hoarsely.

"Aye, and have you not? Then you're free to go, and Tadeus will be asking after you for—*speaking*—to his daughter." Natara smiled. "Especially the words you were speaking to her last night, I hear."

He hid his reaction, he hoped. Belzec could be cruel, but his wife was worse. A bondsman could claim some thin legal protection from his bondholder. A man without a bond, without a clan, was defenseless. All the elders of Smattac were, of course, clansmen. If Tadeus chose to claim that Jazen had made advances to Tiralay, or worse yet—no, the aleman wouldn't say that, it would ruin the girl. But all of Smattac would side with Tadeus. The aleman was one of them, and wealthy. They deferred to him.

From the look of her in the alehouse last night, Tiralay would side with Tadeus. She wasn't about to acknowledge so much as an attraction to, much less any real feelings for, a nobody.

"But I think you'd be better for it," Natara went on. "Give you a place to live out your days."

And work for them for the rest of his life for nothing, instead of the scraps of coin he sometimes got now for bits of extra work. Belzec must have told her about Neesen's knife.

"We've told Tadeus that we're speaking for you," she went on. "You've only to declare it yourself, and it's done. Best you do so quickly, boy." The child struggled to get down, and she swung him up to her hip and looked Jazen over, her tongue running over her lower lip. "You'll not lose by it."

When he didn't respond, she laughed, and left him alone.

The visitors spent the day resting, though the two older ones, Jazen heard, spent quite some time talking to the healer and bought many herbs from her. The two young men wan-

THE FOUNTAINS OF MIRLACCA 27

dered around the village and the fields, spoke to people. Jazen heard about their movements, from eavesdropping on the farmers who stopped by to have a harrow sharpened, who came by for a rake.

He saw for himself when he looked up to see the blond man standing in the open side of the forge. He had just finished the eating-knife for Neesen and was drawing hot wire for the hilting. It was a finicky, careful process, one that Belzec scorned and would likely beat him for wasting his time at, and he was startled at the shadow falling across his work.

The man seemed mildly curious as he looked around the forge, marking the equipment with his eyes. He touched nothing except the side of the wall.

"Hello?" he said quietly.

Jazen put down what he was doing. "Aye? What do you need?" He wondered for a moment if the mule had come lame. If so, it wasn't his fault. He was prepared to defend himself, when he saw the expression on the man's face. It was open, friendly. Not accusing at all.

"I wanted to thank you for shoeing the mule. All four feet too. It was more than you were asked."

Jazen looked around quickly to see if Belzec was near enough to overhear, but the smith was still at the square, setting up for the ceremony. The sky threatened rain; they needed tents to shelter the feast in the square.

"You did a good job. The beast is fussy about it, too. I came to pay for the extra."

But it was to put out Belzec, Jazen protested inwardly. But the man was holding out a fistful of small coppers, more than enough to cover the cost of the shoes, and he nodded quickly, silently, and took them.

"A great day today for your village, isn't it?" the man said, trying to be friendly.

Jazen only nodded, unsure of how to respond. From the reaction of the strangers the night before, they had never even heard of a Welcoming. He wondered what kind of rite this man had gone through. Surely he was old enough.

"Does it happen every year?"

Jazen shook his head. He felt incredibly self-conscious,

standing there in a heavy leather apron and leggings, in front of this well-dressed sophisticate. "Not enough of the right age. Sometimes every year, sometimes not."

"You must have gone through it last year—"

The look Jazen gave him then silenced the blond man's effort at conversation at last. He spent a few more moments looking around, then went away, leaving Jazen alone looking at the coins in his hands.

Taking a deep breath, he separated the cost of the three extra shoes—deducting the profit Belzec had made for overcharging on the first one—and put it in the hollow under the anvil. The remainder Jazen hid with the rest of his few possessions, under the hide-covered straw cot behind the forge and the water tanks. The materials were Belzec's, but the work had been his, after all.

The visitors stayed long enough to be polite at the Welcoming, and then left late the next morning, riding single file down the main path under a lowering sky. Jazen watched them go from the corner of his eye as he sweated over the new fire. The finished knife was set to one side; Belzec had set him to making new horseshoes. While the smith hadn't noticed any missing, he did think he was low on stock.

The rest of Smattac was on the other side of the village, gathered in the square for the feast. Every man, woman, and child of Smattac was there, whether they had a son or brother participating or not. It was a great thing, the Welcoming. All the young boys of the crown village of Smattac coming home as men, ready to have their own fields, their own houses, marry. Have children. Pay their own taxes in their own names. Have a voice and a vote in the village councils.

And he, Jazen sr'Yat, sweated at the blacksmith's forge, hammering a metal rod flat, bending metal to the rough shape of a horse's hoof, over and over and over. Not for him the complex ironwork of gates and windowguards, though he could do that work as well as Belzec ever did; not for him the chance to use the delicate, painstaking skill of drawing wire on anything complex. And never, never the chance to make something important.

No, Jazen sr'Yat made horseshoes under another man's eye, and would never have more than the straw cot behind the forge, and that only until someone saw the little fires spring up with his temper.

The visitors weren't staying for the feast. They had other concerns. They had a place in a world outside Smattac. To someone from the great city of Mirlacca, no doubt, a village Welcoming feast was nothing at all.

There was a whole *world* beyond Smattac, and people lived in it. Traveled through it.

People without any clans Jazen could recognize.

The roan mule's hindquarters disappeared around the bend with one last insolent swish of its tufted tail.

Mirlacca.

A Welcoming that was no welcome.

Tiralay's carefully indifferent eyes.

A stone thrown by a six-year-old girl.

A future of sharpening ploughs for the farmers.

Working a bond, no better than a slave.

Mirlacca.

The place of dreams.

Jazen licked the salt from his lips, tossed his head to get the hair out of his eyes—unsuccessfully—it was damp and stuck to his forehead.

He chiseled another red-hot curve free, caught it with the forceps, smoothed the edges down.

He'd gone through the fields, to the edge of the twisted forest, once. He'd seen the road that led through it, to the Burned Lands, to Hipsola, ten days' journey to the other side. He'd heard Tadeus' tales over and over and over again, and they had given him nightmares.

His dreams the night before had not been of demons, though. They'd been of the sidelong looks when Belzec had said, "We keep good watch."

He let out an explosive breath he didn't know he was holding, and plunged the iron, clamps and all, into the quench tank. Steam hissed up, coated him with more dampness.

He continued holding the metal in the liquid until the cloud of steam was gone and the water stopped bubbling, and then pulled it out again, taking it in his bare hand. It was still very warm to the touch.

The last piece of iron wasn't quite right for a horseshoe—too soft, too many impurities in the ore. Jazen pulled it out of the fire, held it in the air, looked at it critically. It cooled rapidly in the air; a crack was developing, he could see. Swearing, he tossed it aside.

It landed near the pile of raw material stacked at the back of the forge, beside one of the slender bundles of metal, called iyiza, thrown carelessly with the other stock. A finger-joint thick and half as long as his hand, sheets of steel with nickel or other metals, tied together with wire, they were rare and precious, brought back from Hipsola market by Tadeus on his famous journey, and Jazen suspected that Belzec had no idea at all what to do with them. Jazen had heard Tadeus tell him about how the smiths of Hipsola worked them, forging and folding them until the different metals were all one, but the mastersmith had never paid any attention. He'd tossed them back here with the plain ingots, and now the bundles were covered with dirt and debris, like so much dross or waste metal. They had been lying there for two seasons now, and Belzec had never once done anything with them.

Jazen picked one of the bundles up and hefted it. It was heavier than it looked, half the length and all the thickness of his hand, thin, narrow strips of steel and other things. *He* could make something of this.

Still holding the iyiza, he set the clamps against the wall in their proper place, shed the leather apron and shrugged into a ragged shirt, picked up his jerkin and his pouch from the hiding place behind the forge, and set off down the path, following the hoofprints of the roan mule.

Chapter 4

He kept behind the roan mule, out of sight but not out of earshot; the trail led under watery sunlight past the broad, stubbled grain fields bordered by the low stone wall, up through the rocky, bitter sheep pastures, into the first spindly trees that marked the boundary of the land the village had reclaimed. Parts of the land were still barren and black; some of the trees were misshapen, some were strong. Jazen hung back, once ducking into a ditch, but the travelers never looked back.

It was much easier to stay out of sight once the canopy of leaves closed over his head, and much cooler too. After a while it started to rain, soaking already slippery leaves underfoot, making his leather jerkin dark and heavy. He had to run to catch up when the trail was clear, and skulk back when it narrowed and the animals slowed down.

He wasn't used to walking so far. By the time the travelers stopped for midday, he was stumbling tired and almost walked into the little clearing into the middle of the group. He had never been so far from the forge in all his life, and he was cold.

Leaning against the trunk of an old, half-rotten tree, he thought about sitting down. It would feel very good to rest; on the other hand, if he did, he couldn't imagine ever getting up again for anything. He couldn't tell if it was still raining, but water dripped from the sodden branches down the back of his neck.

Perhaps twenty feet away the travelers stood and stretched and drank from waterskins, filled them again from a welling spring. The two young men were trying to build a fire from a handful of sticks to warm their provisions, while the woman and the old man rubbed their backsides, took deep breaths of green forest air, and spoke of maps and trails.

Green sticks, Jazen saw. They were trying to build a fire with green sticks. He smiled to himself. Sophisticated these travelers might be, but *he* knew better than to try to light a fire with green wood.

The sight of it, and the sound and feel of his stomach growling, reminded him that he'd left without any provisions of his own. He couldn't follow behind, starving, forever. At some moment, he'd have to—

"Well, don't stand there. Come eat," the woman called, looking in his direction. She didn't sound in the least surprised; more, in fact, as if she had been aware from the very beginning that he had been following them, and now it was time he joined them.

Now the rest of them were looking in his direction too.

He stepped out from behind the tree, hesitantly.

"Yes, you. Come here and help us with this fire. You do know how to light a fire, don't you?" She gestured at the stack of green wood.

Jazen stifled a laugh and stepped forward, taking the opportunity to avoid their eyes a few moments longer, kneeling at the firepit. Dampness soaked through his leggings at the knees.

"I have a flint," offered one of the young men, the dark-haired one who had been so outspoken in the alehouse. "But the tinder won't stay lit."

Jazen scraped at the branch with his thumbnail; the mark it left was green and moist. Of course it wouldn't stay lit, not with the puny spark from a flint. It needed dry shavings and seasoned wood to catch on. A glance around the clearing, though, showed no deadfalls, only soft, soggy moss. There was nothing there.

They needed a fire, though.

He took the flint and a deep breath, hoping no one was watching. If they were, he hoped they would assume it was just something a forgeboy would know how to do. Usually this happened when he was angry, but sometimes he felt he could actually control it— The green wood remained pristine. Now, of course, when he was among strangers he needed to impress with his usefulness, when he actually *wanted* it to happen, nothing—

A tall tongue of flame licked at the green wood. Over the head of the roan mule, a tree branch rose and fell and snapped itself away from its parent trunk, falling on the animal in a shower of water. The mule bolted, slipping and squelching in the wet leaves. The two young men went chasing after it. The horses, still tied, squealed but settled when nothing else happened.

The green wood blazed merrily, without a hint of smoke.

Jazen looked up through the flames to the woman and the old man, who were gazing thoughtfully at him and at the new fire.

"You'll have to learn to control that," the woman remarked, as if there were nothing unusual in what had just happened. "It's a bit spectacular."

Jazen opened his mouth to deny, to disclaim. The old man was nodding. "Totally untrained, of course. But a useful knack, yes indeed, useful."

Overhead, another branch broke, dumping a load of rain-soaked greenery on top of the blazing fire and on Jazen as well. The new fire sizzled into nothingness.

The woman took a deep breath. "I don't suppose we should have you try it again," she said regretfully. "You'd probably have the whole tree down."

They could not have seen, he thought, as he pulled the wet branches off himself. Not really. "I'm sorry about the mule," he muttered, for lack of anything else to say. Miraculously, there were a few embers left. He blew on them gently, coaxing them with drier scraps the woman brought him.

"Oh, don't worry about that, Meleas is good with animals. He'll have him back here in no time," she said. "So. You're the boy from the forge, aren't you?"

Jazen nodded quickly and poked some more at the fire, which was finally beginning to smoke normally. A nearly transparent finger of flame reached upward.

"Left them, did you?" the old man asked, as if just noticing. "Where are you going?"

Jazen could feel his chest rising and falling, see fire climbing along the white bark of a twig and turn it black. He felt remarkably silly of a sudden. "Mirlacca," he said. "I want to go to Mirlacca."

"Family there, then?" the old man asked.

Of course they'd think he had family. Why would anyone go anywhere if there was no family there to welcome him?

"I think he wants to see the world," the woman said, brushing her hands together. "What's your name, boy?"

"Jazen." He bit off the rest of it. He might be a bastard, but he didn't have to tell the world about it.

She paused, waiting. When he showed no inclination to go on, to provide family and clan and village and guild and oath lines, she filled in herself, as if there had never been any awkward pauses.

"I'm Vettazen sr'Islit, and this old stick is my husband, Firaloy, of the Crown City of Mirlacca. We're exorcists."

"You're what?" Jazen had never heard the word before. Getting to his feet, he looked at them. He was at least twenty-five years younger than the woman, a couple of hands taller; more than that for Firaloy, who was peering at him in mild surprise. Neither of them seemed to regard him as a particular threat. It surprised him. He was a stranger, after all, and he'd been following them.

Vettazen was burrowing into the saddlebags for a pot and a grate to set it upon, moving around the little campsite as if there were no young, strong man standing ever more uncertainly in the middle of it. "We're exorcists," she said, as if everyone knew what that meant.

Filling the pot with water, she set the grate over the fire—"You'll want to look after that, it's going out again"—and made tea, ignoring Jazen's lack of comprehension. Firaloy stood watching her, in fair helplessness, until the aroma of boiling herbs filled the clearing.

"Well, old man, are you going to use your hands to drink from?" Vettazen said. "Get the cups. It's cold here, and the boy is wet and shaking with it." She glanced sharply at Jazen.

"Walked out with only the clothes on your back, I'll be bound. We'll have to do something about that, but it will be a while. Ah, good, here's Adri-nes and Meleas. They got the mule."

"He was enjoying it," the blond one said. "Tried to kick Adri-nes."

The man referred to, dark-haired and disgusted, yanked lightly at the halter of the roan mule. The mule brayed in his ear, as if laughing. The blond man led the errant beast over to the other animals and stood talking quietly to it.

"This is Jazen," Firaloy said. "He'll be joining us."

"Tea!" Adri-nes exclaimed. "Wonderful. I thought I was going to freeze to death." Adri-nes had an odd accent, Jazen thought, different from the oddness of the rest of them; it was more apparent here than it had been in the alehouse.

He reached for the cup Vettazen was holding. She slapped his outstretched hand and handed the cup to Jazen. "Get your own, and fill the pot up again," she said. "I think we have some getting acquainted to do."

Jazen drank deep of the tea, catching bits of herb between his teeth and crunching them. The liquid burned his tongue and throat, warmed him clear into his gut, and he shuddered with the abrupt contrast between warm interior and cold, wet clothing.

Vettazen was watching him through narrowed eyes. "Meleas, don't you have an extra oilcoat? Loan it to Jazen, will you? He's going to catch his death of chill. Jazen, get that jerkin off, and that shirt too. We'll let them dry out."

Adri-nes poured out the remaining tea and refilled the pot with water from the stream. "Fire keeps going out," he announced. "Wood won't stay lit. Jazen, can you get it going again?"

"I don't think so," Jazen muttered, peeling out of the jerkin and shirt. His skin made gooseflesh in the sudden exposure to air, and he rubbed vigorously at his chest and arms, trying to get warm. He thought he could get the fire burning again, in fact, but he wasn't comfortable with the way these people seemed to be taking it for granted. Adri-nes shrugged and tried to feed the flames himself, without success.

"Here, have more tea," Vettazen said. Jazen took it eagerly, and drank half of it down before realizing it was almost boiling hot.

"Put on the oilcoat," she said, taking back the cup. "It's starting to rain again. No, Adri, let the fire go, we need to go on; we can get in a few more miles before we camp tonight. That's right, quench it, though gods know it's beyond me how a place this wet could catch. Let's see now, how are we going to arrange things? Firaloy, get back on the bay—you can use that tree stump—Jazen, you can take the roan; he's tough and you're not heavy—"

"I can walk," Jazen said hastily. He had never ridden an animal in his life. The mule rolled a threatening eye at him.

"Don't be silly, you've been walking for miles," Vettazen said, and hauled herself up onto the back of the brown mare, hauling its head around and taking a few steps down the trail before stopping to wait for her husband.

Meleas maneuvered his own mount in front of the mule. "He'll hold still for you," he said quietly. "He's got better manners than he looks."

Jazen glared at him from under heavy brows.

"You should have seen Firaloy when we started out," the other man said equably. "The old man still can't ride worth demon's tears. Go on—grab the beast's mane and jump up. He's not going anywhere."

Somehow Meleas was between him and the rest. Jazen shot him one more glare, and leaped and pushed and pulled himself up on the mule, settling somehow, and not too comfortably, among the luggage. The roan mule grunted and lowered its head, then sneezed mightily.

"Here, your reins," Meleas said. "He'll keep up, don't worry. He's not that independent. Just don't lean too far one way or the other, and you'll be fine."

Jazen took a deep breath. "Are you sure?"

Meleas grinned, teeth very white against bronzed skin. "Of course." With that he wheeled the mare away, following the others down the trail. The roan mule snorted in alarm and jolted after. Jazen clung to the packs and cursed under his breath. It was a very long way to the ground. He clung for dear life to the reins with one hand and the front packing strap with the other until the mule caught up with the others and slowed into a long, steady walk.

Six hours later the sun was within a span of the horizon, or would have been if they could see it. The woods were thinning, but the sky was still overcast, and lightning licked at sullen gray clouds. The roan mule ran up into the hindquarters of Meleas' mare. She squealed and kicked. The mule ducked back. Jazen fell off.

"Well," Firaloy said thoughtfully, "I think the boy has a good idea there. This is a decent place to camp."

"There's no water," Vettazen pointed out.

"Oh, there's always water about," Firaloy said vaguely. "Over there, somewhere, I believe." He waved one sticklike arm eastward. "Meleas, go find it. Make yourself useful."

Jazen, still sitting on the ground, was not at all sure about rest. He was not at all sure, in fact, about his ability to get up. He looked up to see Meleas standing over him, grinning, offering him a hand. Adri-nes swung off his own animal and shook his head at them, snickering.

"Let him gloat," Meleas advised. "He gets so little joy out of life, you may as well offer him some aches and pains to feast on."

Jazen had no choice but to take the hand; his legs would not obey him. Once on his feet again, with the blood returning to abused limbs, he could not keep from groaning. Adri-nes, having come over to tie his animal beside theirs, chuckled.

"I suppose that's a good enough excuse to skip camp duty tonight," he said, "but you're going to take my turn a few times, I promise you, since I'm the only one with extra blankets. Walk around a bit. Pick up some wood, and we'll see if you can do your fire trick again."

"I have no fire trick," Jazen said, his voice almost as stiff as his muscles. "What do you take me for, a hedge witch?" Better that, in fact, than the other thing . . . The blond man, unpacking, shook his head.

"I take you for a damned poor rider." Adri-nes laughed. "Go on." He turned away. Jazen tried to move, and almost cried out.

Still, it was no worse than a beating from Belzec. He gritted his teeth and stretched up and out, and then forced himself to move, to bend, to pick up bits of deadfall. After a while it got easier.

Everyone seemed to have a task, he noticed, even Firaloy, puttering around the packs and sorting out provisions. Within a very short time the animals were tied to a picket line and munching on grain rations; the fire was set up and sputtering, bedding was spread out, a convenient bush designated for necessary functions. Meleas had found a trickle of water, eastward of the camp, and a large pot of stew sat on the grate, warming to a boil.

Jazen sat on his borrowed oilcoat, toying with the iyiza, sneaking glances at his new companions, wondering if Belzec missed him. They would be celebrating tonight, of course. They might not notice.

Exorcists, Vettazen had said. He didn't know the word, but it had, he thought, something to do with demons. It must, considering these strangers' fascination with the subject. His skin crawled.

"I thought you didn't believe in demons," he said abruptly, startling them. "You said before that they were only stories."

Adri-nes and Meleas looked at each other and at Firaloy, who blinked. "Ah no," the old man said. "I never said they were only stories." He set the cup down in a convenient depression in the ground beside him. "It was your townsfolk said that, as if it would make it true. They sound more sophisticated, so. Even while they teach their young men otherwise in the Welcoming. Your master the smith, though—he knows the truth."

They were the Yaan Maat and where they came from we never knew. They came in the reign of Echesevan the Seventh in the Imperial City of Mirlacca, and they took the souls of the Emperor and his council before anyone knew. There were those who would not believe, in fact, until the bodies of the royal councilors began to rot as they sat and debated in the royal chambers.

There were those who could not be possessed, perhaps one man in ten, one woman in twenty, one child in sixty. In the first years of the Yaan Maat the demons learned they could not de-

vour us heedlessly, and we learned to use magic. And we learned the secret of the mataal, and somehow we learned that demons too could die.

But it was never easy. Never. The demons became more clever, learning to take souls and hide within, learning not to kill their victims right away. But they were never able to share a body for long, and we learned ways to tell demons within our neighbors. We tested them.

Jazen shuddered within himself, looking down at the ground, picking at the sleeve of the dry, dirty shirt he wore. Firaloy's voice trailed off, and Vettazen poked at the stew and declared it ready. The mood was broken by the bustle to pass out bowls, ladle out food, settle and eat.

Jazen was surprised to find he was hungry. He thought he was too tired and too sore to eat, but the stew was hot, good, well spiced, and there were hot roots baked in the coals. By the time he finished the second bowlful he was feeling much better.

"Won't your family wonder about you?" Meleas asked. The blond man was lying on his back, staring up at the moon through the canopy of leaves. Jazen scraped one last bit of gravy out of the bowl and set it aside, reluctantly.

"Not likely," he said, without bitterness. "They're not family." He took a deep breath. Time to say it, admit it, have done with it. "I have no family. I am clanless."

No one exclaimed with shock or horror. Meleas, in fact, nodded awkwardly. "Ah, it's like that, is it? Well, you picked the right caravan to follow. Vettazen is a good woman, and Firaloy—if you have a story or the least scrap of talent or can even sharpen a pen. Firaloy doesn't mind in the least."

Jazen refrained from saying that this was easily the smallest "caravan" ever seen in Smattac, and caught at the truly important thing.

"They aren't your family?" He had thought they were all related, though the younger men were strikingly different in appearance and demeanor; Meleas was solid, substantial, with hair the color of new straw and wide blue eyes, while Adri-nes was slender, quick, dark-haired and dark-eyed and always smiling.

Adri-nes was smiling now, too. "Gods in flame, no. Our families have too much else to do to worry about us, and we like to learn about the old times. I suppose you could say we're 'prenticed to Firaloy, though I'm blest if any of us know what our trade will be."

"Exorcist," Vettazen had said. It felt strange, talking to the others as an equal, being spoken to as an equal. They hadn't even blinked at the idea of talking to a clanless man. They hadn't said what their own clans were, either. There was rather a lot they weren't saying, he thought.

But while he could appreciate their caution with a stranger, he could not restrain his curiosity. "What did she mean?"

He'd never seen someone shrug lying down. Meleas managed it, while Adri-nes collapsed gracefully into a cross-legged position. Jazen looked at him and was reminded of his own rapidly stiffening muscles.

It was, it seemed, a look Adri-nes had seen before. "Don't worry," he advised cheerfully, "you won't know what soreness is until the morning. But a couple of weeks from now you won't even feel it."

"I'll be dead by then."

The two laughed, but it was sympathetic.

"Tell me what she meant," Jazen repeated. The older couple were spreading out more bedding on the opposite side of the fire, far enough away that they might not be able to hear. "Are they looking for demons?"

"Gods in flame forbid," Adri-nes said devoutly. "No, they're looking for the old stories. The old spells. Firaloy is a historian of the old times. Vettazen studies the old spells. She collects manuscripts for the palace library. Firaloy tries to figure out what makes them work."

Meleas did not contribute to the conversation, staring up into the darkness.

"Is that what an exorcist does, then?" Jazen asked. He was feeling his way through the discussion, more aware than ever that the two men were holding something back, something they didn't know him well enough to tell him yet. It made him profoundly uneasy. "Collect spells?"

"Among other things."

THE FOUNTAINS OF MIRLACCA 41

"They're witches, then," Jazen said. "And you—"

One of the horses whickered uneasily; Meleas looked over his shoulder at it and muttered something. "They're not witches, and neither are we," he said, turning back. "Though I could use a good love spell sometimes. Vettazen and Firaloy are, I don't know . . . historians?"

The word made no more sense than "exorcist" had. Jazen seized on what he understood. "Demons?" he suggested, trying to make it sound as if it might be a joke.

He was relieved to see it taken as such.

"They study history and magic," Adri-nes said, folding his arms behind his head. "They collect stories. That doesn't make one a Yaan Maat."

Jazen was silent for a little while, listening to the quiet movements of people and animals, the crackling fire, the chirr of insects. The stars came out one by one as the sky turned from blue to black.

"How can you live from that?" he asked at last.

The two men looked confused. "What do you mean?"

Jazen was confused in turn. "Belzec forges metal to sell to those who need it. Farmers raise grain to make bread, sheep for meat and wool. But who needs stories? You can't eat them, can't cut with them. How do they live?"

"How do they earn, you mean," Meleas said. He paused, choosing his words carefully. "I really couldn't say. Perhaps the palace library acts as their patron."

Jazen had no idea what a library was, or a patron, and decided that he would wait to find out. He had heard storytellers in the alehouse, trading news and tales for a night's bed and food, but he had never heard a tale that would buy a mule.

"Where are you going, then?" he asked. *You.* Not *we.* He was not a part of this little band, not yet.

"To the Wasted Lands," Adri-nes said, moving over to the other side of Meleas and stretching out on a blanket. "Firaloy has been talking about the Wasted Lands for months now."

"What does he want there?"

Adri-nes yawned. "Gods know. To find out if anything's left, I think. I suppose we'll find out when we get there. We usually do.

"As for me, I'm going to sleep, and I suggest you do the same." With that, he rolled over, his back to Jazen.

Meleas was already snoring peacefully. On the other side of the fire, Firaloy and Vettazen were shapeless lumps of shadow. The fire itself was guttering, almost out. Outside the circle of its light, something made a noise, and the brown gelding snorted. Jazen jumped. In response, the fire flared.

There was nothing there. Nothing but trees, and night, and the sound of insects and the breathing of horses and Meleas' snoring. The tiny crackling of the fire was far from the rumble of the forge fire, carried none of its concentrated heat. There was no wall to curl up against.

There was no Belzec with his family on the other side of the wall. No Smattac.

Only the forest, and four strangers.

For a long time Jazen thought about Smattac, and Tiralay, and everything out of his past, and he wondered why he was lying here, in the rain, in the forest, among strangers.

It was a long time before Jazen slept.

Chapter 5

Jazen opened his eyes to the smell of cooking meat and boiling tea. For a moment that was the only sensation he was aware of, and he savored it.

After a moment he realized he was cold, much colder than he had ever been in the morning, and he remembered where he was and reached for his blanket.

He tried to reach for the blanket. His muscles froze in place. He smothered a scream.

Adri-nes stood over him, laughing. "I told you you'd be sore. Get up and move, or you'll freeze that way."

Jazen lay there, thinking of the comfortable heat of the forge fire on a winter morning. If he breathed carefully, he might trick his body into thinking it had spent the night on his own cot—

Adri-nes leaned down and waved a plate of stew a hand's-breadth in front of his nose. Jazen's nose twitched. The plate came closer, bathing his face in the aroma of hot food. Jazen closed his eyes and tried to move his hand again.

Adri-nes held the plate a moment more, then deliberately placed it a few feet away, within sight and smell, the steam rising in white billows. "If you want it, you have to get up."

Jazen thought about murder. He shifted his head minutely to watch Adri-nes swagger away to squat down beside the fire and the other three travelers, all busy eating, all looking perfectly at ease. He thought about flames, and wondered how Adri-nes would like it if his breeches caught fire. But Vettazen would probably suspect it wasn't natural. And Jazen didn't really have any control over it anyway.

He got up.

It took perhaps three times longer than usual to get to his feet, and then stagger behind the bushes to relieve himself. By the time he came out again the food was no longer steaming. He picked up the plate and forced himself to stand upright and walk over to the fire. Adri-nes looked up at him and grinned.

"Look who's here," he said amiably. "That's cold. Let me get you some warm." He rose to his feet in one smooth, enviable movement and took the plate away. "You should move and stretch," he advised. "Arms up and around. Kick. Move."

Jazen stared at him as if he had lost his mind.

"He's right," Vettazen said, taking the plate from Adri-nes and scraping the stew back into the bubbling pot and stirring it. "Move around. You'll feel better."

Some time later, back on the mule and moving through the thinning trees, Jazen had to admit they were right. While his back and buttocks and legs were sore and stiff, at least he was fed. The stew was warm in his belly, and he was more willing to contemplate his companions with some objectivity. It was made easier still by his position, once again, at the end of the line of pack animals.

At the head of the line, Meleas and Adri-nes alternated the lead position, trotting sometimes out of Jazen's sight. The two of them rode easily, Adri-nes with more skill to Jazen's inexperienced eye, turning the sorrel mare in tight quarters with a minimum of fuss. Jazen watched and tried to imitate the other man, shifting his balance; it was difficult, wedged between sacks of grain. When Adri-nes caught Jazen watching, he always smiled cheerfully and waved.

Meleas rode with less flash, quiet and steady, one hand resting on the long dagger scabbarded in his belt. The blond man was stolid and quiet and much less likely to laugh at Jazen. Meleas never looked at others in the party except when he addressed them; for the most part he kept alert to the surrounding forest. It was Meleas who found the path again when it appeared to branch, dismissing the way Adri-nes had taken as a deer trail. When the dark-haired man came cantering back a few minutes later, he was laughing, acknowledging the mistake.

Vettazen rode like one of the sacks of grain slung over the roan mule's hindquarters, only upright, sagging and swaying minutely with the movement of her animal. She was more likely to exchange a quiet word with Meleas, shake her head at Adri-nes, and keep going. Sometimes she tugged absently at the gathered material of her split skirts, shifting herself in the saddle.

Firaloy barely seemed to notice where he was, or indeed that he was even on a horse. He followed Vettazen and stared absent-mindedly into the treetops, wrapped up in layers of leather and wool, and every time his horse shook its head Jazen held his breath, expecting the old man to fall off. He never did. He never even seemed to notice.

Two more pack mules came next, plodding, carrying more than their share of the load because Jazen was riding their brother. Occasionally they voiced their resentment in low rumbles. Jazen wondered what would happen if bandits broke out of the trees and attacked the little party. He could imagine Adri-nes making a grand stand, like one of the heroes in the tales, waving a sword around—and getting it caught in the trees—and Meleas with his back against one of those trees, fighting with quiet efficiency. He could not find a place for Firaloy or Vettazen in this playlet, and as for himself—well, as for himself, he would be lucky not to be dumped onto the ground and lie there stunned while great battles took place around him and the roan mule bolted all the way back to Smattac.

"Why are you smiling at last?" Adri-nes asked, coming up beside him in a wide place on the trail. "Or is the pain so great you're screaming to yourself?"

"No." Jazen realized suddenly he had forgotten the pain. "I was thinking about bandits."

"And this is amusing?" Adri-nes leaned almost into Jazen's lap to avoid a branch and straightened up again.

"Have you ever had trouble with bandits?"

Adri-nes shook his head. "We're no rich merchant caravan. Just an ordinary little family party, of no interest to anyone."

His tone sounded odd. Jazen studied him, puzzled. "Rich merchant caravans have mercenaries to guard them. You'd be easy to defeat."

"Where did a forge boy learn such skill in tactics?" Adri-nes responded, lifting his eyebrows.

Jazen blinked. There had been no hostility in the other man's voice; Adri-nes sounded as if he were teasing, if anything. At the same time, there was enough truth in the words to sting, and Jazen simply shook his head. After a moment Adri-nes spurred his horse away to the front of the little party.

Perhaps it was true, and they'd never been attacked. But he'd heard the stories about bodies found barely rolled off the trails, stripped of all they had; about wild men and evil men living in the woods by their wits and other men's gold. Adri-nes, he concluded, was either a fool, or knew something he wasn't saying. In either case he had just made it clear that he considered himself every bit as separate from Jazen as any of the people of Smattac ever had.

For a moment he remembered again the warmth of the forge fire, not as sleep-dazed confusion but as regret. Belzec would be roaring as loudly as his own bellows; Natara, his wife, would be brisking around her hearth with lips pursed tight, calling him ill names; Tiralay—

It dawned on him suddenly that he would never see Tiralay again, not even passing by at the well, and he wondered, panicked, if it were too late to turn back, to pretend this bizarre adventure had never happened.

Then they broke through the trees, into the sunlight, into the beginnings of the Burned Lands.

Ahead of Jazen, the party had stopped, riding animals and pack mules leaving their single file to move up beside each other, staring out over the new landscape with as much interest as the humans they carried.

To the south and east, as far as Jazen could see, was rubble and white sand. To the west rose blue mountains, abrupt, as if they had been shoved upward by a giant hand, leaving a face of sheer cliff with debris fallen at its feet. On closer look he could see the cliff was not, perhaps, quite so sheer, and it was dotted with scrub trees, giving it a speckled appearance. The mountains were ugly and unforgiving, and much, much easier to look at than the devastation that lay at their feet.

Firaloy moved his horse forward, letting it pick its way along the wide path that appeared to lead from the forest trail. The rest of the party fell in behind him, looking about them as they rode, Jazen moving up with the other riders. In a few minutes they passed between two long, irregular rows of stone. The path became rougher. More loose rocks turned under the animals' feet. The roan mule snorted and threw up his head as he missed a step, and Jazen grabbed for the baggage straps.

The rows of stone were walls, Jazen realized, walls that came no higher than his knee, and the path they followed was a road, a road that at one time had been paved. Tiny goldenbells grew in the cracks.

All around them, the remains of a city stretched out, as if a sword had slashed through and cut it down. Heaps of unrecognizable rubbish and trash were swept into corners.

Jazen cleared his throat. "What is this place?" he called out to Vettazen, riding in front of him. No birds startled into flight as the sound of his voice; nothing lived here but the goldenbells. His words were lost in the steady clopping of hooves.

He opened his mouth to ask again, but Vettazen glanced back at him and raised one hand. He took it as a warning to silence and settled back against the packs, looking about him as the roan mule patiently followed the others.

They rode along what once had been a wide road, so wide there was still a clear path through the rubble. From time to time he guessed that other, narrower side streets had led off from it. The stones were yellow and white, darker brown or black sometimes along one side or another. He looked for bones, but there were no bones; there were no bodies. Whatever had happened here had happened too long ago, or had been too terrible, for bones.

Tadeus had never spoken of a ruined city in the Burned Lands. A fountain, he'd said, and blackened stones; but he had never told a tale of a place like this. This city had held five times as many people as Smattac, and now it was empty even of birds.

The roan mule walked into the hindquarters of Vettazen's mare, and flattened his long ears and brayed in protest when the mare kicked at him for his familiarity. Firaloy and Vettazen had stopped, exchanging a few excited words, pointing at invisible landmarks. Adri-nes and Meleas had already dismounted and were looking closely at the ground, nudging at crumbling building stones with the toes of their boots.

Jazen slid off too. He was surprised to discover he could stand, could even move. Stretching cautiously, he looked around. The mule, chastened again by Vettazen's mare, snuffled disconsolately at a patch of goldenbells and rejected them.

Meleas and Adri-nes examined a stack of rocks. Firaloy studied a map. Vettazen stretched, too, and joined her husband. Her horse followed, nose reaching for the belt pouch.

Looking around, Jazen was unable to see anything remarkable, as opposed to the rest of the ruins they had been riding through for the past several hours.

"What is this?" he asked again. "What are you looking for? What happened here?"

The two younger men glanced up. "Ask Firaloy," Meleas said briefly. He cast a quick look over his shoulder, as if someone might have overheard him.

Jazen raised his eyebrows. Ask Firaloy, indeed. Firaloy, the aged, bemused taleteller?

Well. Why *not* ask Firaloy, indeed.

Firaloy kept his gaze on the map, tracing an invisible path with his fingertip, his thin lips moving silently. Jazen waited for the space of several breaths.

"He won't answer," Vettazen said, behind him. "He's busy. You could ask him later."

"Or, perhaps, I could ask you now?"

"No," she said briskly. "I'm busy too. You can help, you know, if you'll stand right over there and hold this beast out of my way." With that she put the mare's reins in his hands and pointed to a clear space some yards away.

"But what are you *doing*?" Jazen began. But she gave him a light push, and he found himself watching the four of them from a distance as they trotted back and forth between Firaloy with his map and various spots the old man indicated. The mare investigated him, too, but he had nothing to give her and she quickly lost interest in him.

"Well," he muttered philosophically, "at least you're all consistent." He resigned himself to simple observation.

After a while he began to see a pattern to their movements, and amused himself attempting to predict where Meleas, Adri-nes, and Vettazen would go next. They trotted from place to place, checking position with Firaloy, picking up stones and looking beneath them and then coming back and going out again in a different direction. There was never anything at all under the rocks.

Finally Adri-nes, carefully shifting a small pyramid of debris, yipped in triumph. Firaloy called a halt, and the three searchers returned to him. Jazen watched, puzzled. They did have something, after all, little flimsy stuff, like cloth almost, but too thin. Vettazen waved him over to see.

It was thinner, more fragile than parchment, covered with thin brown marks. Jazen held it between his fingertips; the wind caught at it and tore it half out of his hand.

"Careful!" Firaloy admonished. "It's paper. Amazing, simply amazing, that it's lasted so long. You've done very well indeed, Adri-nes."

"What use is it?" Jazen asked, still confused.

"It's something the Yaan Maat used. You are holding a genuine artifact of the Great War—"

"*What?*" He let go as if the fragile stuff burned. Unfortunately it stuck to his fingers, and he shook his hand frantically, trying to get rid of it. The other four yelled at once, trying to rescue it.

"Will you please calm down?" Adri-nes said through his teeth, protecting his discovery from further mishandling.

"How—how do you know it was—" Jazen began, trying to rub the feel of the stuff off his hand.

Firaloy sighed. "This place our maps call the Wasted Lands, and your friends in Smattac call the Burned Lands, was once the Yaan Maat city of Heza. Somewhere near this spot was the house of one of their great lords. I had hoped to find more than this, particularly considering the story your aleman told. I suspect he was exaggerating, or perhaps took a different route.

We can see clearly the effect of the final battle here, however."

He waved his hand around him. Jazen glanced quickly at the black and yellow and white landscape, and then his attention was drawn back to the scrap of paper, as if to a snake. This place was not, indeed, as Tadeus had told of it. Where was the fountain? The blood? But at least there was the paper—

"What are those marks on it?"

"Those marks—" Adri-nes stopped, looked at him oddly. "They're writing. Don't you know what writing is?"

"I've seen it," Jazen said. "What's it for?"

Tiralay had shown him once, one night late in her father's room of business. Jazen felt no particular shame that he could not understand the marks on it; only Tadeus, and perhaps another of the elders, could read a little.

Vettazen raised one eyebrow. "You don't know?"

Meleas, standing behind Jazen, muttered, "That does it. She'll have you reading in a week."

"What for?" Jazen muttered back, baffled.

"That's what she *does*," Meleas returned. "You'll see."

The paper seemed to be all that Vettazen and Firaloy wanted from the dead city. The party spent the night in a dry camp among the rubble of the square, suffering from dreams. The next day they moved out and across the Burned Lands, south toward Mirlacca.

The land changed. Now there were the bones Tadeus had described, crumbling to black, rotten ooze under the animals' feet. They disliked it, throwing up their heads and picking their hooves up gingerly, spooking at the wind. Now, too, there were pieces of rusted, old-fashioned armor. The urge to examine them and see how they were made was easy to ignore.

It was all a battlefield, Firaloy said, riding beside Jazen that morning. The old man nodded to a skull, kicked loose and rolling by the roan mule. *All this place. Here was the last great battle between men and demons, where the Yaan Maat stood defiant, and the men who learned their demon magic turned it against them. Never before, and never again, will all humankind be so united as they were then. As they are now, lying dead on this field.*

Not even ravens circled the Burned Lands.

The great dukes of the north came down with their armies, each of them ten thousand men in armor that gleamed, banners that glowed. Mirlacca's duke—he was but a duke then; he was Emperor after, taking back the throne—brought his army too. The lean men of the desert came, the soft men of the south and west. They all came. They all fought. They all died. And more came, and more.

After humankind finally defeated the Yaan Maat, they fell upon each other, until there were only a few left, and chief among them was the Duke of Mirlacca, who named himself Emperor and placed a crown upon his own head.

That was two hundred years and more ago since they broke the back of the demon lords, but the bones still lie in the Burned Lands, and no one has the heart to claim them.

How could they tell, Jazen wondered, if the bones came from a man killed by demon magic, or by the followers of an ambitious duke? Two hundred years later, the skulls were sightless either way.

What troubled him more was the thought that their kin had left them here in this land, in a place where grass did not grow or insects sing, where the mules and horses kept their heads high and moved quickly, eager to get away. They had kin, all of them, they must have had. And they left them, as if cursed.

Looking about him, Jazen could see bones, white slivers stark against ratted, sickly grass everywhere, as if the dead had not even the grace to sink back into the land. Not even the earth had wanted them.

He felt a sudden kinship to the bones.

That night they found a well in the middle of nowhere, and trusted the animals to tell them the water was pure, and drank it gratefully.

Seven more days it took them to travel through the Burned Lands and out again to living fields, and then they came to Hipsola, as if they had gone in circles and returned to their beginning. It looked like Smattac, down to the well in the village square; there was a forge, a wide, dusty main street defined by two ruts, bordered by trees, even a man recommending an alehouse. Jazen suffered a stab of homesickness; then he saw the forgemaster, a twisted, small man, and remembered Belzec.

They swung down in the street, and a wisp of a child appeared to lead the animals away.

Inside, the alehouse looked like Tadeus' too, so much so that Jazen was startled to see a young man instead of Tiralay coming forward to serve him. That reminded him of his last sight of her, testing his coin. He had money enough, barely, to pay for a meal, he thought. Vettazen watched him fingering his pouch uncertainly. He wasn't sure how far away Mirlacca was, exactly, but he would have to eat when he got there, and there wasn't much . . .

"Put it away, boy," she said comfortably. "Adri-nes, Meleas, now you. I suppose you eat as much as they do. You can't eat much more, lords know."

She seemed to mean it. Jazen looked uncertainly from her to Adri-nes, who was already reaching for a bread bowl, and Meleas, who patiently waited his turn, and Firaloy. Vettazen nodded again. "Go eat, boy."

The stew was considerably better than trail food; even the hollowed-out loaves of bread in which it was served were still soft inside. Jazen finished three of them before realizing he was full at last. He looked up to find Vettazen observing him, eyebrow lifted. "Perhaps I was wrong about that."

Jazen blushed. Vettazen laughed.

That night, uncomfortably sharing a musty, low-ceilinged loft with the two younger men, Jazen stared at the roof beams and tried to imagine Mirlacca. "What's it like?" he said at last, frustrated.

Adri-nes groaned and pulled a corner of blanket over his head. Meleas, who seemed to know what Jazen meant, said, "Mirlacca? It's a city."

"As big as the city in the Burned Lands?" Jazen could not imagine a place so huge as that, alive. Filled with people moving about, roaring with the sounds of life.

Adri-nes snorted.

"Much larger," Meleas said. "Much, much larger."

"It can't be," Jazen protested. "How could so many people

live in one place? They couldn't raise enough to feed themselves."

"They trade," Meleas said. "That's what makes it a city."

"That and the Emperor," Adri-nes added, finally giving up and coming out from under his blanket. "The Emperor makes a difference."

"*You* would think so." Meleas was not really agreeing, Jazen thought. There was the mildest edge in his tone. "Because of the Emperor, there's the palace, of course. It does take up quite a bit of room. And all the court, buzzing around, vying for precedence and influence.

"But more important than that is the Great Market, and all the lesser markets. Farmers bring in grain and animals from miles around, and merchants from all over the empire, and even farther, bring finished cloth and jewels, weapons and pottery, perfumes, spices—"

"Everything you would expect to find in a market, in short." Adri-nes was, perhaps, making a bit too much of his boredom. "Are we going to recount the wonders of Mirlacca all night?"

"I wouldn't know what to expect to find in a market such as that," Jazen said. He had decided long ago that there was no point in pretending to more sophistication than he actually possessed; better to display his ignorance and have it cured than try to hide it and have it exposed.

"Surely you had a market in—what was the name of that place?"

"Smattac. And yes, there was a market there." It seemed very small now, and very long ago since he had walked through the square of Smattac, carrying a yoke across his neck. "Every hand of days, the season market, for new crops. And once in fall and once in spring, the peddlers come." They would be coming soon, in fact, with their hand-drawn carts and shabby goods, setting up around the well, vying for custom. Tiralay would go from one cart to the next, laughing, teasing the young men into buying her ribbons and needles, a length of cloth or a pretty toy—

"The Great Market is open all the time, not just once every five days. The lesser markets too, though of course the caravans from farther out, the duchies and the other lands, come mostly in the fall.

"Mirlacca is a lovely city. It has gardens, flowers. The palace. Great houses and lesser ones."

"Fountains," Adri-nes added sourly. "Don't forget the fountains."

"Well, yes." Meleas sighed. "There are the fountains."

"He'll find out about the fountains soon enough," Adri-nes said. "Unless you talk all night. And then you get to explain to Vettazen and Firaloy why we start late in the morning."

"I suppose he's right," Meleas agreed, smothering a yawn.

"How long before we get there?" Jazen asked, feeling dazzled.

"Who knows," Adri-nes muttered.

Meleas only snored.

Chapter 6

A week later Jazen was beginning to get used to the stretch and pull of new muscles, and the roan mule seemed resigned to its live burden as well. He was getting used to the idea that Firaloy would never really notice him, that Vettazen made a good morning-stew, that Adri-nes was quick and impatient, and Meleas was tolerant and quiet.

He was also getting used to the idea that they were all interested in magic. In demons.

No one else had ever spoken of demons so easily in Jazen's hearing. He listened intently, waiting for the tales told in Smattac about demonspawned babes left behind to grow up and work evil on trusting humans, about men who never even knew they were demons until the day the demons flared up and took control, about demons who flitted from life to life, eating humans from the soul out until they crumpled and fell to dust. In Smattac, such tales were told quietly, late at night, where the light from the fireplace licked at the faces of the storytellers, each in turn, one by one, adding stories to the stories, speaking too softly, they thought, for a young boy to hear. They would tell their tales and glance into the shadows, and he would wiggle back from their seeking eyes, denying them.

Firaloy told no such stories.

He told history.

The Yaan Maat first appeared, to the best of our knowledge, six hundred years ago. We do not know to this day where they came from, though it is suspected their nation must be much like ours. Still, before the Yaan Maat, we had only the small magics of the herb witch, the seekers and healers. The Yaan Maat came to us and brought their magic with them, and for four hundred years we struggled to survive long enough to learn their magic and defeat them.

Chen Mayaus was the first to discover the link between the souls of the Yaan Maat and the mataal, the flat ovals and discs in which they live in between possessing humankind. It is said he managed to destroy a handful of mataals before the Yaan Maat found him and took him, a hundred of them at one time tearing his knowing mind apart.

Lez-nes was the one who fought possession long enough to tell us what it was like to share one's body with a demon—the demon named Quaz. The scholar Chualt speculates in his "On Knowing Demons" that Quaz allowed it because he enjoyed the effect on the family as they realized their brother was living still.

Chualt is, of course, mistaken; we have no evidence that Quaz or any other demon truly realizes the depths of human misery. On most other points, such as the storage of the mataal, he is quite sound.

It was a different kind of story. As Jazen listened during their journey, he realized that there were a number of folk like Firaloy; people who did no work with their hands, but spent all their time studying and arguing about demons.

Once the Great War was over, the magic of the demons was burned, buried, shut away, denied as, for a while, the demons' very existence had been denied. Oh, there were always small things that remained to remind humanity that evil had walked among them, leftover spells and backlash magic; but let any man, any woman practice magic, true magic, strong magic, and they were like to burn.

Only now could those like Firaloy, under the guise of history, seek out magic, and Jazen could not help but wonder why.

Now we are in a time where those who call themselves wise laugh at the idea of magic. They call students of the Yaan Maat fools, frauds, charlatans—but it is to us that they come late at night to have their fortunes told, for love potions and poisons.

THE FOUNTAINS OF MIRLACCA

There are those who can provide what they seek, but if they do so too boldly, they run the risk of being named demon....

"Well," said Meleas, riding beside him, "why not?"

Jazen tilted his head. "Why should one run such a risk? If there are no more demons, no more magic, why bother?"

Meleas' lips twisted. "Fair enough. Well, look you. In the great battles, the demons were defeated, right enough, and they left. But what's to say they've all gone? What if they come back, and us without the memory of how to deal with them? We don't know how to defeat demons any more."

Jazen had heard, often, Tadeus deriding Belzec for superstition. Most people in Smattac shared Tadeus' view, even while they told their children stories about abandoned babes, and let them throw stones. This studying, though, made good sense. No one ever said demons never existed, after all, so it was possible that they might still. He wondered what Tadeus would say to that.

He knew the answer Belzec would give to destroying them, though. "You burn them," Jazen said. "Everyone knows that."

Meleas turned white, swallowed hard. Jazen felt a sudden quivering in his skin, as if a chill wind had bitten through his clothes. Meleas was suddenly remote, grim, as if he were seeing something from memory, something that carried more pain and more anger than he could bear. His fair skin was pale, his eyes like chips of blue crystal.

His voice, however, was reasonably steady. "If you burn them, how do you make sure the demon doesn't escape the flames to possess someone else?" he asked. After a while, he went on, "This we know: demons need humankind, but they're not like us. They're . . ." The blond man paused, looking for the right words. The words would not come, but he stumbled on. "Spirits, perhaps. Spirits who are bound to the mataal, until they can find a human host to feed from like a leech. When the host dies, they seek another, or return to the mataal. Or so says Firaloy."

"Destroy the mataal," Jazen said promptly.

"So then they *must* possess a human being."

"Then how *do* you kill a demon?"

Meleas, gazing down the wide path before them, said nothing for a long time. "With magic," he said at last. "Demons are creatures of magic, on magic and on blood they feed, and with magic they can be destroyed."

Jazen licked his lips, driven to ask one more question, a question he wasn't sure he wanted an answer to. It was hard to say the words, hard to address anything to the man riding next to him. "Have you destroyed a demon?" he whispered at last.

Meleas didn't respond for a moment. When he finally turned to look at Jazen, his eyes were burning. "Not yet."

Up ahead, Adri-nes was riding beside Firaloy, quiet for a change as the old man spoke to him.

Jazen swallowed. "Have you ever—seen a demon?"

Meleas nodded jerkily. "Yes. I mean—" He cut himself off, shook his head.

"How can you tell it's a demon, if it's in a human being?"

Meleas drew in a long breath, and then shook his head, repudiating the question. Jazen opened his mouth once more, and Meleas kicked his horse into a canter, leaving Jazen and the roan mule behind.

They were, Jazen decided, all entirely odd.

Six days later the little party broke camp very early, wending their way through a small pass with barely enough light to see the path underneath their animals' hooves. Jazen expected them to stop for an early rest break at one of the farms which came closer and closer together as the soil grew richer, but they pressed on. All of them were tired now. Even Firaloy was silent, hanging grimly on to his saddle; Vettazen kept glancing at the sun, her lips thin, and pushing on.

The land was softer as well as richer here. Jazen had never seen so many fields under cultivation at once; the farms were scattered, houses standing alone in the middle of the fields instead of all together in one place. The crops were tall and green. The houses were neat and tidy and whitewashed, sparkling in the sunlight with roofs of gray or red stone. There was more traffic on the road, too: people coming the other way, on horses, in carts drawn by oxen, men and women dressed in the same colors Firaloy and Vettazen wore, children in short tunics running back and forth, getting in the way. A little girl who looked very much like Eri Weaver's-daughter pulled away from her mother's hand and stood in the middle of the road, under the roan mule's nose, shrieking.

The mule tossed its head and brayed.

The child, who had just noticed the mass of animal and man bearing down on her, screamed in real fright this time, echoed by her mother. Jazen sawed frantically on the reins. The mule, who had long since stopped, casually snapped the reins out of his rider's hands and brayed again, indignant, before lowering his head to rub an abused mouth against a foreleg.

The mother ran up to snatch her child out of impending danger. The drivers of the three carts backed up behind her added their curses to the tumult. Jazen, with no way to move the mule—who was in no case inclined to move anyway—kicked uselessly at the slack bags hanging at its sides, turned red, and wished himself anyplace but on this road. The rest of his party, the older couple and the two young men, were on the other side of the carts, staring back at Jazen as if wondering why he was still sitting there. Finally he slid off the mule, grabbed the cheekpiece of the bridle, and hauled the beast off to the side of the road so the carts could pass. The mule chose to cooperate.

Vettazen glanced at the sky, shook her head, and spoke sharply to Adri-nes, who trotted over to Jazen, dismounted, and scrambled in the mule's saddlebags.

"Extra set of reins," he explained. "Next time you do this, but Vettazen is upset. She wants to get moving."

Jazen watched as Adri-nes made quick, competent work of replacing the leather. "Why such a hurry?"

"Got to get there before noon, or we won't be able to water the animals. Don't worry about it, we'll make it."

"To Mirlacca? Why won't we—" But Adri-nes was already mounted again, wheeling his horse back up the road, and Jazen had no choice but to scramble back up on the mule before the animal took it into its head that it was being left behind. Jazen was more respectful, now, of how he tried to guide it.

The road twisted and turned, the houses becoming fewer, then suddenly more numerous as the hills rolled and softened into yet another valley.

One more turn, past one more cluster of buildings behind a

high wall, and the road broadened and smoothed under their animals' hooves, and ahead of them lay the city of Mirlacca.

Jazen pulled the roan mule to a stop and stared open-mouthed, his head moving back and forth as he scanned from horizon to horizon of the Miralat Valley. He had thought the city of the Burned Lands was large, compared to Smattac. The city of the Burned Lands would vanish into the smallest of the suburbs of Mirlacca. Smattac . . . Smattac, where he had lived all his life, the measure and template of community . . . Smattac was very small indeed.

Before them spread Mirlacca, Throne City of the Empire of Miralat, stretching from the half-circle of mountains on either side of the pass to the gray sea defining the horizon. The docks were abuzz with ships. The travelers were too far, too high to see the people who must be there. All he could grasp was the size and number of the buildings spread out below him everywhere he looked; they could not even be contained by the city walls. Outside their protection, houses huddled, trailed into the valley. A few of the taller buildings in the center of the city were of golden, weathered stone. Most were paler, newer. The new construction gleamed.

The city was built on hills; miles across the valley from the party's vantage point a golden dome caught the noonday sun and shone like one in a fairy tale. "Emperor's palace," Meleas said laconically.

The mule started moving again. Jazen let the reins lie slack as he tried to grasp the size of the place. Meleas had told him of markets, and gardens; there were no gardens here, not on this side of the great walls rising up in front of him. They were still high enough to look down into the city, and he could see the buildings crouched close together, and an almost visible odor arose from them. As they moved down the trail to the main road, the wall came closer and closer until, abruptly, Jazen was too close to see anything but the wall itself.

Ahead of the travelers a coordinated troop of a dozen riders in quilted tunics of yellow and purple rode in double file, clearing a path in front of a sedan chair borne by four men. The chair passed so close to Jazen that he could have reached out and touched the silk panels, tied closed to conceal the occupant of the chair. The bearers were bald except for a single braid of hair in the center of their skulls, and wore only loincloths. Their bodies, tawny and glistening in the noonday sun, were muscled like Belzec's, only smoother, and without scars.

The opening closed up behind the rear guard, and Jazen turned to see Vettazen looking both irritated and resigned. "We're not going to make it," he heard her mutter.

The little party continued to force its way through the crowds and up to the great gate.

The Great Eastern Gate of Mirlacca stretched three times Jazen's height. It was made of timbers hewn from whole trees and bound together by iron bands, hinged to solid stone walls. He found himself wondering how they had been forged, and if even Belzec, who called himself a master blacksmith, could imagine how to handle so much metal, how to shape it to his will. They passed a party of guards, standing lazy in the sun, and proceeded into the shade past the doors.

The walls were nearly as thick as they were tall. The shade was a welcome relief. For all the traffic between the walls, the roadway here was free of debris; the animals' hooves rang cleanly on the flagstones. They passed over a neat row of holes; Jazen looked up to see a lattice of nails the size of his fist, with wickedly sharp points, hanging over his head. He kicked the mule forward, crowding up on Meleas, to get out from under it.

Abruptly, they broke out on the other side of the wall, inside the city. Ahead of them, a wide plaza stretched, oddly empty considering the fountain that played cheerfully in its center. The horses, scenting water, picked up their pace. Jazen was startled to see all four of his companions steer their animals away from the fountain and down a broad street bounded by the awnings of shops and merchanters.

"Why aren't we stopping?" Jazen asked Meleas. "Can't we get a drink here?"

Meleas glanced at the sky, imitating the look that Vettazen had been giving the skies for the past two hours. "Not now," he said. "In a while. We might as well go home first."

It made no sense to Jazen. It made no sense to the animals, either, and they had to be physically pulled away from the splashing water as Vettazen led the way down an alley. The roan mule, last as always, ignored its rider and headed for the fountain anyway. Sawing frantically at the reins and casting a frantic eye at the disappearing pack animals, Jazen tried to haul the mule's head around.

He succeeded beyond his wildest dreams when the mule, who had been stretching its head down, bounced back with a startled snort, almost rearing up, and wheeled to follow its companions. Jazen, fighting to remain on the animal's back, caught only a glimpse of a sudden ruby streak in the water. By then the mule was plunging after its fellows, and once again its rider was hanging on for dear life.

"Told you it was too late for a drink," Meleas said, still laconic.

"What in the name of flame—" Jazen gasped, still fighting the mule.

Meleas only shook his head. "Let's go home. Then we'll tell you all about it."

PART 2

Mirlacca

Chapter 7

The fountains of Mirlacca ran with human blood every day at noon.

It had been so for as long as anyone living could remember. All the scrolls said so; indeed, it had been so for two hundred years and more, since the city had been gripped by the terror of the Yaan Maat. Then, one could believe, it would make sense for the fountains, the aqueducts, the sewers, to run red. But even after the Yaan Maat were gone, the fountains gushed forth blood, every day at the same time, all over the city.

Vettazen sr'Islit rolled the scroll up and tapped it thoughtfully against her teeth. The scroll was from Irzlebet, a town west of Mirlacca. It purported to contain spells the side effect of which might be to turn water to blood. It was one of a large pile of messages awaiting her and Firaloy upon their return.

As far as she could tell—and she could tell quite a bit by this time—the "spells" were nothing more than the ravings of a demented mind—perhaps someone seized by a demon and then abandoned by it. Such had been known to occur; for example, the Archives contained an account of a demon who took possession of a human being dying of some loathsome disease. The demon had abandoned his prey almost immediately. There was great debate as to why; since being possessed by a demon invariably debilitated the host in any case, Firaloy held that this case showed that demons were capable of experiencing their hosts' anguish, but wished to inflict it themselves, as a variant to Chualt's theory about the demon Quaz. Chezayot, of the desert kingdom of Elzael, scoffed at this theory, asserting that the particular human merely "tasted bad" to its predator.

Vettazen herself held no opinion either way, while recognizing that Chezayot's theory at least had potential; if humans could be made to "taste bad," perhaps demons could be discouraged from possessing them at all.

That was neither here nor there. She made a mental note to have Adri-nes inscribe one of the simpler-looking spells from the descriptions, perhaps substituting a more modern formula. It should be well within his capability, as long as he wasn't distracted by women or politics. Meleas could bundle up the rest of the scrolls and deliver them to the others in the city.

That left Jazen. Neesen said the boy had talent, and Vettazen had felt it herself. But he was a complete innocent in the clutches of Adri-nes and Meleas. It was a good thing the two of them were basically decent most of the time.

Vettazen shook her head, looking around the upper room of the house. It stretched the whole length of the building and half its width. The inner wall was covered with cabinets and shelves, the floor reasonably clear but for the tables, the chairs, the empty birdcage. No one had been in here for months, and it showed.

It was dusty, motes dancing in the last rays of sunlight shafting through the high windows under the eaves. A film of gray coated the table in the middle of the room, the bookshelves, the apparatus stacked carefully on the working shelves. A couple of webs stretched in the corners.

She hated housework. Perhaps that would be a use for the boy, at least until Firaloy could determine the source of the power in him. That it was there, not even Meleas, usually blind to potential in human beings, could deny. Neesen had been right about him, of course. There was talent there.

She'd been pleased and surprised when he'd followed them from—what was the name of that flameless place, Smattac? The people of the border towns were insular, narrow-minded, and suspicious of strangers; it was odd that the boy had the courage to walk away.

Firaloy took it for granted. He was too busy combing through the bits and scraps of information they had gathered to notice if they had picked up a whole troupe of hangers-on and farrier's boys. Even now he was oblivious to the dust, seated at his own table on the other side of the room, eagerly examining the broken chips of a mataal with an unusual pattern found in the Burned Lands. The boys had carried their luggage upstairs, dumped it in a pile beside the door, and gone downstairs to the kitchen to reacquaint themselves, in the case of Meleas and Adri-nes, and to meet, in Jazen's case, Rache-who-cooked. Neither Firaloy nor Vettazen had bothered to unpack. There would be time enough for that later, after all.

Reluctantly, Vettazen admitted that there was more to work on than could be done in one day, or many days. Meeting with the rest to look over the pickings, see what the situation was at Court, see if that merchanter was yet inclined to lower his price on the place in the Street of Jewelers. Best to get the clothing aired out, and find a place for Jazen to sleep, at least; Rache would have food ready, and like as not they would all look to their beds immediately after, even the young ones. It had been a long trip.

The pile of messages and packages scooped up from the table in the front room of the house needed attention, too. There had been at least one silk-wrapped packet. Vettazen regarded the pile now in front of her and stifled a yawn.

If she started reading silk, she'd feel obligated to take care of things immediately, at least to eliminate the trivial things. The messages and pleadings from the nobles, seeking magical assistance in their petty romantic and political maneuverings—assistance never publicly acknowledged, gods knew—could wait, at least until tomorrow.

First things first, and the first thing should be finding a place for the boy to sleep. Or—no, surely Adri-nes and Meleas would make sure he had a bath first.

He would need clothing, too. He couldn't wear that ragged tunic here, not if he lived in this house.

It was like having a child of her own, she thought. She and Firaloy had never had children; they acquired them instead—adopting, fostering—polished them somewhat, sent them out into the world. Some of them had real talent; years ago, one of the first, a little girl, had stayed with them three years before going on to study with Chezayot. Firaloy had been disgusted, but even he had to acknowledge that the girl's gifts in foreseeing were beyond their scope, and Chezayot was better equipped to teach her.

Unfortunately, she had learned too well and not well enough to see in air and water, and had been burned for a demon in the desert-town riots a year later. Chezayot had barely escaped with his life. Since then, Vettazen had tried to convince the southerner to come to Mirlacca and stay with them, but he was nearly as stubborn as Firaloy himself. He liked his own home, his own place. They were the same reasons Firaloy had given when Chezayot invited them to move south.

Vettazen sighed. She was too old to take on another child at her age. The boy Jazen barely had any manners—he still glared sometimes from underneath that mop of dark hair, as if he expected them all to turn on him.

She could trust Meleas and Adri-nes, at least, to civilize him, if he lived long enough under their attentions. Perhaps he might even teach them a lesson or two. In any case she had no intention of mothering the boy. Just now she had more important things on her mind. She had a guild to create.

The three young men sat on the edge of the Western Fountain, gnawing on hot-meat sticks and watching the life of Mirlacca go by. It was edging into winter, a season, so they said, of bitter cold and snows as tall as the city walls. In two months, Jazen had learned much more about the people who had taken him in: that the neighbors scorned them as false mystics and seers; that a small but steady trickle of strangers regularly came to visit Vettazen behind closed doors, often leaving after an hour with troubled looks on their faces; that Firaloy spent great sums of money on books and scrolls, and had a wide correspondence; that all of them spent much time seriously discussing magic. Adri-nes had even shown him some verses he claimed were spells he'd written, and Vettazen seized on them as primers in her ongoing efforts to teach Jazen to read. Nothing mystical ever happened as Jazen stumbled his way through the words scratched into the wax tablets, but they all seemed quite serious about it.

THE FOUNTAINS OF MIRLACCA

He, for his part, still had not mentioned how he saw imps in flames. He wasn't sure yet whether they were all mad or not. The fact that they accepted him, offered him friendship, food and clothes for his back, and a roof over his head, was important—but if they were all as crazy as rumor made them out to be, it could all vanish in an instant, and they might consider him as mad as themselves, or worse, ask him to prove what he saw. He wasn't sure he could. He had never really been sure the imps were real.

And if they weren't, that *did* make him as mad as they might be. He was not yet prepared to pay in that coin; what he saw in the flames was still too personal. Instead he did whatever small tasks Rache gave him. He suspected he was doing a goodly share of Adri-nes' and Meleas' work too, but all of it together was easier than a single day at Belzec's forge, and no one offered to beat him. Therefore, he was perfectly happy with this odd crew, for however long the situation lasted.

"That's the chief cook in the Earl of Sillamar's house," Adri-nes said, swinging one leg idly. The pointed toe of his leather slipper scuffed at the seed-heads of grass tufting from the base of the fountain. "He makes a very good chicken-in-wine."

"Your brother says, no doubt." Meleas was not impressed. Jazen was—though less now than he had been the day he'd found out Adri-nes was a scion of a noble, albeit minor, house.

"Who is the Earl of Sillamar, and what does your brother have to do with it?" Jazen swallowed a mouthful of meat. "I didn't know you had a brother," he added after a moment.

Adri-nes grinned merrily. "Oh, I have a dozen brothers, all older than I am. Why do you think they'd let me study with Firaloy? They barely know I'm gone. And as for who the earl is, well, he's the earl. Of Sillamar."

"And what is Sillamar?" Jazen asked obediently. In the three months since their arrival in Mirlacca, he had become used to Adri-nes' habit of leading him down the fool's path. He absorbed the information the other man let fall in dribs and drabs, since it was mostly reliable.

The Western Fountain marked the center of the Great Western Square—a great, thick stone bowl and central pillar with three jets of water arcing out of the top. The square itself was bounded by the public baths on one side, food shops—the source of the meat sticks—on another, with aromatic spices and herbs sold on the remaining two sides. Each shop had two shutters, one opening downward to display the shopkeeper's wares, the other opening upward to provide shade; banners or flags or strips of colored cloth hanging from the top shutter provided color and light. A door at the side of each shop led inside, if the merchant was inclined to try to lure the customer inside. The square was one of Jazen's favorite places in the city. The three young men came here often, and often sat, and watched, and enjoyed the sweet smells. The square reminded Jazen of a hive, with human bees crowded in with each other, crawling over and around one another, each busy about its own essential business.

It was said that the world passed through the Great Squares of Mirlacca. One could see citizens of a hundred cities here, hear two dozen languages. Even the pack animals were strange sometimes, long-necked humpy things that even Meleas kept clear of. The money-changers argued over coppers and silver and gold in a myriad of coinages—and in forms other than coins, too: little plaques from Elzael, coils of wire from some place even Adri-nes had never heard of, jewels and packets of rare spices. The three friends often sat and speculated about where people came from and why they came, each guess more outrageous than the next. Jazen was growing used to the idea that even the most outrageous guesses of all might actually be true.

"Sillamar," he prompted.

Meleas laughed.

Adri-nes merely smiled and waved at a serving-maid. She waved back. "I think you're capable of carrying on this conversation without me," he said, sliding off the rough stone edge of the fountain. "Besides, it's nearly noon."

Noon. Meleas and Jazen both edged off the stone ledge as well, Meleas looking for a likely serving-maid of his own, while Jazen watched the water, enthralled.

The water of Mirlacca came, they said, from underground

rivers, came up clear and clean and cool, ran deep in the fountain, sparkled in the air. It tasted sweet and pure.

And every day, at noon, the fountains of Mirlacca ran red with blood.

Adri-nes and Meleas barely noticed. They had lived with it all their lives. One could tell who was new in the city, it was said, because they drank at noon. Jazen was fascinated. This was real magic, not the silly words Adri-nes strung together, not the framed crystal shield in Vettazen's room, not the dusty books Firaloy pored over; this was real magic, one could feel it sticky on the fingertips, smell it hot and metallic, even taste it if so inclined—and Jazen had once, on a dare. True citizens of Mirlacca saw it every day and barely noticed. Jazen wasn't yet so blasé.

It began sometimes with drops, drops that did not fall from the air but were there, suddenly, spreading from dark red to thin pink in the water, more and more swirling, darker; at other times the sprays of water, bright against the sky, jetted suddenly as if from cut throats, the liquid thick and smelling of metal. In this season, the water along the rim of shaded fountains was often edged with ice, even at noon, and Jazen had watched more than once globs of blood appear underneath, pushing up against the ice, which itself gradually turned red too. It took, mostly, only minutes for all the water to turn. Animals approaching would veer away, as if horrified.

It was water again, always, never more than an hour later. Between one moment and another, the blood would be gone. Jazen watched, trying to catch the moment, and never managed to see the transformation. This time, too, the blood became water again, between one flick of an eyelash and another.

Chapter
8

Jazen looked around. Adri-nes was long gone; Meleas too. He shrugged. There was time to spare. If he went back to the house in the Street of Scribes, Vettazen would likely want to give him more reading lessons or, if she were otherwise occupied, as she often was, she would turn him over to Rache for something to keep him busy. There were more interesting things to do.

He reached down to the pocket in the side of his boot and pulled out the iyiza bundle. There was more that Vettazen had taught him, reading from the old scrolls and books, than she ever knew: there had been a spell there, an old spell from even before the time of the Yaan Maat, that mentioned iyiza. Those words, at least, he had memorized, even if he couldn't read them himself as yet. They had to do with metal, and flames, and this, together with the bundle of metal he had taken from the forge in Smattac, had some time past given him an idea. Adri-nes and Meleas' departure had given him another opportunity to pursue it.

He slid off the wall and stepped around the apprentices and maids lining up to fill buckets for those shops and houses without piped water, heading for a narrow alley beside the baths.

He still didn't know his way around the city as well as his two friends. Every day he ventured farther, saw more, and retreated back to the house to try to assimilate all that he had seen and smelled and tasted and felt. There were parts of the city where guildsmen clustered, working in brass or cloth or

THE FOUNTAINS OF MIRLACCA

leather, jewels or weaving or pottery, wood or stone or glass; there were places where no one worked, but only lived in great houses; there were streets with nothing but alehouses, market streets and little squares near the gates where the produce of the farms outside the city was brought in every morning and spread out on tables for the inspection of the affluent. There were markets for animals, too, birds and sheep and oxen, horses and mules, markets for fodder and for trappings for animals and carriages.

The people of Mirlacca bought the same sorts of things as the people of Smattac, only more and of greater variety. Jazen could spend hours wandering in any one of the markets, marveling at the different kinds of fruits and vegetables, oblivious to his companions' urging to move on, to go elsewhere, to see more. He lingered at the potters' stalls, watching the towers of clay rising like magic from between their hands as the wheels spun, smiling as the towers became vases or goblets or plates. He asked questions of the weavers, making faces at the smells from their vats of dye. He stole samples under the indulgent eye of the cheesemakers. He passed by the pools of the public baths. Once addicted to the experience of warm water and soap, he much preferred a long, luxurious private soak in the bath in the house in the Street of Scribes, with no one to stare at him.

This time, though, he did not pause at the wonders around him, waving only at acquaintances as he passed; he was heading for another corner of the city, one found by accident while wandering alone, a place in some ways that was a bit of home in the middle of Mirlacca.

He could smell it and hear it well before he got there; the tenor clanging of hammers on hollow metal, the scorched aroma of quenched steel. The Street of the Forge, he named it to himself, and never troubled to find out what the people who lived there called it. It didn't matter. From the time he first heard the music of it, his palms had itched for the shaft of the hammer, the arm of the bellows. And there was one there who saw and recognized the hunger in his eyes for what it was. He had to bring his own metal, though; Gilé was a working man, and had no steel to spare for experiments. That was not a problem. The metal, he had.

The iyiza was less a bundle of whisper-thin metal plates and more blade, now, though no one who did not work metal would know the difference. He had tested it in the fire, pounded the different metals into each other, so that now it was a misshapen striped block.

Gilé nodded to him as he slipped behind the broad display board and back to the hearth; there was nothing working just now, and Jazen could have the anvil and hammer to himself while Gilé, balding Gilé with three teeth and the cunningly crafted linked chain of a master metalworker about his neck, haggled with young and old over his edged wares under the three-striped shade of his booth. Gilé made good, workmanlike knives with leather-wrapped hilts for eating, better quality for protection. Selected customers, Jazen knew, were privileged to see and buy the beautiful knives, the slender, keen blades with hilts of etched gold and jewels hidden away in the locked case in the back. Jazen had been permitted to see them, once. Gilé had watched him with narrowed eyes to see if the peasant boy would be moved to snatch away one of his treasures, worth more money than Jazen had seen in his entire life. Instead he had tested the blade, set aside in scorn a particularly elaborate piece to admire instead a relatively plain edge that could shave a baby. After that, Gilé made him free of the forgefire, showed him how to work the metal, heating it, twisting it, melding the plates into one another, notching and reheating it. It was a different kind of forgework than he had ever done before, and he gloried in it.

Meleas and Adri didn't know; it was Jazen's secret, his link to the past, the familiar, with the added bonus of Gilé's genuine admiration for what he could do, and willingness to teach him more.

Even so, Jazen glanced over his shoulder at the burly craftsman before drawing the cherry-edged metal out to place it on the anvil. Out of the corner of his eye, he could see imps dancing in the fire, the same imps who had danced when he made small things for Belzec. The first time he had seen them in Gilé's fire, he thought he was cursed. After a while, he began to wonder if every forgefire held demons, even if only he could see them.

If so, perhaps he, who was supposed to be demon too, could make them work for him. Perhaps his magic was in the iron box of a forge.

He could not remember the meanings of most of the scratches on wax that Vettazen showed him, but he could remember the meaningless sounds of the incantation as her finger traced each line. Now, in the heat of the metal glowing on the anvil, throwing sparks from the blows of his hammer, he could repeat them, saying lines over again where he misremembered, trying to smash the glittering fire-devils or at least catch their wings with the steady hammerfall. The blade stayed red much longer than usual, he thought, and the hiss as he quenched it had all the sounds of protest.

The knife would have a hidden tang, a double edge. He tapped it out with the peen, let it cool, folded it back upon itself, heated it again to the proper color, over and over and over again. Annealing, grinding, hardening, tempering, listening to the metal sing to him . . .

The tapping hammer stretched the length of metal out too, and out, and out three times its length, and he folded it back upon itself and began again, and again, and again, watching the nickel glisten through the steel, before trying for an edge. He was focused on the peen, the hammer, the heat, and the metal, and paid no heed to the passing of time, the movement of Gilé back and forth as he served his customers, the heat of the fire and the aching of his shoulders as he changed hands on the hammer. Once or twice, with the murmured meaningless words, he smashed a demon squarely into the material of the knife, and felt a triumph beyond words. He did not even feel the harsh grin on his face as the weapon took form for him. Not now the heavy blows to force metal into itself, but the loving, endless taps to coax it into a fine edge, finer than anything he had ever done before. His own sweat fell onto the blade and sizzled, and the hammer tapped there too, as if sealing a part of himself within it.

A sudden loud rattle finally broke into his concentration, and he looked up to see Gilé folding the now-empty display shelf up into a wall, pulling a net of metal links down behind it. He straightened, disappointed; one did not work a forgefire in a closed-in place.

Gilé nodded. "I would have let you work on, boy, but 'tis nightfall. Long past time for honest men to go and eat and find their beds. You'll have another chance." He came over and looked at the blade lying on the anvil, picked it up in the tongs and inspected it. "Aye, it has merit. One more session, perhaps, and you'll be hafting it. Will you sell it, then? I might be interested."

"No," Jazen said without thinking, then paused. When he'd stolen the bundle of metal to begin with, he'd planned to sell whatever he could make of it. Now he couldn't understand why he had ever thought such a thing. "But I . . . I cannot give you more than thanks for this." He swept a hand, indicating the anvil, the fire, bellows, tongs, all the accoutrements of the smith.

Gilé smiled, understanding. "Ah, well, you raise me in my customers' eyes. There's nothing the lordlings like more than to see their inferiors sweat for their sake." His voice held equal parts of humor and irony. "They think you work for me. And you might, you know, if you wished it. Do you?"

Jazen looked at the smith, holding his breath as he considered. Gilé was not Belzec. More, Gilé did not know he had no family, and even if he did, family and clan seemed to count much less here than in Smattac.

But there was Vettazen, and Firaloy, and even Adri-nes and Meleas, and there was much to see yet of the city of Mirlacca. If he 'prenticed now, he would never see a hundredth part of it.

"I thank you," he said humbly, wiping the moisture from his forehead and putting his tools away. "But I have . . . obligations elsewhere."

Gilé nodded philosophically. "As you say, boy. Though I swear you must have a strange master, who lets you go from his own forge to work at another man's." He chuckled at Jazen's reflexive jerk of alarm. "No, peace, I'll ask no questions. And I hope you do come and finish your pretty work here, and perhaps lure a few more customers to me. But not

THE FOUNTAINS OF MIRLACCA

tonight, boy. And not tomorrow, either. I have work of my own to do, to make more of this and that for their silver and copper. Go now, get you home. It's late."

It *was* late. Jazen had never been out after dark in the city by himself. Always before he had been with Adri-nes or Meleas or both, sometimes exploring the shadows between the street torches and sometimes walking escort for Vettazen or Firaloy to some house or other. He was not, exactly, afraid of the dark, but he did not need tales from Adri-nes or the more reliable, if drier, reports from Meleas to know trouble could lurk there. He paused in the street before Gilé's shop to get his bearings, and was startled to see how different the quarter appeared in the deepening dusk. The Street of the Forge boasted only one torch, at the end that terminated in the square. He headed that way, trying to look as if he knew where he was going.

The square held a fountain too, and at this hour the only other living thing was a dog, carrying a dead rat in its mouth and warning him away with a growl before slinking into an alley. Jazen paused to sniff the water before dousing his head and neck to cool himself—it was water still, of course. The evening breeze caused a pleasant chill on his skin, and he briefly considered stripping himself and dousing his entire body—but night or not, it was still a public square, and while Adri-nes, drunk, might do such a thing on a dare, he, Jazen, was much too aware of what others might think—or do to him as a result of their thinking. Sighing, he sniffed the breeze deeply. It carried the sharp, foul taint of the tanners' quarter in the southwest part of the city. He turned his back to it and took the widest street available, picking and choosing his way among the twisted, narrow ways that led eastward.

Chapter
9

The kitchen at the back of the first floor of the house on the Street of Scribes was large enough to hold a great-table; all six of the household ate there without respect to position. Rache was setting out meat and bread when Jazen entered. She threw him a sour look; the housekeeper was not known to favor any of the young men. Doubtless Jazen had delayed supper again.

Firaloy was already seated at the head of the great-table, and gave him a vague nod. Adri-nes, dressed in his best tunic, came down the steep flight of stairs from the second floor, followed by Meleas.

"Where did you go?" Meleas inquired as they seated themselves on the long bench.

"Somewhere entertaining, no doubt," Adri-nes said, his nose wrinkling delicately.

"Eat quickly and clean up," came Vettazen's voice, behind them. "I'll want you to come with me this evening."

The three young men looked up, startled. "Late for visiting, isn't it, my lady?" Adri-nes said, clearly reluctant to participate in whatever Vettazen had in mind.

Vettazen smiled. "Do I gather you have other plans for the evening?"

Adri-nes hesitated, his fingers brushing the fine fabric of his sleeve. "Well, I did have a previous engagement . . ."

"You need not come. Meleas and Jazen will do as well, I think."

Adri-nes nodded and settled down to eat, evidently satisfied. Meleas, as usual, said nothing. Jazen paused in the act of

THE FOUNTAINS OF MIRLACCA 79

pulling apart a piece of bread. "Where are we going?" he asked, dipping the raw brown edge into the gravy swimming in the platter.

"To the palace." Vettazen gathered up her skirts and settled in the great-chair, a match for Firaloy's, at the other end of the table from her husband.

Adri-nes choked on a mouthful of bread; Jazen froze, wide-eyed. Meleas continued to methodically chew and swallow, but even he was watching Vettazen now.

"I am summoned by Lord Lasvennat," she said unconcernedly. "He asks to know what we learned on our journey, and if there is aught we can do for the Heir. And I, in turn, will ask about the house we are promised."

"Lasvennat? The Emperor's Heir?" Adri-nes sputtered. "In the palace? The *Emperor's* palace?"

Vettazen raised an eyebrow. "Aye. As Lasvennat has none of his own, and the Emperor's Heir lives nowhere else. But you were otherwise occupied this evening, as I recall; I wouldn't dream of keeping you from some previous appointment."

"I can break it," Adri-nes said.

"There's no need. Jazen and Meleas are escort enough; it's not so very far."

"But at night . . ." Adri-nes protested, as if seeing some great opportunity slipping from his grasp. "You'll need all of us. For consequence."

Vettazen smiled. "Oh, I think two will be enough. It's not as if we have such great importance, after all."

"You won't if you don't assume it." From protest, the dark-haired young man had gone to his feet, to argument. "My lady, you need all of us. More, even."

She shook her head, decisive. "Not this night. Besides, there's the chance we'll cross your oldest brother's path, and that I think would not be best for either of you. Next time, perhaps." The last was offered with a hint of sympathy for Adri-nes' disappointment. "Finish up, you two," she went on, directing her words to Meleas and Jazen. "And find Jazen a good tunic, not something with holes burned in it. We may not have consequence, but we have whole clothes, at least."

Jazen accepted the gentle rebuke in a daze. The palace? The

place where the Emperor lived? He had seen it, from a distance—from across the great square. The three had not dared venture closer to the guardsmen at the gates. Now *he* was going to enter those gates? Enter the palace walls himself?

Meleas nudged him, glanced sidewise at the homely plate before him with its rapidly cooling pool of gravy and grease, with carrots and green things poking up between the chunks of beef. Jazen fell to it, ravenous, and wiped the last bit of gravy from the corner of his mouth just as Meleas finished his own meal. "Go clean up," Meleas told him. "I'll get your clothing."

The water-house took up nearly a third of the small garden. It was divided into two parts, the larger for bathing, the smaller for elimination. The bathing side had two large tubs, both of which could be used either for bathing or washing clothes. Jazen stripped and twisted the handle on the pipe overhead.

The water was cool, but not icy, as the stream beside Smattac had been. The first time Vettazen had told him to get a bath he'd been shocked, not certain what to do. He'd been sure he'd die of it, until Meleas pointed out that it wasn't so different, after all, than swimming in a river. But rivers never had metal tanks with fires under them to heat the water. Jazen sank into the long tub, immersing himself with a sigh of pleasure and scrubbed away the sweat and stink of the forgefire.

"Leave yourself some hide to wear," Meleas advised, coming in and placing a pile of clothing on the bench running along the side of the room. "And be quick about it. We'd not do well to be late."

Meleas, always impeccably neat in any case, had already changed, to a dark red tunic and black hose, with a particolored red and black surcoat over all.

"Will we see the Emperor?" Jazen asked, sloshing water over himself to rinse the soap away. He tried to imagine what the Emperor, legendary ruler, pinnacle of power, must look like. Back in Smattac, he had barely been aware that such a thing as an emperor existed. Here, the six-starred seal of the imperial house was everywhere, and wealth and power were a pervasive presence in the city. The Emperor was supposed to be a man like other men; Jazen couldn't see how that was possible.

"I doubt it," Meleas said laconically. "I hear he has a cold."

He did not wait for a reply. Jazen stepped out of the tub and let the water drain away, reached for a towel and dried himself off, throwing the towel onto a bench in sudden panic that he was delaying matters. The clothing left for him was of the same style as Meleas', but in dark yellow and blue. He pulled it on and ran out the door, still tugging a low boot on one foot as he went.

Meleas, waiting for him in the front room, handed him a traveler's torch, identical to the one Meleas carried himself. Jazen took it, straightened his tunic, and looked around for Vettazen.

Adri-nes watched, moping, then brightened suddenly. "You'll need a knife," he said. "Something besides that meat cutter of yours—wait." Moments later he came dashing back into the room, carrying a belt with a scabbard.

"Flames," Jazen said, awed, as he tucked the unlit torch under one arm to draw a long fighting knife partway from its sheath. The blade was twice as long as the one he was crafting at Gilés. "It's almost a sword."

Adri-nes shook his head. "No, no, you use it *with* a sword. But you don't need that—you couldn't use it anyway. You've just got to have *something* if you're going to the palace. Here, give me that torch and put it on . . . hurry, here comes Vettazen."

Jazen wanted to ask Adri more, about where they were going, who they would see, how he should act, whether they would enter the palace through the Great Gate—Adri would know these things, he had noble blood, he could advise them, surely—but there was no time.

Vettazen was coming down the stairs, one hand against the wall to keep from tripping. She had changed her accustomed split skirt and overblouse for a long blue dress, belted at the waist with a wide strip of leather worked with brass buttons. She looked the three of them over, making no comment, but Jazen finally got the belt properly in place and looked up triumphant, and her lips curved briefly.

"Very well, my brave boys, let us go and impress them all, shall we? And Adri, keep the hearth warm for us."

Even Meleas flashed a smile at that one.

Jazen had hoped that the haughty guardsmen at the Great Gate would stand aside and bow as Vettazen went by. He was disappointed. The three of them walked ever upward to the square, and then, not even approaching the mustachioed, silk-clad armsmen, followed a mostly empty street nearly half a mile along the palace wall. At last they came to another entrance in the stone wall, larger but not otherwise more imposing than the door to the house on the Street of Scribes, without any guards at all.

Jazen looked to Meleas, confused, but Vettazen brushed past him and knocked hard against the plain, unpainted wooden panels. The blond man looked unperturbed, but then, he always did.

Within the space of three breaths, the door had creaked open. A tall shadow stood in the opening. Jazen flinched, his hand straying to the hilt of the scabbarded knife.

"Vettazen sr'Islit to see Lord Lasvennat," she said briskly.

The shadow moved aside at once, and she marched in, followed by a dour Meleas and a gawking Jazen.

The Great Palace of Mirlacca was, at first glance, not even as impressive as the house they lived in. It seemed to consist of a room too small to hold four people.

The shadow resolved itself into an armed porter, head and shoulders taller than either Jazen or Meleas; when he held out his hand for their weapons, Jazen followed Meleas' lead by meekly surrendering the knife, belt, scabbard and all, hoping only that he would see the harness again before he left. The man wrapped the belt and placed the whole on a shelf behind himself.

The porter made no effort to guide them farther. Vettazen was already heading out a door at the other end of the room, not waiting for her escort to catch up with her. Their footsteps sounded odd, hollow somehow.

The little room turned out to be an anteroom to a long, broad corridor. The floor was tiled with colored stone set in patterns of red and yellow and blue, matching the woven tapestries draping the walls. Tall, narrow pointed windows alternated with bright banners hanging limp, high over their heads. A bird called from far up in the rafters.

They were not the only ones in the hall; men and women and even children in servants' liveries and badges, and others wearing no such livery but no jewels, either, marked their passing by. Jazen saw one young girl in black and white giggling at him, and schooled his expression to match Meleas' blank impassivity.

"Somebody's daughter," Meleas said out of the corner of his mouth. "Don't smile at her."

Jazen had no idea that a building could be so large. The hallway seemed to go on forever, broken only by doors, open or closed, equally ignored by Vettazen. Jazen lagged behind more than once to peer at the people, the mysterious things they were doing, and had to run to catch up and ask Meleas what he was seeing.

"Have no idea," he responded laconically. "Never been here before, myself."

Ahead of them, Vettazen chuckled.

Vettazen knew where she was going. After ten minutes of walking, or fifty banners, she made an abrupt turn and went through another door that looked like all the rest.

The door led to another hallway, with a long spiral staircase. Vettazen proceeded up the stairs without pause. Jazen, who had never even seen stairs before coming to Mirlacca, nearly fell on his face trying to watch where he was putting his feet on the tapering surfaces.

The staircase led to another, smaller corridor at right angles to the first, with more doors. And there were yet more doors, and more corridors, and more stairs, until Jazen was thoroughly bewildered.

Vettazen paused before one more door, one painted blue and gold, with glossy panels trimmed with shallow carvings of flowers. This time, instead of pushing her way through, she knocked softly.

The door was opened silently by a serving-man wearing matching shades of blue and gold—nearly the same colors

Jazen was wearing. Vettazen moved past without speaking and stood in the middle of the room, next to a table polished to a high gloss. The table was empty save for a quill and inkpot and a bell made of jewels and crystal.

A set of double doors, made all of translucent green glass, led out into a garden, with grass and trees and a small fountain bubbling merrily in the middle of it all. Jazen started over to look more closely, enthralled equally by the idea of so much smooth, clear glass and by the idea of a garden growing on what surely must be a rooftop.

Meleas caught at Jazen's sleeve and tugged lightly, indicating the two of them should stand in a corner of the room, beneath a painted panel flanked by plain, unworked curtains of a heavy crimson fabric. The panel showed fantastic creatures, dragons and winged men and great insects, some of which Jazen recognized from tales, apparently having a picnic at the edge of some sylvan river. The images gleamed and sparkled, as if the dust of jewels had been mixed into the paints.

The painting, and the room itself, was lighted by a dozen torches mounted on brass poles, with polished fans behind them reflecting the light upward. Jazen found himself studying the torches rather than the extravagant furnishings they illuminated, trying to figure out how the reflectors were kept free of soot, and so missed the entry of Lord Lasvennat through yet another doorway leading from an inner room.

It could have been no one else; only a lord would wear such lace, worked so fine with threads of gold and silver. Only a lord would wear so many jewels, stitched onto satin and silk and the leather belt that crossed over his chest, or the fashionable, sparkling blue powder in his hair. He glittered as he moved, gathering the light and throwing it back at them in reflections of his grandeur.

"Ah, Mistress sr'Islit. I was wondering when you would grace me with your presence again." He was carrying a sheaf of papers, and set them down in an elegant fan on the table.

It took concentration to look past the gleaming and see a rather ordinary-looking man with hot dark brown eyes, wearing tall heels on his boots to make him eye to eye with Jazen. He had a mole on his left cheekbone, and a long nose, and a

THE FOUNTAINS OF MIRLACCA

quiet voice, his accent precise. He sounded as if he had been trained to sing his words as easily as speak them. He was, Jazen had heard, one of the most powerful men in the empire.

Vettazen did not curtsy, but she did not stand close, either. "My lord."

She didn't particularly like the man, Jazen thought. He wasn't sure how one dared like or dislike someone so high; he glanced at Meleas out of the corner of his eye, not wanting to attract attention by actually moving. Meleas was watching Vettazen and Lasvennat intently.

"I understand you have discovered some small items on your travels which may be of interest," Lasvennat said offhandedly. "Something which may provide diversion for His Highness, perhaps."

"May His Highness continue to enjoy the best of health," Vettazen said, as if it might be a rote response. Then she went on. "We are still examining them. It takes time, as you know, my lord."

The glittering man laughed aloud suddenly. "Time to pass them among your fellow . . . historians, I take it, and for you all to read them and quarrel over the meaning of a symbol or a pen stroke?"

"We would not wish to present something which was not completely understood, my lord."

"And how much more quickly it would go if you only were closer together, had all of your books and scrolls in a single place, accessible to all. Is that it, mistress?"

"Of course it is, my lord. But we make progress; we have found a place that is mostly suitable—"

"Or that most of you think suitable, which is a far different thing, I gather?"

Vettazen smiled slightly. "Of course, my lord."

Jazen found himself holding his breath. He could feel the threat in the air between the two of them. They were engaged in a dangerous dance, and mirrored each other, move for move. He could not understand why; they were speaking of commonplaces, of nothing.

"Well then, let me see the results of your last journey"—he emphasized the adjective with delicate menace—"and perhaps some additional funding may be found." He turned away to the table, as if taking for granted that Vettazen would produce whatever it was that he wanted.

What he got instead was a soft murmur from the woman, a *pop* in the air over the table, and a flare from the three nearest torches. He jumped back, the image of sophistication slipping badly, and spun around to Vettazen, fury in his eyes.

Vettazen murmured again, and moved her hand. The torches flared again, higher, and a small cloud appeared over the table, with miniature lightning crackling within it. Lasvennat turned back in time to see a small deluge soak his sheaf of papers, before cloud, lightning, rain, and papers all disappeared.

The torches continued to roar for some moments before returning to their accustomed levels.

Lasvennat's mouth worked convulsively, and he made three tries to speak before succeeding.

"Was this . . . something you learned on your travels?" he said at last.

"No," Vettazen said composedly. "It's something several of us managed to develop over the past two years. We could probably have done it more quickly, of course, but the post riders are slow in the winter. I am sorry about the papers. We haven't completely defined the extent of the effect, though one of my colleagues in Triez, on the coast, has been working on that. Or at least so he said in his last letter," she added thoughtfully. "Before we left, six months ago."

Jazen stared at her as if a full-sized, flame-breathing dragon had materialized before his eyes. This was what Vettazen and Firaloy collected in those piles of scrolls—collected, learned— and taught? This was not mere history, mere marks on paper. This was real magic, the stuff of witchcraft and demons and stories, worked casually before his very eyes. He remembered the imps dancing in the flame of the forgefire. If this was real, then so were they— The only sound in the room was the crackling of the torches, and the rustling of the lace at his lordship's wrist. Jazen could not tear his gaze away from the short, stout figure of the woman in the center of the room. This was the woman who tried to teach him the sense of marks on paper, who scolded her absent-minded husband for forgetting his medicines, who planned a day's meals with Rache . . . who trafficked with demons. . . .

He stood in the palace, wherein lived the Emperor, who was powerful beyond imagination, in the greatest, richest city that could possibly exist, and he could not move for the terror of this practical house-wife under whose modest roof he had lived for the past two months, who stood innocently in the center of the room facing a wealthy, powerful nobleman without so much as blinking, because she, she commanded the power of *demons*—

He knew Vettazen and Firaloy studied magic; they had said so. But he did not know, did not believe they *worked* it.

The little thunder was, in its way, far more frightening than the imps that danced in his forgefire. Those, after all, had been around all of his life. This, this was *magic*.

He glanced over at Meleas, to see his companion looking at him sidelong. Meleas had not been surprised.

Squeezing his eyes shut, Jazen took a deep breath and then opened them again, determined to remain steady.

"I should like very much to see the working for that," Lasvennat said, his voice nearly back to normal. "It's quite a shame, actually, that it takes so very long to perfect these things."

"Oh, it's far from perfect, my lord. And it's only a minor problem. We hope that it will lead us to a better understanding of the whole phenomenon, of course."

"Of course . . . I can purchase the site you've identified—" Suddenly the nobleman seemed to hear the tension in his own voice.

"I'm very sorry, my lord, but my colleagues wouldn't feel at ease with such an arrangement. They prefer to remain independent of any one lord's favor, much as the guilds are." The balance of power in the room had decisively shifted, from the glittering lord to the plainly dressed woman with her hands folded comfortably over her soft, protruding abdomen.

The lord was silent, the fingers of one hand absently tracing patterns in the dampness remaining on the gloss of the table.

Vettazen was silent too, watching him, bright-eyed.

And she was using that balance to bargain with a nobleman in the palace of the Emperor of Miralat.

And the nobleman was chuckling softly now, rubbing his fingertips together, nodding. Wry. "I trust, then, like a good guildsman, you have set a fair price on this particular example of your research?"

Vettazen inclined her head. She was smiling too, a smile Jazen had never seen before and was not inclined to see again. "It represents a considerable advance on our understanding of weatherwork, my lord, and the shared efforts of many of the best historians of the era."

Beside him, Jazen felt Meleas jerk slightly.

Lasvennat did not appear to take notice of the change in the woman's demeanor. "Well then. The price should be appropriate."

He smiled thinly, reached out for the crystal bell sitting on the table. It was still wet from the demonstration, and he hesitated before grasping the bell to ring it sharply, once.

Before the shrill echo had faded, a young man stepped from behind the wall hangings and came forward, to stand deferentially three paces from the nobleman.

The young man—a boy, really—was at least two hands shorter than Jazen, still gawky and coltish, but in his broad shoulders, not yet filled in, was the promise of more size when he matured. His eyes were the same deep brown of Lasvennat's, his hair unpowdered, straight and raven dark. He had been out in the sun too much recently; his skin was fair and an angry red showed across his face and the backs of his hands. The color was visible up his arms as he gave the nobleman a graceful salute.

The boy was wearing clothes of very good quality, not as fine as Lasvennat's but enviable nonetheless, in soft browns and russets. He showed none of the pain he must be suffering from the rub of his tunic against the burn that presumably covered the rest of his body.

For jewelry he had no more than a plain linked chain of soft gold around his neck. A single link from that chain might buy a good horse and all its harness; Adri-nes had pointed out such chains to Jazen once, saying that bondsmen often wore all their worldly fortunes in such manner. Jazen had thought it a reckless way to wear a fortune, since it could be easily lost. He thought, too, that the bondsmen of Mirlacca were richer by far than free men in Smattac.

"I will sponsor your guild to the Emperor Himself," Lasvennat was saying, "and sell you the building and land you require, if you will meet *my* price."

"And that is, my lord?" Vettazen asked evenly, though Jazen thought he detected an undertone of eagerness in her words. Lasvennat didn't see it.

"Make available to me the results of your research. Leave open to me your books. Provide me the results of your studies. Show me your discoveries."

But Vettazen was shaking her head. "My lord, did we not just discuss this matter? We cannot be an instrument in the politics of the Court."

Lasvennat smiled again. "Then to the sponsorship and the land, let me add yet another incentive: you may take this boy into your ranks, and train him as you will. I have reason to believe he has some small talent. And it is not every guild which includes in its members those of . . . noble connexion."

The boy remained impassive. Beside Jazen, Meleas took a sharp breath. He made a small, voiceless sound of protest. Vettazen's bargaining face slipped fractionally, revealing shock.

But she had already stepped around the table and to the intervening space to look deep into the boy's eyes. "My lord has, of course, no small skill himself, but, of course, you cannot allow yourself to become part of a mere guild." There was no sarcasm in her words, only the brisk and practical tone she used to direct her household, to organize a shopping expedition in the markets, to strike a camp. "We are greatly honored by your offer."

She was speaking as if the boy were a plucked chicken she was evaluating and bargaining over for dinner, Jazen thought, indignation swelling on the boy's behalf. But Meleas' presence beside him provided restraint; the blond man was paying very close attention to all three of the participants in the little scene before them, and Jazen followed his lead.

Vettazen had taken the boy by the chin, was tilting his head back and forth to see his features better in the light. The boy stood silent, tolerant, though he stood nearly eye to eye with her.

"What is your name, boy?" Vettazen asked.

"Cadan, mistress." His voice cracked on the second word, slipping from soprano to baritone, and he flushed even redder for a moment.

"Hmmph." Vettazen lifted the gold chain with one finger, not looking at it but into the boy's dark eyes instead. She seemed satisfied at the reaction she found there, and let the metal fall again to his chest.

"My lord," she said, turning back to Lasvennat, "you know what you ask is impossible, though you offer us the imperial seal itself. Were we to accept your offer, we would be no guild at all, but your school. We cannot function so; no guild functions so. Every guild has a sponsor, and the payment is three gifts in open court at the sponsoring. More than that I cannot do; more than that we may not do."

"Need they know?"

Beside Jazen, Meleas allowed himself a soft snort of derision.

Vettazen allowed herself to become angry. "My lord, be sensible. How could it not be so? If you sponsor us, sell us land, how could we deny it?"

There was a long pause.

"Are we at an impasse, then, mistress?" Lasvennat said at last. He flicked his fingers at Cadan, who stepped back, nearly to the curtains from which he came. In so doing, the boy glanced over at Jazen and Meleas, and for a moment, Jazen felt a chill creep down his spine.

I do not know you, he thought, *but I will. Not now, but someday.*

"My lord, I came this evening with wares to sell you, as any tradesman may, and you have honored me greatly with this interview. You honor us further by your offer of involvement in our work, but we have made our position plain, and surely you understand. The ways of the court are more tangled than any demon's spell, and we do not wish to become entrapped by them."

With Vettazen's words, Cadan stepped even farther back into the shadows, effectively breaking the thread between himself and Jazen. Jazen turned to look at his teacher and the nobleman. When he looked back, Cadan was gone, the tapestries hanging limp against the wall again. Jazen took a deep breath and let it go, slowly. It was his imagination, of course. It was being in the palace, that was it; everything was new, rich, strange. Even some nobleman's bastard carried an aura of menace.

"And the boy? Do you find he has no aptitude for sorcery?"

"We are not sorcerers, my lord. We are students. We seek to learn so that we may root out the remaining tendrils of the demons in our land, and be prepared should they come again. The magic itself is only a path to that."

Lasvennat's expression was patronizing. "I do forget you call yourself ... exorcists, is it not?" In the space of a breath his manner changed, so that he was bargaining in the same marketplace as the woman before him. "Very well. This weather spell of yours is an amusing oddity. It may be worth a gold piece."

"It is worth twenty, my lord."

Jazen's jaw dropped. He glanced over at his companion. Somber Meleas was struggling to restrain a smile. "Bargaining," Meleas breathed. "Watch."

"But such a small spell. Such a small area."

"Presumably with the strength of the magic worker, the area increases." Vettazen didn't follow her remark with any such flattery as, *My lord is well known as a strong man*, or *Surely my lord can make great things of this*. "I did not wish to risk a larger backlash spell."

"Ah yes, the backlash." Lasvennat's interest heightened. "For this, now ... a spell of rain and thunder ... the backlash would be—ah, of course, the torches."

Vettazen nodded. "Aye. Or sometimes wind. A dust devil in the hallway, or in the courtyard, perhaps."

"Backlash?" Jazen mouthed.

"Later," Meleas breathed back.

"So with great rain, a great fire, or a great wind. An interesting effect."

"And well worth the gold, my lord."

Lasvennat chuckled. "Done then, woman. I look forward to your presentation gifts—a fortnight hence at the Presentation of Guilds, at the Court of His Imperial Majesty Addonat the Fourth, Emperor of Miralat, Lord of Mirlacca of the Fountains."

Chapter 10

"For every spell there's a backlash," Meleas said later that evening around a mouthful of Rache's berry tart. They were sitting at the great-table in the kitchen, telling Adri-nes about their adventure, and as usual, the three of them had found another reason to eat. "The greater the spell, the greater the backlash." The blond man licked a dribble of purple berry juice off the side of his hand.

"Lasvennat fancies himself a sorcerer," Adri-nes added. "He collects spells." Adri-nes was sitting sideways on the long bench, one leg stretched out, one knee bent, with an arm hooked around the bent knee to balance himself.

"But that was one of *yours*." Meleas grinned. "I recognized the words. That was the spell you wrote yestereve, from the notes from the Burned Lands."

"And it actually worked." Adri-nes grinned. "Wish I'd been there to see it."

"*You* wrote it? Does that mean you can do what Vettazen did?" Jazen asked. He had seen Adri-nes laboring over scrolls, muttering to himself, as Jazen muttered, trying to make sense of the marks on parchment. Jazen wasn't about to admit that Adri was doing considerably more than struggling with words, though he was beginning to have second thoughts about competing with the dark-haired man for the favors of the local girls. Anyone who could call lightning—

Adri-nes shook his head. "Me? Haven't the talent to cast a spell across the room. I can *write* them, though. I'll have to ask Vettazen to do it for me. I want to see what it looks like."

"But she sold it," Jazen said, bewildered.

Meleas snorted, just short of spraying the table with berry juice. "Do you think a spell is like a horse? No, she didn't. You can't sell knowledge, only buy it. You always keep it."

"Our Meleas is a philosopher," Adri-nes said, reaching for the last tart. "As well as being rather gifted himself."

Startled, Jazen looked back and forth from one to the other, feeling whiplashed. "Gifted?"

"With animals. He can talk bees from their hive, or make a wild horse dance, can our Meleas." Adri-nes shot a look at Jazen, laughing. "Ah, never say you didn't know! Who else can talk to that damned mule?"

Meleas, nose deep in a mug of brown ale, flushed red but did not deny it. "No backlash," he mumbled, putting the mug down. " 's better than your stuff."

Jazen swallowed and wet his lips. He knew they studied history here, and demons. But that they actually worked spells, and spoke of it so casually— He felt as if a curtain had been torn down between himself and the other two, and the men he had come to consider his first friends were suddenly revealed again as strangers, as much as Vettazen had earlier in the evening. "Aren't you afraid they'll call you demons?"

"Who?" Adri-nes said. "The city folk?" He studied Jazen for a moment with a sudden sympathy. "This is Mirlacca. Here we have all manner of things, sorcerers, herb witches, exorcists—we could have Yaan Maat themselves walk down our street and no one would notice."

"Not quite," Vettazen said, coming in from the front room. "Did you leave anything of that tart for anyone else? I thought not. Greedy boys."

"What of that boy, what was his name? Did he have any gift?" *Do I?* Jazen thought. Did dancing, cursing imps count? But he could only *see* them, not summon or control the things.

Vettazen shrugged, reaching across Adri-nes for the jug. "And you left me dregs here, too. Thank you, that's most kind." She took another mug from the shelf high on the wall and poured the last of the ale into it, shook the empty jug and handed it off to Meleas. "The boy has some gift. Not surprising if he's the blood he looks to be. But we're not mad enough to take an own son of Lasvennat, not now. Besides, there isn't room."

"Why not?" Adri-nes demanded. "There's only the three of us."

"Chezayot is sending four more in two months, two girls and two boys—and you'll be keeping your hands *off* the young ladies, or have sorrow, I promise you." She shook her head. "Flowers and fire alone know how we're going to feed you all, but there it is."

"And where are we to put *four* more students?" As usual, Adri-nes was asking all the questions, in a tone not quite rude but confident of an answer. Jazen was still bemused by the idea of more people in the house—more witches—exorcists—

Vettazen smiled. "In the new and first Guildhouse of the Guild of Exorcists in the Imperial City of Mirlacca, that's where. In a fortnight we shall be presented to the Emperor Himself and receive our charter from his own hands. Though he pretended otherwise, my lord Lasvennat has persuaded His Imperial Majesty that it might be amusing to sponsor a faux guild—but whether Addonat the Fourth believes us false or not, it still gives us standing, and gives us imperial protection." She smiled, the sort of smile that Rache wore while beheading chickens. "There are those who won't be happy about that.

"And you will all be expected to work harder than any of you have ever had to—except perhaps you, Jazen, since you at least had an honest upbringing." She finished the last of the ale. "And we begin tomorrow, with the sun. So to bed with you. Tomorrow we begin something new."

That night Jazen lay on his cot beneath the open window, staring out at the few stars that managed to sparkle through the layer of smoke that hovered in still air over Mirlacca, trying to sort out what had happened.

Adri-nes, of the sharp brown eyes and sharper tongue, carefully chosen clothing and precise sword—Adri-nes wrote *real* spells, not just copies of ancient texts. Inside that room in the palace Jazen had felt the rain against his skin.

Meleas, quiet blond Meleas, was "gifted" with animals. And if Adri-nes wrote real spells, then it seemed likely Meleas had a real gift too, and his way with the roan mule, as Adri had said, was no accident.

Vettazen spoke to noblemen as if she were their equal, and worked magic before them. And it was she who spoke to them, he thought, because Firaloy could not be bothered to leave his beloved books.

He had no idea if Firaloy could do what Vettazen had done that evening; he was willing to wager that whether he could or not, Lord Lasvennat *thought* Firaloy could, and more. Perhaps the old man could. Or perhaps he was as Adri-nes, unable to cast spells but very great at creating them out of the bits and scraps of magic left behind by the Yaan Maat?

Where did a forgeslavey from Smattac, a boy-man of uncertain age, no name, no clan, no *nothing*, fit in with all this? He had no gifts. He couldn't even read. All he had of his own was a half-made knife, fashioned of metal stolen from the only place he'd ever known as home. He was cursed with delusions of imps in his forgefires, and when he spoke the words of a spell he didn't even believe in them. Not when he had seen a thunderstorm and lightning within gilded walls, called by human will. That was *real* magic.

And yet they all seemed to accept him, take him for granted.

A scratching in the eaves over his head told him that even amongst the magic, Mirlacca still had everyday vermin.

Perhaps there was a place for him after all.

They had a fortnight before the Presentation. It seemed to Jazen to be a very long time, not worth the expression of absentminded worry on Vettazen's face when she came into the kitchen the next morning. Rache was scrubbing out the cookpot and glared at her, jutting a long chin at the covered dish in the middle of the table. Vettazen ignored her and set tablets and styli in a heap before the three young men.

"Adri, Meleas, time to make lists. Jazen—no, not yet, I suppose. But don't go anywhere, I'll find something for you to do too." As an afterthought, she dug into the dish for a flat cake, scooped jelly over it, and bit in. "Clothes, to begin with, for the procession. Adri, you must know someone—not too expensive, mind, and something they can use again."

The stylus dug a deep hole in the wax. Adri-nes stared down at the white ridge as if he couldn't understand what had happened. " 'They'?" he repeated, as if he'd heard something he didn't quite understand.

"Jazen and Meleas. And Firaloy and myself, of course." Vettazen put down the cake and scrubbed a smear of jelly off her cheek. "Adri, you know that you can't go to court."

Adri-nes' head snapped up so fast, the single lock of black hair that usually hung in his eyes flopped back over his head. "And why not, my lady?" His accent, brittle and precise, was stronger than ever. "Is there some reason I am denied participation in a royal presentation?"

It was not, Jazen could tell, wholly unexpected. Meleas groaned and hid his face in his hands. Vettazen sighed, contemplated taking another bite of the flat cake, and changed her mind. "Adri, your family will be there. Some of them, at least."

Adri-nes drew back his head and stared at her, and for an instant Jazen was reminded of Lasvennat. Adri had the same air of freezing, insufferable arrogance.

Vettazen stared back, her gray eyes mild. "No, no one is saying anyone would dare deny even the youngest member of the House of Derlai vn'Sai Khor has a right to enter the imperial palace and take his place before the throne. I'm saying only that quite a few other members are likely to be there, and one or two of them might not be happy to see a member of that august family in a guild train."

Jazen looked from Vettazen to Adri and back again, stunned. "House of Derlai vn'Sai Khor"? Adri-nes? Adri-nes, who chased servingmaids in the marketplace?

He had no idea what the House of Derlai vn'Sai Khor might be, but the name together with the blazing anger in Adri's eyes and the spots of red high in an otherwise white face led Jazen to believe that perhaps his friend was rather more than just a minor noble, as he had offhandedly referred to himself. He wondered whether Derlai vn'Sai Khor—or perhaps it was vn'Sai Khor, or even just Khor—outranked the Earl of Sillamar. At this moment, Adri-nes did look like someone who outranked an earl.

"I chose this," Adri-nes said, very softly. "Of my own free will, I came to you for the weighing of what gift I have. I have taken and I give to the best of my measure, and if that is not enough, my lady, to win me a place in this guild the equal of anyone's . . ."

Vettazen heaved a deep sigh and held up her hands. "Oh, all *right*. All right, Adri. But you have to remember they'll make trouble if they see you."

Adri deflated suddenly, the spots fading and normal color returning to his face. "I want very much to be a part of this, my lady."

"Then you'll have to get clothes too, won't you? And find a carriage for us, as well. We'll have to have consequence upon consequence, I fear. Difficult, with only the five of us, but I'd rather not bring in Rizard and Demachee at this juncture."

"Two carriages," Adri said definitively, getting up. He seemed willing to pretend the dispute just past had never happened. "I know someone." He snatched up the tablet, still unmarked save for the gouge in the wax, and left quickly.

Jazen looked large questions at Meleas, who shook his head and shrugged. Vettazen, meanwhile, finished her flat cake and went on with her list of instructions.

"We'll need the gifts—books, I think, suitably obscure so my lord Lasvennat can spend many happy hours trying to translate them, and we'll need to get good covers for them. Can't have shoddy sponsor gifts, after all. We're going to look pathetic enough as it is."

"Why?" Jazen was unable to remain still any longer. "Why should we look pathetic?"

"Because our presentation is just one out of every guild in the city," Meleas said dryly.

"This happens every third year," Vettazen said. "All the guilds in Miralat come for imperial recognition and renewal of their charters. New guilds are recognized too. All the Court is present to witness. So it will be very large, very confusing, very chaotic. I do hope Adri's brothers aren't there," she added as an afterthought. Draining her mug, she added, "I expect the two of you to be available when we need you for fittings, and we'll need to practice, no doubt. It's going to be difficult enough to get Firaloy there."

As she left, still muttering to herself, Rache snorted and slammed the cookpot onto its drying hook, making both Jazen and Meleas jump.

"Oh, it's going to be *such* fun," Meleas said, shaking his head in denial.

It was too much too suddenly for Jazen to comprehend. The palace? The Emperor? Derlai-whatever-she-said? "Meleas," he said hesitantly, the drive to *know* battling with the deeply instilled reluctance to ask a direct, personal question, "is Adri really—"

Meleas snorted. "Oh, yes, if it means anything to be a thirteenth son of a fairly ancient house. Don't let him bother you; he climbs up on his ancestors' tombs like that sometimes. Doesn't mean much. If you want to shock him out of it, call him 'my lord.' Works most of the time."

"Are *you*—"

Meleas looked taken aback. "Me? Noble, you mean?" He laughed. "Not likely. *My* father was an estate keeper in Chaynoos." He stood up, clapped Jazen on the shoulder. "Come on, let's go out while we still can."

The next few days blurred together as Vettazen and Adrines consulted over great matters such as guild colors, banners, silks, symbols, and precedence, while Firaloy hid in his study and Rache slammed pots and ladles with increasing violence. Tailors came, and for the first time in his life Jazen was fitted with clothing made specifically for him, a pale blue silken shirt and quilted midnight-blue tunic of the same material, snug-fit breeches of the same dark blue, and good leather shoes. Vettazen came in at one point to see him standing bewildered with his hands in the air as others fitted and measured, and told the tailor to make three more sets in more serviceable fabrics while he was at it. "I'm tired of seeing you bursting out of Meleas' old things," she told Jazen.

The days rolled past too quickly, until the appointed time came and two open carriages rolled up at the end of the street—the Street of Scribes was too narrow to accept a wagon and horses—and the five of them gathered to ride to the palace for the Presentation of Guilds. The three young men were dressed exactly alike, with thin gold chains around their necks—"Don't break it, you clod, we have to return them after"—and Vettazen was resplendent in a long, dark blue gown with a belt of flat metal squares hanging low over her hips. Firaloy sported a long coat and a soft cap with a fine feather to it. They all, except Adri-nes, looked rather uncomfortable, Jazen thought. Adri-nes managed to look supremely at ease, except perhaps for the thin chain. His attire and bearing really demanded more jewelry. He passed Meleas and Jazen long staffs with banners wrapped. "There. You'll be carrying these during the Presentation—it will give you something to do with your hands. Firaloy will have the scroll, of course—

"Who's got the gifts?" he added abruptly. "Meleas, do you have them?"

"No. I thought you, or Vettazen." Meleas was only slightly discomposed, and that only because so many around him were excited. The whole population of the Street of Scribes had gathered round to see them off to the palace; people who had never acknowledged their existence before now eager to talk to them, to touch their new clothes.

Adri stepped back to confer quickly with Vettazen and Firaloy, returned with a large package and a look of exasperation, and stepped lightly up into the first carriage, turning to take the banners and store them in place against the bench.

Jazen followed him uncertainly; he had never ridden in a wagon before, and certainly not one with cushioned seats and polished wood and doors in the sides. Meleas came too, sighed resignedly, and took the seat facing backward. Jazen twisted around to see Vettazen helping Firaloy up into the second carriage, and then the hired driver snapped his whip and the carriage jerked forward and Jazen almost landed in a heap on the floor. "Steady," Meleas remarked.

They rumbled over the cobblestones the long way around through the broader streets, joining other carriages as they went. People shouted down at them from the windows and balconies and from the street as they passed, waving, tossing things; Adri cursed as a particularly sticky confection landed on the seat beside him, and he had to sit on the edge of the

THE FOUNTAINS OF MIRLACCA

bench to avoid it. They were delayed several times as larger processions moved in place ahead of them, banners flying, carriages and wagons painted gaily.

"Should we unwrap these?" Jazen asked, indicating the two poles.

"No, we haven't been formally recognized yet," Adri told him. "Afterwards, we will. I wish we'd get moving. We'll probably be there all night at this rate." He glared at a metal contraption from the Tinsmiths which pulled in front of them, sending their drivers' horses into a momentary fit. Meleas half-rose, then settled back again as order was restored.

They had begun at the third hour past the fountains' turning, and it was twilight before they made their way into the Great Square. Jazen was surprised to see how quickly the line of transport moved; as each conveyance arrived at the palace gates, the occupants disembarked and disappeared inside without crowding or confusion. He discovered why when their own carriage arrived; there was no time to look around when the dreaded guardsmen made it clear that no conversation would be tolerated. The three young men barely had time to snatch up the banners and the package and get out of the carriage before the driver had whipped up his horses and was moving out of the way.

The guards attempted to move them along into the building; Adri-nes put on his noble persona to give them enough time to make sure Firaloy got safely down, clutching the scroll. Vettazen hopped down behind him, and then the five of them were moved briskly into the Great Hall.

The hall echoed with the shouting of guildmasters trying to organize themselves, the tuning of horns and pipes by musicians, the pleas of imperial servants attempting to create order out of chaos. Around the perimeter of the room, enterprising guildsmen had set up food stands for those too rushed to eat before the ceremony. The smells of sausages roasting over improvised firepits mingled with those of bread, straw underfoot, too many people jostling each other. Jazen, still clutching his banner staff, tried to see everything and still keep track of Vettazen and Firaloy.

"There are *horses* over there!" he said, nudging Meleas. "Look!"

"I know," Meleas said briefly, pulling him out of the path of two large men pulling a cart filled with carefully polished marble busts. "Horsebreeders have a guild, too. Lot of good it does them."

"Why?"

"*Everybody* breeds horses. Get back over here while we figure out where we are and what we're doing next. If you lose us in this, you'll never find us again."

Vettazen was engaged in a heated debate with a supercilious woman wearing an imperial sash and carrying a senior chamberlain's mace. Firaloy, standing next to them, was looking over the seam of his sleeve, making it quite clear that he had no part in the debate. Adri interrupted the chamberlain's tirade and the woman threw up her hands and marched away.

Vettazen gave Adri an exasperated look. "You do realize, young man, that you're going to have to decide—"

"Adri-nes!"

The young man actually flinched. Jazen craned his neck to see around a large member of the Weavers' Company. The man who called Adri's name was a more mature version of Adri, taller, dressed in better clothing and, at the moment, far more self-possessed than Adri-nes. He had the same dark hair, clear brown eyes, high forehead. The resemblance was quite startling, in fact; he even had the same bright red spots on an otherwise pale face that Adri had when *he* was furious.

"I *thought* I might find you here," the newcomer snapped. "I hoped you wouldn't go through with this, but no, you're determined to shame us before the very throne itself, aren't you?"

"Oldest brother," Meleas said laconically, in an aside to Jazen. "The one we didn't want to run into."

Without waiting for a response, the brother turned on Firaloy. "And you have the utter gall to bring him here and make him a part of your chicanery? You think that people will see that a vn'Sai Khor lends your so-called spells countenance and that will somehow give you credibility? You scheming, swindling, thieving old—"

"Bentane, stop it!" Adri shoved the precious gift package into Meleas' hands and grabbed his brother's arm. "This is none of your concern!"

Bentane moved, twisted, and shoved Adri away. "What my family does is my business," he responded. "That you choose to associate with charlatans and frauds is my business. That you drag our good name in the mud, so that respectable people use it as a joke, is most certainly my business. I want you to get out of here and get home where you belong."

"I won't." The two of them faced off at each other, and Jazen wondered with appalled fascination if they were going to start a fight, just when the procession of guilds had finally begun to move into the Throne Room, to be called one by one in order of precedence to recognize their sponsors and renew their charters. At their end of the line, the most junior societies were still jostling for position with the groups who, like themselves, had not yet been formally recognized. Vettazen was watching the two scions of vn'Sai Khor and glancing over at the line too. They could not afford to lose their place, not now.

Adri's hands were clenched at his sides, and the effort he made to keep his voice even showed. "Bentane, I have had our mother's permission for this for years. You are the one creating a disturbance here, not I."

"Our lady mother was taken in by their so-called magic!"

"I won't discuss it with you now."

"I won't permit you to be a part of this farce!" Bentane reached out, intending to pull Adri-nes away from them.

"Oh dear," Meleas remarked conversationally. "That was a mistake." At the same time, he looked past Jazen at the members of the Horsebreeders' Guild, who were holding the product of their craft quiet with some difficulty.

Adri kicked his brother.

Meleas whistled sharply.

One of the horses, already sweating with panic, rose straight up in the air, shrieking. People scattered. Vettazen guided Firaloy over to an opening in the line, gesturing for the three to follow; Meleas paused only to make a short detour past the animals, patting them as he went by. It seemed to calm their nerves.

Hardly anyone noticed the oldest son of the House of Derlai vn'Sai Khor curled up on himself on the flagstone floor of the Great Hall, while the youngest slipped into the processional line.

"Just to minimize the damage," Vettazen observed as they sorted themselves out, the three young men taking places before her and Firaloy, "Adri, I'd like you to take a banner and be inconspicuous. Meleas, you do the presentation, please. Jazen, just follow along and do what Adri does—or no, Adri, do what Jazen does; he seems a bit more dependable this evening."

Adri looked as if he might protest. Vettazen's lips thinned. Adri acquiesced. The parade moved onward, slowly.

"Do you think he might come after us?" Jazen asked under his breath.

"I hit him as hard as I've always wanted to," Adri whispered back with vicious satisfaction. "I don't think he's going anywhere. In fact, I hope he's already married, because he's not likely to be interested in siring heirs after tonight."

Jazen grinned and shifted the weight of the banner pole as they moved ten more steps forward, to the doorway of the Throne Room.

The Throne Room was roofed by the gilded dome that was the central landmark of Mirlacca. The floor was polished mosaic, not covered with straw. It was a cavernous space of arches and beams, the walls covered with frescoes and sculptures in high relief, flags everywhere, and every fifty steps a small fountain, bubbling merrily. Jazen sniffed the air as they passed one such, and realized with a shock that the clear liquid was wine, not water.

"Of course not," Adri whispered in response to his exclamation. "Wine doesn't turn. These are the clear fountains."

They continued moving down the center of the room, pausing as each guild in front of them made their obeisances, received their charters, bowed, and was escorted from the room. Jazen couldn't see, as yet, the throne itself. There was more than enough to see in the crowds lining the perimeter of the room, all the nobles in furs and silks who profited from the sale of raw materials to the guilds and merchants while pretending they never sullied their aristocratic hands by dabbling in trade.

"Don't gawk," Adri warned Jazen, standing rigidly beside him. "Perfect Court face."

"What?" Jazen almost turned to him.

"No expression. Don't let anyone know what you're thinking or feeling. You've seen it all before, and you're bored with it." Adri was speaking out of the corner of his mouth, his eyes straight ahead.

"But I haven't," Jazen protested.

"Quiet," Vettazen said from behind him.

Jazen shut up and paced self-consciously forward, holding his bound banner. Several of the groups in line ahead of them also held tied banners; they were also to receive their charters this evening, he guessed.

The line was long enough to curve around, and he could see the throne at the other end of the room now, and the man who sat upon it, dressed in purple shot with gold, his collar trimmed with thick, soft furs in seven colors. It came to him suddenly that he was looking at the Emperor of Miralat, the lord who held the power of life and death over all in that room, over all the nation, even as far as tiny Smattac. It was this man's whim and life that were the obsessive focus of every plot, scheme, and intrigue at court. All that mattered was who could talk to him, who could influence him, who had his favor.

He looked like Firaloy, only older.

Next to him, on a lower chair, sat a boy of perhaps ten years, who looked pale and exhausted. Dried spittle clung to the ermine trim of his collar. It was the Heir, whose health was the second—no, more often the first—subject of interest from kitchen hearth to bathhouse gossip, for Addonat IV was old. There was no one else to take the throne when he was gone. Addonat's son had lived long enough to sire this child, and then died, unmourned by father and country alike.

The boy was dressed in the same shade of dark blue that the Exorcists wore, without the ice-blue to set it off. Blue was predominant tonight; Jazen wondered how many people knew ahead of time what colors the Heir would wear, how many chose their hues in an attempt to compliment him.

Behind the Heir stood his mother, a sticklike blonde with a mouth that pulled down. Jazen could not recall what her name was. Her importance lay solely in her son, over whom she had no influence any more, according to rumor. She looked as if she knew it, and resented it; her hands grasped either side of the back of his chair as if she would shake it, and him, into paying attention.

Around the imperial family, clustered at a respectful distance, were the sponsors and the members of the Emperor's council. Among them stood Lasvennat, not in the first rank but standing modestly back, rather closer to the throne than not.

They paced forward again, and Jazen could see the pattern of movement as the presentations were made, kneeling, speaking, bowing. Moving up to the throne, where the sponsor held the precious charters out to the Emperor, who touched the scrolls of vellum with his fingertips so that the sponsor could make the presentation in his imperial name. Sometimes the Emperor actually spoke to the guildsmen. Jazen could feel his hands sweating on the pole as they moved forward again.

And again.

And again, and around the curve so that they were facing the throne directly; and then they were next. The guardsman who was unobtrusively controlling the movement of the line waved them on, and Meleas strode forward, Adri-nes two paces behind him, and with a nudge to his back from Vettazen, Jazen sr'Yat was striding down the length of the Imperial Throne Room to come face to face with the Emperor of Miralat.

Twelve paces from the steps that led to the center of power for the empire, Meleas stopped and went to one knee. So did Adri-nes, with Jazen half a beat behind him. A herald announced, with some incredulity, "On behalf of the Exorcists of Miralat, Lord Gan Lasvennat prays the recognition of His Most Puissant Highness Addonat the Fourth for their guild."

A titter spread among the onlookers. Jazen dared to glance up to see the assembled sponsors laughing to one another, and Lasvennat stepped forward, taking a scroll from Cadan, who stood in the squire's place behind him.

THE FOUNTAINS OF MIRLACCA

"Exorcists, my lord?" It was the Emperor Himself, and he too sounded amused.

"Lasvennat insults the honest guilds of your empire with this nonsense," someone else, hidden deep in the throng of councilors, said. "How dare they presume to the same status as legitimate guilds? I know these people. They're nothing but imposters, swindlers, fakes, preying upon honest men with their claims to working magic."

The unknown speaker had the sympathy of many of the onlookers, it appeared. He sounded like a relative of Adri's. Jazen looked quickly at his fellow banner-bearer. Adri was staring into the middle distance, expressionless: court face.

Lasvennat listened to the murmurs of agreement with an odd smile upon his face. "My lord, lords and ladies, even thieves have their masters and apprentices," he said at last. "Who among us can deny that there was once magic in the world? These are students of that time, and who wish to organize themselves to better pursue that interest."

A hush spread through the room as more people realized that this would not be the automatic, mechanical presentation that the rest had been.

"Do even our historians require the protections of a guild, then?" Addonat IV inquired.

Behind him, Jazen could hear Vettazen and Firaloy stirring in protest. This was not supposed to happen; Lasvennat was supposed to have ensured all would go smoothly. Surely it could not go wrong now. Surely the Emperor would not embarrass Lasvennat publicly—

Surely not. Jazen wondered suddenly if there were other messages here, for other people. If the Emperor allowed one of his great lords to be challenged so publicly, perhaps Lasvennat was not so powerful after all.

"My lord, the first purpose of a guild is to police itself. Surely anything to do with magic should be policed."

"The nonexistent requires no oversight," the dissenting voice said, from out of the crowd— And perhaps someone thought Lasvennat *should* be embarrassed.

"To say a thing is nonexistent," came Firaloy's voice from

behind his banner bearers, "is to say it never existed at all. Do you then deny the Yaan Maat?"

Another murmur swept the crowd, and beside Jazen, Adri-nes inhaled sharply between clenched teeth. Once Firaloy became involved in a debate, the old man quickly forgot where he was and to whom he was speaking.

Addonat chuckled, and the answering voice of protest was abruptly silenced. "Let it be so," he said. "We are not neglectful of our own history, and we do not see the harm." He waved a negligent hand.

So simply, it was done. Meleas presented the three gifts, the books bound in the best white leather, to Lasvennat, who took them with eager hands and passed them back to Cadan. Lasvennat took the scroll and knelt before the Emperor, who touched it. Lasvennat then strode between Jazen and Adri-nes to deliver the precious scroll directly into the hands of Firaloy, who pressed his lips to it and then passed it to Vettazen, who did likewise. Adri-nes reached up and untied their bound banners, letting the blue-on-blue silks shake free and hang limp in the still air of the Throne Room. Lasvennat withdrew to the crowd of sponsors, and the herald waved them off to follow the others in the long line.

Whatever challenges or warnings had been made among the great ones no longer mattered. The Guild of Exorcists was a reality.

PART 3

The Guildhouse

Chapter 11

"This," Vettazen said, brushing dirt from her hands, "is the new Guildhouse of the Exorcists of Mirlacca."

Meleas and Jazen traded a look, and Meleas lifted a skeptical eyebrow. Adri-nes stifled a yawn.

They were standing in a broad, dusty street at the top of a hill in the northern part of the city, somewhat apart from the residential quarter where the noblemen kept their city houses, in front of a gate set in a high wall. The gate was solid timbers, painted red, to a point well above their heads; the rest of it, half as high, was a series of roundels set a hand's-breadth apart, braced at the top with a curved brass rail. The sun was barely up; they stood in the shadow of the wall across the street, shivering.

"This is the place where we will live and study, where we will gather our books, learn and exchange learning, where we will find the secrets that will allow us to defend ourselves against the return of the Yaan Maat." Vettazen gestured at the blank wall with a grand flourish.

As always, Meleas seemed to withdraw inside himself at the name of the demons. Remembering the city in the Burned Lands, Jazen asked, "Do you really think they might come back?"

Meleas turned, his bright blue eyes suddenly hard as stone. "What makes you think they ever left?" he snapped.

Jazen flinched, remembering their conversation on the journey to Mirlacca, so long ago. "I meant, in armies," he said, trying his best to placate the other's sudden anger.

Meleas chose to be appeased, or at least to defer the argument.

Adri-nes, listening, stepped closer. "Preparation is all," he chirped, his voice considerably brighter than his yawns would have indicated.

The interruption was enough to ease the moment of tension. Vettazen, oblivious, pulled a large brass key out of the folds of her skirt and inserted it in the keyhole, which was the only interruption in the bottom two-thirds of the gate. "Blast the thing," she murmured, panting as she wrestled with it. Within the gate something grated and clanked. The gate remained unyielding.

"Well," she said, looking at her three escorts. "Don't just stand there. Push."

They pushed.

The gate of the new Guildhouse creaked open, and the three of them stepped inside and looked around at their new home.

"Disgusting," Adri-nes pronounced.

The great gate opened into a courtyard which had, by its looks, been abandoned for decades. Things had died in the corners; wind and weather had drifted leaves and branches in man-high piles. Grass grew up between those cobblestones still left intact. Shade trees wilted along the walls. The rim of the fountain was cracked and badly stained. Rats and squirrels skittered through debris.

Through an archway directly in front of them, the main building, many times the size of the house on the Street of Scribes, could be seen. The doors stood ajar and sagging, as if torn from their hinges, and more debris was piled in the opening.

Off to one side, another, wider, taller opening led to a stable area. Meleas wandered over, looked inside. "Room enough for a dozen horses, maybe more," he reported over his shoulder, disappearing into the shadows. Jazen paused, torn between following him and going with Adri-nes and the woman into the main house.

Vettazen paid them no attention, marching directly through the archway and inner doors.

The front hall was in the same neglected condition. Thick

THE FOUNTAINS OF MIRLACCA

cloth hung in tatters from the walls, letting in some light from high windows; the remains of a long-dead fire still occupied the fireplace. The stone floor was still in good repair, the flagstones uncracked; Jazen could feel the chill of it through the soles of his boots. Opposite the fireplace, two stone staircases wound upward to a higher floor, their wooden banisters splintered and broken away. On either side of the stairs, holes in the walls indicated where doors had been.

To Jazen, it was far grander than the house on the Street of Scribes, worlds beyond anything in Smattac; indeed, for size, it equalled anything he had seen in the palace itself, save for the Entrance Hall and the Throne Room. From the glow in Vettazen's eyes, she shared his opinion, pivoting in place and looking around as if imagining the wide hall filled with light and sound and people.

Adri-nes, on the other hand, was not impressed. "Flames, what a mess," he said between his teeth.

"It will clean up well," Vettazen said, starting up the stairs.

At least, Jazen thought, they weren't likely to crumble under her, being of the same fabric as the bones of the house. The angle of the sunlight struck through the windows, lighting the hallway at the top of the stairs.

There was vast space in this house, courtyards and rooms and corridors, a dozen large chambers in the front part of the first floor alone, a well-lit audience room on the level above, and more floors above that. Jazen went from one to the next, leaving Vettazen and Adri-nes to explore on their own.

Some of the nooks and crannies still held furniture, tables or beds or cabinets. Some had doorways that led to still more rooms, but without a torch Jazen was disinclined to venture into the darker ones. Off and on he could hear the voices of the others, comparing notes; Meleas came up to join them, exclaiming over some new discovery.

In the farthest reaches of the second floor Jazen found a large bathing room, with rotted wooden tubs and good pipe, and made a note to himself to find out how the builder had managed to bring water *up* for his luxury. Just outside the door he found yet more steps leading to a tower. Following them up, and up again, he came at last to a door which led out to the roof. Stepping out on the flat section of the roof, next to a high turret, he looked out over Mirlacca, for his first view of the city as a city since the day he had entered her.

Mirlacca, Imperial City. Young Mirlacca, most of its walls and houses built within the last two hundred years; brave Mirlacca, the scars of burning and battle barely recognizable any more. Off to the west, glowing in the morning sun, on a hillside higher than his own, the palace loomed over the city, walls and tall blocks of masonry, steep roofs, and the single gilded dome, catching the light and casting it back across the city. Stretching before him, as far as he could see, were buildings of all shapes and sizes, white and rose and gray of the stone they were made from, masonry barely parted by the gleaming of a wide river winding from the mountains to the docks. He could see gardens green and fruitful, squares where people gathered, temples where they worshiped, markets where they traded, all veiled by the white dust rising where the masons and builders continued to raise stone walls.

He had not realized before that the city in which he lived was so new. The image of bees in a hive came back to him, each cell of the hive a house or a shop or some other pulsepoint of the city, humming with life, constantly building itself, expanding endlessly. . . .

"Nice view," Adri-nes remarked, stepping out beside him. "We could have rooms up here, I suppose."

"Long way from the kitchen," Meleas said, peering over the darker man's shoulder.

"More privacy, though."

"Aye, but what's it good for? There are rooms over the stables."

"Oh, of course, you'd want to be there." Adri-nes paused. "We could each have our own room here, you know. Even with four more, we could each have our own."

Jazen turned to look at them, bewildered. Adri-nes' words made no sense to him. A room of his own? Shared with no one? Like his space behind the forge, but with walls and a door and a window so that he could see all the wonder of Mirlacca, spread before him like a rich honeycomb, dripping with gold and human adventure?

Vettazen came out of the door to join them, panting. "There you are. I'm afraid there's nothing left to hire people to help clean it up; it will be just us, and Rache, of course, until we can find or develop something else to take the eye of Lord Lasvennat or somesuch. But it will do, I think." She grinned at them, an uncharacteristic expression that made her look years younger. "It will definitely do. Don't you agree?"

The three young men, each in his own way, indicated agreement.

"Then perhaps we'd best get to work. Not least because we've sold the other house, and the new owners expect us to have it clear within the month, and we need room. It's not just us, of course. There's Chezayot and his four, and Tiris and Dalzen have agreed to come. They'll probably have students too. We'll never hear the end of it, once Chezayot and Firaloy start at it.

"But we have a guild, and guild rules with it, and the rules say the 'prentices do the sweeping, so go you and find brooms and get to it."

"Are we really 'prentices?" Jazen asked, dazed. Apprentices were so far from forgeboys, so far from bondsmen—they got paid, they learned a trade—what trade could magic be?

"It seems so," Meleas answered dryly.

"You *are* so," Vettazen assured him. "Apprentice Exorcists from this day. So get you to work."

Firaloy peered uncertainly at the twelve young ones seated before him on benches, chairs, even pillows on the floor, in the newly refurbished refectory of the Guildhouse. They were ten boys and two girls, from all over Miralat and beyond, each trained by his or her own master or mistress in a particular discipline, a particular mode of study. Vettazen and Rizard had persuaded the others that formal training was needed. Firaloy wasn't certain that the system they'd always used was at all unnatural, but the other masters had all met, all decided, and now he had to leave the records from Ilec still unread, in order to talk to these children.

Not children: apprentices. A round dozen of them, from all corners of the empire and beyond, culled by their masters, sifted for the signs of talent. From the littlest, Demachee's Alissa, red-haired and intense, sitting cross-legged on the floor because they didn't have enough chairs yet, to Mikal, Dalzen's arrogant son, his arms crossed across his chest and a bored, supercilious expression on his face, and all the others in between: Rayd, Netchame—Adri-nes, Meleas—he had no idea what all their names were.

He didn't know what to say. They looked up at him with eagerness or wariness or impassivity, each according to their nature; they ranged in age from ten years to twenty-two, he thought. And each of them had, in some respect, some aspect of magic.

He could feel it in each of them, could see the glow of it in their eyes. They had the gift, if not the knowledge. They had the power, if not the means to use it. The idea of taking responsibility for all these young people frightened Firaloy suddenly, and he hoped he wouldn't have to deal with them very much. Let the others teach. He only wanted to study.

The light of the afternoon sun was weak, pouring through the high windows and making broad stripes across the young faces, the brown and black and red hair. They watched him, waited for him to give them wisdom.

The wisdom was back in the books, he thought, and he heartily wished he was back in the new library, reading and gathering more of that wisdom for himself. But there was no help for it. He only had to do this once, he reminded himself.

"Two hundred years ago," he began softly, "humankind defeated the Yaan Maat. But we did not destroy them utterly. Demons remain among us. . . ."

His audience stirred uneasily, sharing glances.

"There are those who will tell you that this is ancient history, that there are no more demons, that to be possessed by a demon is a myth. Some of you know this is not true." He could not bring himself to look at young Meleas, whose blue eyes remained cool and steady upon him, even when others looked over at him.

"There are those who say there remains only magic, for those with the strength and will and gift to use it. There are many who say that magic itself no longer exists.

"They are wrong. They are all of them wrong."

He licked his lips, took a deep breath. The memories pressed against him, and he pushed them away, and he looked in particular away from Meleas.

"Magic remains. But so also remain the Yaan Maat.

"We know—we have the records—we know it is a dreadful thing to be taken by a demon, to be trapped within one's own flesh as an observer, unable to speak or act for oneself, until the body burns up from within, and dies.

"We know—for we have those records too—that there is a way to destroy the demons, in their own form, in the form of the mataal, even in the flesh of their human victims. But it takes great strength, great discipline, and long training. It has been done. It must be done again. And again. And again, until we are safe, and the Yaan Maat destroyed.

"We have brought you here because we believe you can be trained to help us exorcise the demons from our world. It is not an easy task. Some of you will die."

He was grateful for the broad table that was set between himself and the apprentices. It provided no kind of barrier to the surge of power that came from them. They did not believe they could die. They were the young, the strong. Each of them had been chosen by a scholar, by a teacher, for the flicker of talent hidden within, for their potential. For their gifts. Even those who were unsure of those gifts were sure of their own immortality. They were very young.

"We will begin, today, that training. Each of us will contribute what we may to you, from our store of knowledge. But one day you will have to go forth, each of you, by yourselves, to gather yet more knowledge, to seek out both demons and more like yourselves who can be taught how to destroy them, until we are sure, to the limits of human knowing, that the demons are gone forever."

He stopped. He didn't know what else to say. They were so young. So very young.

Chapter 12

By hard winter most of the Guildhouse was clean, if not yet habitable. They had even got the clogged fountain in the stableyard working again, and watched with justifiable pride as the first gleaming sparkles of water rose up in the air. It was not a proper house without a fountain, Adri-nes remarked.

Like all the other proper fountains of Mirlacca, the water turned red at noon; it was Jazen's job to fill the kitchen casks before then, and more than once he won a scolding from Rache when he forgot and the midmeal was delayed. Rache made much of her added burdens with all the new people in the house. Though more than twenty people lived in it, the house still echoed. Rache drafted any of the students walking through the huge kitchen for help with roasting and baking, claiming with some justification that she could not do it all herself. She got no help from Vettazen or the seven other, older inhabitants. The housekeeping tasks, too, fell to the younger people, who despite their lofty status as apprentice exorcists spent most of their time scrubbing walls and floors, sweeping up debris, cleaning up the garden and stable.

Each student had his or her own room. Jazen was relieved to find he was not the only one for whom this was unimaginable luxury. One or two of the students took it for granted, though, and Mikal-who-studied-with-Dalzen-his-father (he seemed to think this would impress the others) claimed to have seen it long before in a vision. Mikal liked to wear jewelry with little pieces of metal—he said silver, but Jazen knew them for tin—in the shape of suns and moons and stars, hammers and wells; he liked to affect an air of mystery and portent. He often could be found sitting in the windowsills, watching birds, and would slide down nodding to himself as if he had seen or heard something terribly important. Jazen considered the man an ass. Meleas said that insulted asses. Jazen, after some thought, conceded the point.

The first rooms cleared were the library, for the books, and the workrooms, for the Masters—the men and women who spent their time with the books and the parchments and in the debates over magic and the Yaan Maat. Adri-nes had once thought he might be part of that class, expecting his talent for developing spells to be of import to them. He was rapidly disabused of it. The Masters, male and female, were far beyond anything he had done.

"Chezayot made a dragon today," he informed the younger group, his face still pale. "And he took me on a tour of its insides. Said it would do me good to have a different perspective on anatomy."

"So?" said Rayd, a young man who studied with Tiris. "I was doing dissections when I was ten. What of it?"

"Have you ever tried to keep your footing inside the stomach of a live dragon?"

The thought gave all of them pause.

"Dalzen has notes on an exorcism he did in Fres Meut," Mikal announced. "And the victim survived it, too." He sneered at Adri-nes. "Dragons are nothing. They're imaginary. Dalzen's been dealing with *demons*."

"It didn't feel imaginary to *me*," Adri-nes muttered. Jazen could measure his friend's disconcertment by the fact that he failed to take offense. It was well enough; someone else would no doubt do so before the evening was over. Mikal was that kind.

A room of his own notwithstanding, Jazen wasn't sure he liked living in the Guildhouse with all these new people. Vettazen barely had time any more for his reading lessons, and he still couldn't keep all the Masters straight; all their pupils filled the great room that was both kitchen and refectory with noise and discord each night and after lessons, as each of them tried to prove that his or her own particular teacher was the smartest, the wisest, the most powerful. And all of them seemed to have some gift or other. He'd had no idea there were so many demon-gifted folk in all of Miralat. Beside them, his own doubtful knack for seeing imps in forgefires was not even worth speaking of, and he knew they wondered what he was doing among them.

He had not been able to get away to the Street of the Forge for a long time now, since his visit before they had purchased the Guildhouse, in fact. His iyiza knife was still half-made, and he had never had a chance in peace and quiet to see if the spell he'd tried to set into it would actually work. He thought perhaps he should finish making the knife before trying it out, but he wasn't sure he remembered it all anyway. And there was the matter of the backlash magic associated with that particular spell, too; he had no idea what that might be. Backlash was a topic they all had pounded into their heads endlessly. Magic released danced wild—and dangerous.

"The measure of great magic is not what spells you can cast, but whether and in what fashion you can control the backspell."

It was one of Rizard's maxims; Rizard was the youngest of the masters, a man not too much older than the 'prentices. Every spell had a backspell. The very best of the masters could control and use the backspell to reinforce the power of the spell itself. But backspells were unpredictable. Ninety-nine times out of a hundred, a given spell would be associated with the same backspell. The hundredth time something totally new would happen. Not even the masters themselves could always obtain the results they expected. Much of their work was directed toward trying to understand the side effects of spells.

After lessons, whether lectures or individual study with their respective masters, the students gathered in the refectory, much to Rache's disgust. More often than not, several of the senior members of the Guild would be there too, trading gossip over hot tea. While there were pipes to carry heat all over the Guildhouse, the kitchen was still far and away the warmest place to be when, as now, snow fell thick day in and day out.

"The man is mad," Vettazen was saying, sweeping past the cluster of young people to the kettle bubbling over the large fire. She and the youngest master ignored them all. "He says demons are gone, and magic is safe, and he wants full access to all our workings. I knew that was what he was after."

"And he would do with them—?" Rizard had a habit of prompting answers to questions he already knew the answer to, in order to educate the rest of the audience. The practice annoyed some of the older Masters, along with wearing his long, exquisitely curled hair gathered in a mare's-tail at the nape of his neck, and the three rings, sapphire, emerald, and ruby, that he invariably wore on his right hand. He never flaunted them, never raised his voice; he was always quiet and always, spectacularly, *there*.

Vettazen knew about his particular teaching method, and as far as Jazen could see, it didn't bother her in the least to cooperate. She pitched her voice a little higher, the better to carry to the whole group sprawled over the benches at the various tables. "The Duke of Seven Banners has been overthrown, his crown city occupied. To the best of our knowing, the entire family was killed. It is a matter of some interest at court to know if this is true. Especially to our petty little Lord Ritash, who is a distant cousin, and imagines himself suddenly the heir to an independent principality. He thinks he can use our magic to see what really happened, and probably assassinate whoever's sitting in the ruins," she said. "As if he had the talent to do so! The man can't even make a cat sneeze."

"Well, neither can I," said Rizard mildly.

One of the apprentices choked. Rizard was regarded, even among the pupils not his own, as one of the most powerful of the masters.

"The difficulty is that he's been telling others at court that it's dangerous for *us* to have the knowledge while *they* do not," she went on. "The letter I had from him this afternoon was a threat, no less."

"I don't like being threatened," Rizard said, his tone unchanged.

"Oh, dear," Meleas said, barely loud enough for Jazen to hear. "Someone's going to die of it, I fear."

The remark startled Jazen, jerking his head around. But Meleas merely widened his eyes, innocently, and glanced past him to the two Masters.

"We'll have to take steps," Vettazen fretted. "We can't afford to be seen as a threat. We *aren't* a threat, blast them."

Meleas snickered softly.

"But perhaps what we know is?" Rizard shifted, moving a bench away; he made room for Vettazen to carry two full plates of stew over to the table that Jazen and Meleas occupied, next to Adri-nes and assorted others. Rizard looked at the two of them, and they hastily relinquished their places to give the Masters room. The other apprentices made themselves busy on whatever small tasks they had brought to the warmth of the refectory, pretending not to listen.

"They couldn't assassinate someone, could they?" Jazen asked Meleas. "Not as far away as Seven Banners?"

"Dalzen could," Mikal said pompously. But he was careful not to say it loudly enough for Vettazen or Rizard to overhear.

But instead of answering immediately, Meleas nudged Jazen and nodded to the door. Jazen followed him out and through the greeting hall, but stopped as Meleas reached for the garden door.

"Are you crazy?" he asked. "There's a blizzard going on out there, and you haven't even got a cloak on."

"I'm only going to the stables," Meleas said reasonably. "And it's just as warm there as it is in the kitchen."

"Stinks worse, though."

"No, it doesn't."

Giving up, Jazen pursued the other out the door, taking only enough time to pull it shut behind him, and went slipping and sliding diagonally across the courtyard to the stableyard. The skim of ice on the fountain was still pink; it was only half an hour past noon, but the sky was dark and lowering, and the wind bit through his heavy shirt, the little needles of snow biting at him like so many mosquitoes.

He almost tumbled over Meleas in an effort to get into the stable and out of the wind. Meleas pulled him away from the door and shoved it closed against the swirling snow.

"See? It's warm. And it doesn't stink of Mikal, either."

And it was warm, with the heat given off by the horses,

peacefully munching at hay in their stalls. The stable smelled of hay and horse and mule, manure and leather and grain, and it glowed golden from the light of the lamps, set in lipped recesses in the walls to keep them from accidentally being knocked over and causing a fire. Jazen took a deep breath, stamping his feet to free them of snow and ice, shaking his hands to get the blood flowing again. It really wasn't so very bad at all. His opinion of Meleas went up another notch.

"What did you mean, 'someone's going to die of it'?" he asked. "And *could* they assassinate someone?—And why *would* they?"

Meleas took a horse blanket from a rack against the wall and spread it on a bale of hay, threw himself down on it, and worried a long golden stalk free to chew on thoughtfully. "Oh, only that I wouldn't like to threaten my lord Rizard," he said, staring up at the beams of the ceiling. "Yes, I think the Masters could do that, if they wanted. They can do a great deal."

One of the horses stuck an inquiring nose over a stall door and whickered.

"Not yet," Meleas said, answering the animal. "Finish your bran, or you'll colic again."

Jazen shook his head. He ought to be used to it by this time, but seeing Meleas speak to an animal as he might to a human being, and worse, seeing the animal behave as if it understood him, bothered him more than he liked to admit. This was the "knack" Adri-nes had told him about, months ago. It still seemed unnatural and demon-tainted, somehow, perhaps because it was so very matter of fact.

"*Is* Rizard a lord?" he asked, changing the subject. Unnatural Meleas might be, but he was also willing to answer any question that came into Jazen's head.

"I think he is. Adri would know, but he hasn't said. Rizard *acts* like a lord, though, and no commoner would wear those rings so openly."

Jazen made himself another couch on more of the stacked bales. "So what has that to do with someone dying?"

"Only that if you threaten a lord, they usually see that you don't do it again," Meleas said simply.

Jazen shivered inside. "Vettazen said the court thought we might be a threat," he pointed out.

There was a long pause, broken only by the grinding of equine teeth and the occasional stamping of a hoof or swishing of a tail.

"Aye," Meleas said. "And we are, you know. We must be either stronger than they are, or so impotent that they dismiss us. And if we're impotent, we can't do what we're here for."

"What *are* we here for, really? To kill people as far away as Seven Banners so Lord Ritash can be a duke?"

"We are here," Meleas said, his voice quiet as always, "to find demons and destroy them."

"Demonspawn!" Eri Weaver's-daughter yipped, throwing stones at him as he struggled to balance the copper buckets on the yoke over his shoulders.

"There haven't been demons for two hundred years," Jazen said sharply, forgetting for the moment all he had heard and learned over the past months. "They're all gone."

"My mother was taken by a demon," Meleas answered, his voice still quiet, still calm. "I watched her die of it. It took almost a year. Twice after she was possessed, she was able to speak to me herself. The first time she told me she loved me. The second time she asked me to kill her."

Jazen could barely breathe. "Did . . . did you?"

"If I had killed her, the demon would have taken me." There was another long pause. "Instead she died, and the demon moved on to my little sister. Firaloy came then. He burned the mataal in a cursefire, and tried to cast the thing out, but it was too late. My sister died, too. The demon—" Meleas took a long breath, continued as if he were telling a tale about someone else, as if it didn't really matter to him, "We don't know exactly what happened to the demon.

"I asked him to teach me how to destroy them. He brought me with him to Mirlacca, and I've been studying ever since." He sighed quietly. "I may not have the knack of it, though, whatever it is. My gift is animals. I'm very good at keeping rats out of the corn."

Jazen closed his eyes. He had never had a mother, or a sister, or any family he could call his own, but he could feel the loss in Meleas' measured words, taste the bitterness the other man did not permit to change his tone.

"Well, you *have* a gift," he said. "And perhaps one day the animals you speak to will destroy demons for you."

"One day," Meleas agreed. They were quiet a while longer. Then he added, "What's *your* gift? I'd thought I'd know it by now, but I don't."

Jazen bit his lip. "I don't know. I don't know if I even have one or not."

"Oh, you must." Meleas rolled over and propped his head on his hands. "That's one of the things Firaloy and Vettazen are best at, finding people with gifts. Take Adri, for instance. He can't work magic to save his life, but he can write spells that work.

"Not everyone has a gift, of course, and of those who do, some don't have much to work with. But they can find it if it's there, and I don't see why they'd have taken you in if you didn't."

I'm demonspawn, Jazen almost answered, but didn't. Whether it was true or not, it would be unkind to say, now that he knew more about the source of Meleas' hatred of Yaan Maat. But it still might be true. All those gifts and knacks that they spoke of, that all the exorcists pored over and boasted of so gleefully, all of them, according to the wisdom of Smattac, were demon-taint. All magic was, from the headache-curing spells of Neesen the herb witch to the dragon an exorcist contrived to teach anatomy.

Of course, according to the wisdom of the more sophisticated Mirlacca, they were all fraud, too.

"It has something to do with fire, surely," Meleas went on. Jazen wanted to tell him to be quiet, to tell him he didn't want a gift and if he had one, he didn't want to know anything about it, but it would jar Meleas out of his mood, and Jazen let him go on. "You can always get a fire started. And you were always running off to that forge, before we came here."

"I worked at the forge in Smattac," Jazen said defensively. "It's what I know."

"Oh, I know. You gave Bang-tail a new set of shoes. But

after you left Smattac, you kept seeking forges and fires. There's your gift. You should work on that."

"I don't think I *want* magic," Jazen said, momentarily panicking. "It's demon-born. It's evil." *And if I am demonspawn, and work magic, everyone will know. I don't know who I am. At least you knew your mother.* But he couldn't say that to the other man. "Why would anyone want anything to do with it?"

Another long pause. The wind rattled the stall doors, and the filly at the end of the line of stalls snorted and kicked at the stable wall in magnificent alarm. "Oh, shut up," Meleas yelled at her affectionately. "It isn't going to eat you.

"It isn't going to eat you, either," he went on to Jazen, "as long as you learn how to control it. We learned in the wars that we couldn't defeat the Yaan Maat with bows and lances and spears. We had to find humans who could use magic to do it.

"I don't even think magic belongs to the Yaan Maat. I think it's been around all along, and we just never needed it before. And if we're going to be prepared for the Yaan Maat to come back, we'd better know as much as we can. You need to study. To be prepared."

How can I study? Jazen thought angrily. *I'm in a house full of scholars!*

"I'll bet," Meleas went on, as if talking to himself, "I'll bet there are smith spells in the library. We could look for them."

Jazen's lips tightened.

"Better yet, we'll make Adri-nes find them. He knows more about what's in there than anyone else, even the Masters. We'll see if we can find a spell you can work, and maybe that will tell us what your gift is."

Meleas seemed pleased with his solution. Jazen shook his head. "I'm not a scholar or a priest. I can't read. Much," he amended, giving credit to the hours spent sweating over alphabets with Vettazen.

The blond man blinked. "Oh. Well, don't worry about that. You'll learn it. I don't like it much myself, but I learned, so you can too."

"What do I need it for anyway?" Jazen was surprised at his own belligerence. "I'm no scholar."

"Mostly so you can find more books for the rest of us. Maybe even write things down for *other* people to read." Meleas grinned. "Think of it as making some other poor sod's life miserable. Someone like Adri, for example." He laughed, and unwillingly, Jazen joined him. "Don't worry. We'll find a spell to start you out on, and give it a try." He got up, brushed the straw off his breeches, and held out a hand. "After all, you're one of us." He paused, struck by the expression on Jazen's face. "You really are, you know. So you'd better find your magic. We've got standards to maintain."

Chapter 13

"What's it supposed to do?" asked Alissa, climbing up on a hay bale and sitting cross-legged. She'd discovered Adri-nes searching the library, coaxed the story out of him, and demanded the chance to participate. Jazen wasn't too upset by her involvement; at least it wasn't Mikal, or Rayd. Alissa never looked down her nose at him, and treated him much as she did all the rest of the apprentices—as slightly impractical older brothers. She was, however, insatiably curious.

"It's a finder spell. You place this spell on something and then you can call it back to you." Adri-nes shook the hair out of his eyes and looked over the list of ingredients, checking them off in the pile in front of him. "Have any of you cretins seen my raven's foot? I should have made a spell pouch for this—" Spell pouches were a series of bags sewn onto a common backing, so that elements could be kept separate: herbs, stones, chalk, candles, whatever might be required to create the proper atmosphere, the proper focus, tune into the proper elements of the stream of magic.

Rizard, tired of having to assemble spell-makings every time he wanted to try something new, had designed the pouches, and the rest of the masters, except Firaloy, had adopted the idea.

Firaloy refused to have anything to do with spell pouches. He claimed they narrowed perceptions; if the makings of a spell were all ready to hand, he argued, there was no incentive to try new combinations, new components, and the search for new ways to use magic would be correspondingly restricted.

THE FOUNTAINS OF MIRLACCA

Jazen had no position on the debate. He was an apprentice. Vettazen told him to make spell pouches, and he made spell pouches.

"I thought it was supposed to be a smith spell," Jazen muttered to Meleas.

"All the smith spells use fire, and I'm not going to let you do a fire spell in the stable," Meleas returned. "Alissa, where's the chalk?"

"Here," she said, pulling out a piece of white chalk the size of her fist. "Does he have to do the circle, or can I do it?"

Adri-nes hesitated. "I think he has to do it."

"You mean you're all going to watch me do this?" Jazen was ready to forget the whole idea.

"Well, of course we are. We're going to do this, too, one of these days. Don't be silly." Alissa stuck out her lower lip and blew strays hairs out of her face. "Help me move this stuff, or you won't be able to do a big enough circle."

With Alissa directing, the men moved bales of hay and straw, sacks of grain, a honey wagon, rakes and brooms, and saddle racks. When they had finished to her satisfaction, Meleas groaned. "What a mess! We're going to have to get all this moved back when we are finished."

"He needs the room. All right, Jazen. You can begin now."

The three men exchanged glances over her head, careful not to laugh.

"Well? What are you waiting for? Come on. We don't want to be late for dinner."

This, at least, was an argument that made sense. Jazen looked around once more at the bare dirt and walls of the tack room. It didn't seem like an appropriate place to deliberately set out to do magic, somehow.

Especially not with an audience watching eagerly.

Still, everyone had to start somewhere.

He took a deep breath, digging his fingers into the lump of chalk, feeling it crumble under his fingertips, and leaned over to define a circle. Out of the corner of his eye, he saw Adri-nes draw breath to say something. To correct him, probably.

Before he could stop to ask what he was doing wrong,

Alissa planted an elbow firmly in Adri-nes' ribs, and nodded fiercely to Jazen.

They had heard about this over and over in lectures, but never tried it before, not on this scale. Jazen looked down and saw that the line wavered; a rock had interrupted its continuity. He dragged the chalk over it and continued, describing a circle large enough to enclose all four apprentices, with room to take perhaps five long strides from one side to the other.

Circle complete, he set the chalk aside and moved to the middle of the circle, took the half-made iyiza knife in his hands, and focused on it.

Magic, Firaloy had said, was will, will focused in such a way as to change some piece of the world around oneself. Those with the knack, the ability, could use the spells left by the Yaan Maat, and the spells created by humans since, to help focus the will to a particular outcome.

This knife, as yet half-made, was a part of him. Inherent in it was all the craft he knew. In its shape, as yet unrefined, could be seen its final purpose, the double edge, the length, the long tang waiting to be set to a handle. One could already tell it wouldn't be a simple eating-knife, used for the table; it had another destiny in store.

As this metal had taken heat from the fire, had glowed, he had seen imps dancing along it, singing, laughing, chortling to themselves as they had looked up at him. And when he had pulled the metal from the forge and set it on the anvil and slammed the hammer down upon it, they had dodged the blow and cursed him for it. He had struck the metal again and again and again, stretching it out, folding it back on itself and pounding it over and over and over again, folding it back, giving it back to the fire to glow and take on a life of its own.

Around him he could feel his friends—yes, they were his friends—watching anxiously, willing to help him, wanting to help him, their need for him to succeed as palpable as the length of metal in his hands. Adri-nes dark and shadowy, Meleas light and solid, little Alissa fierce and determined and flickering like flame itself. They held hands, linking themselves, wanting to somehow link to him but not doing so. This was his test. Only his.

He was saying words now, words he scarcely heard or remembered or paid attention to. He was telling the knife its story. The pattern in the metal was his pattern, of his making. There was no other blade in the world like this one, and without his skill, it was nothing. If he could focus his will on the spell as he had on this knife—

He could feel it. He could feel magic rising. The hairs on his arms rose up to the power. It moved to his words, to his focus, to his will. All of it, the power of it, the wanting of it, held within the rough circle, contained within the storage area, brought forth from himself and the power around him and poured into the metal in his hands. He told the knife its tale, its origin and making and destiny, how it would one day be completely finished, a part of him, a part of his past, and his future, the one part that might be refined in the fire but would remain always, essentially, Knife.

Drops of sweat from his forehead had fallen on the blade, sizzled on the blade, dropped on the little demons and drowned them and slowed them as the blows of the hammer had been unable to do, slowed them until the hammer had caught them and crushed them into the metal, demon and sweat and metal and will all made into Knife. His knife. The best that his skill could create, unfinished as yet.

The words of the spell.

The memory of the fire.

The focus of his will.

It was a part of him.

Part of him.

It would not leave him. He would not lose it. And when it was finished, perfect, knife and spell and magic, it would come at his call.

It would. He could feel it. Imbued with the power of the awkward spell, the unskilled sorcery, he could feel it still, with all the strength of his will; the will that had allowed him to survive alone among a people who were never alone, never uncertain, who always knew who they were; the will that he had summoned to walk away from all that he knew to enter into a life alien and strange, to not only survive but thrive; the will that caused him to reach out and cause the world around him to conform this small piece of it to *his will.* . . .

"*Demonspawn,*" *Eri Weaver's-daughter screamed* . . .

Suddenly the knife was molten hot in his hands, and he dropped it with a shocked cry.

The spell of the spell was broken as he stared down at his hands, watching them redden and swell, looking down to see the wisp of smoke as a scrap of straw caught under the half-made blade turned to ash.

Around him, Meleas and Adri-nes and Alissa broke apart to come close to him, not yet daring to touch him, to see if he was hurt.

The strength drained out of him suddenly and he sat down, his legs buckling.

"Jazen? Are you all right?" Alissa was the first to touch him, her hand light on his shoulder, on his face, raising it up to the torchlight. "Adri, open the door, get more light in here."

"We'll freeze," Adri-nes protested, but he stepped past the chalk circle to open the door to the light and the wind and the swirling snow.

And, as it happened, to Vettazen and Rizard, standing outside the tack room door, reaching to open the door themselves. The four young people drew apprehensive breaths.

The two Masters swept past Adri-nes and into the rooms, taking in the remains of the chalk circle, the pale, tense face of the boy-man sitting on the floor, the two standing over him, intent and protective.

"And do we need to inquire, exactly, what is going on here?" Rizard asked.

"Nothing," Jazen mumbled, putting one hand out to try to get to his feet. His palm landed on the tang of the knife, and he flinched at the warmth still remaining in it. His hand closed over it and he staggered to his feet. "There's nothing here, I was just . . . and they, they weren't doing anything."

"But my dear boy, the place stinks of power." Rizard's elegant nostrils flared. "Can't you feel it?"

Jazen could not. He was far too numb. He could, however, see the recognition in the eyes of his companions, and the awareness in the newcomers. They could tell that power had been raised in this place.

He couldn't tell whether he was sick with disappointment at his own inability to detect it too, or giddy with triumph because if it was there, it was there because he, Jazen sr'Yat, of no clan and unknown parentage, had caused it to happen.

"Jazen," Vettazen said, her voice brisk and practical as always, "what in the name of flames and flowers were you trying to do?"

"He wanted to find his gift," Alissa, equally practical, told her. "He didn't know what it was. I think he does now. I *think*." The last was added doubtfully, as she glanced at Jazen sidelong. Meleas stood close, to catch him in case his swaying got out of control.

Jazen shut his eyes against the temptation to strangle the child.

"That isn't exactly what we were asking," Rizard said. "What spell were you casting?"

Adri-nes cleared his throat, nervous. "It was, er, one of mine."

"One of . . . *yours*?" Rizard's eyebrow arched high in disbelief.

"It was a good spell," Adri-nes responded, indignant. "It worked!"

"Did it, now." The Masters' heads swiveled as one to look at Jazen.

"Let me see that knife." Vettazen held out her hand in peremptory fashion.

Reluctantly, Jazen handed it over. It was cool enough to handle now. He watched it with an odd hunger as it turned end to end in Vettazen's square, capable hands, as she passed it over to Rizard for inspection. The younger Master tested one as-yet-unhoned edge, made a surprised sound as a line of blood appeared on his thumb.

"It's sharper than it looks," Jazen said. At Rizard's glance, he added, "sir."

The Masters traded looks.

"What was the intent of this spell?" Rizard asked, still holding the knife lightly in the palm of his hand.

Jazen licked his lips. There was no help forthcoming from Adri-nes or Meleas or Alissa. Spells were the responsibility of those who cast them. He had heard Vettazen say that, but until now had not realized just what it meant.

"I wanted it to come when I called," he whispered.

"Did you?" Rizard pursed his lips, considering, then laid the blade down on the beaten earth at his feet. "Call it, then."

They were all staring at him. Waiting. And he was looking at the piece of metal on the ground and trying to think of the right words, trying to recapture the feeling of rising power pouring into the blade, and . . . and there was nothing there, nothing at all.

"Jazen?" he could hear Adri-nes say, pleading. Adri, too, had a stake in this. It was his spell, after all.

If they would just stop *looking* at him . . .

He reached out his hand, flat, as if pleading with the knife to rise up from the dirt and slap itself into his palm as the knives of assassins were said to do in the tales.

For a moment, the knife stirred. And it was not his imagination; he could hear the indrawn breaths of the people around him as it twitched, careless as a cat, considering. He could feel his eyelids stretching wide as he stared at it, willing it to move again, to come to him. He could feel himself focused on it, pulled toward it.

But the knife did not move.

After long moments, Rizard sighed. "Well. This was not, perhaps, the most successful of your experiments?"

The apprentices looked around at each other, guiltily.

"I think some discipline is called for here," Vettazen said grimly. "And perhaps some training, as well. I shall expect all of you, after dinner tonight, to present yourselves in the upper hall; I think some basic exercises would be appropriate."

"So long as they involve dusting," Rizard sighed. "The hall is *such* a mess, isn't it?"

The Masters left. After a long moment, Alissa brushed her hands together and said regretfully, "I suppose this means mop buckets, too. I'd better see about that."

Adri-nes nodded. "It should have worked. I thought it *did* work. I felt *something,* didn't you, Meleas?"

Meleas shrugged. "Apparently we were wrong, at least this time." He and Adri-nes turned and moved to the door.

Jazen leaned down to pick up the recalcitrant knife, and yelped in surprise. The blade was hot again, as hot as if it had just been pulled from the fire—

—but this time, his hands did not burn.

Chapter 14

"I think it's silly," Rayd said. "Tiris never asked me to do anything like this." The twelve apprentices were all seated at the refectory benches, with old scrolls, parchments, razors, rulers, and writing-blocks before them. The blocks held inkpots and quills and polishing-squares made of animal teeth. The Masters assembled had decided that the young people needed more than mere exercises, and the most useful thing they could do would be to make fair copies of every book in the library.

"I agree. There's nothing of value in this." Mikal sneered, shoving himself back from the table and gathering unheeded glares from the others sharing his bench. "Why should we be punished just because the yokel can't work a simple piece of magic? This is copyist work. Any clerk in the marketplace could do it."

Adri-nes paused in his careful lining of a piece of parchment and said softly, "What would a clerk want with it?"

"What do *we* want with it?" Mikal responded, snapping his fingers. A shower of sparks appeared in the air over his head. "*Some* of you may need such childish exercises. *I* do not."

"What would you do, then?" someone else asked from farther down the table.

"I'll find some spellwork of my own. Not this trivial stuff. Real magic. That'll make them notice."

"Do you think you could work one of these?" Adri-nes challenged. He had a set of wax tablets beside him, and in be-

THE FOUNTAINS OF MIRLACCA

tween copying was making notes about the scrolls he worked on.

Mikal hesitated. Adri-nes laughed, turning back to his work. Mikal said abruptly, "I'll bet I'll work one before you ever will."

Adri shook his head. "That's no bet. We all know where my talent lies."

"Well, before Jazen does, then. Before *any* of the rest of you!"

Adri shook his head. Meleas, though, looked up and said softly, "I'll take that bet. How much are you willing to risk, southerner?"

The rest of the apprentices held their breath, looking from one of them to the other.

"Three goldens and all my silver," Mikal said. "I'll work one of the Great Spells before that yokel does. Probably before he even learns to *read* them."

"Done."

"And I, too," Alissa piped up. "Against you, Mikal."

Even Adri-nes looked startled. But Meleas turned back to his work, humming to himself. Mikal, too, settled back and started scraping a parchment clean, finally tearing it and giving up to stomp out of the room in disgust.

Jazen, trying desperately to make sense of the scroll held down by weights in front of him, half-listened to the squabbling. He could puzzle out some of the words on the leather, but most of them were merely marks. His fist was white as he clutched the quill, its point hovering over the scraped surface of the palimpsest. A drop of rusty ink gathered at the feather's tip and dripped onto the yellow-white surface, spreading a bit as it soaked in. He bit his lip. Would the mark mean something? Would it change something?

He would never finish this, never. All of them could do it, all except himself; even little Alissa could copy the exercise without effort—indeed, she had been the first to finish it, since she spent no time protesting it to begin with.

Now she tapped Jazen on the arm, and he jerked around, covering the scrap of parchment with his arm to prevent her from seeing its blankness.

"You can't think in here," she said, making a face at Mikal's back. "Come with me."

"Where?"

"Vettazen's study. It's quiet there. She's at the palace."

He might as well fail there as elsewhere. As he got to his feet, he saw Meleas watching, and nodded to him. To his relief, the blond man came to join them. Adri was deep in his own project, and shrugged off the invitation.

"We're going to Vettazen's," Alissa informed him, and the three of them slipped out the back way and up the stairs to the rooms on the third floor, which were reserved for the Masters.

"I don't understand why we're supposed to do this either," Jazen said under his breath as they opened Vettazen's door. "Mikal's right, damn it. It's copyist work. Why ask all of us to copy out bits and pieces of scrolls?"

"Because the more copies there are, the less likely the information is to be lost." Vettazen was seated at her table. "And as you scribe words on parchment, if you're fortunate, you scribe them into your memory as well."

"Begging your pardon, mistress," Meleas said for the three of them. "We didn't know you were here."

"We thought you were—"

"She wouldn't have gone alone—"

"And why not?"

The three apprentices looked at each other, thinking of thieves, thugs, magic, and realizing that there really was no reason Vettazen, Guildmaster, should not go anywhere she wished, alone.

"Oh, come in. You can stay if you'll build up that fire. What are you working on?"

"Herb lists," Meleas said promptly. "I had no idea there were so many plants in the world."

"And I was copying out the poisons that could be made from them," Alissa added primly. "Dreadful things."

"And you, Jazen?"

He shook his head. "I don't know." He tossed the scrolls down on a small table next to the wall case, and turned to the stack of wood by the fireplace, pulling out three new logs.

THE FOUNTAINS OF MIRLACCA 139

"I'm useless at copying. I might as well make your fire for you."

Vettazen merely looked at him, without contempt. "Then I expect your friends will have to help you. You have no objection to being helped, I trust?"

"Of course we'll help," Alissa said, pulling up a chair, sweeping her skirts aside and curling up into it. "Meleas?"

Meleas paused. "Mistress, may I ask one question?"

Vettazen sighed and rubbed the bridge of her nose. "Only one. I have work of my own to do, you know."

"Will this copy-work really help us destroy demons?"

"Yes. Not immediately, perhaps. But when the day comes, you'll be glad of it." A small smile quirked the corner of her mouth. "Aye, even lists of herbs you never heard of."

After a long moment, Meleas nodded sharply and turned back to Jazen and the girl, pulling up a stool beside them. "Let us see, then."

Sounds became symbols. Sounds made words. Symbols made words. Alissa found a tablet and a stylus for Jazen to practice with, shaping and rubbing clean, rubbing the surface thin and spreading the soft wax even again. After a while the scroll and shift of lines became almost familiar, as Alissa pulled scrolls and books off the shelves at random, setting him to find the symbols, as Meleas drilled him over and over, patiently, on their order. They were no closer to copying his assigned scroll, though, when Vettazen came over, a new torch and a new scroll in hand, and dropped the scroll on the table in front of them.

"Look at this one," she advised.

Jazen picked it up and unrolled it. It was the one Vettazen had been trying to teach him from earlier, the scroll with the spell he had chanted in the stable. He could recognize some of the words—

He could recognize some of the words. His head jerked up and he stared at her, mouth open.

"Now you see?" she said. "That's what words are for. Now copy it out."

She turned away, affecting not to hear when Alissa leaned

over and said, "And make an extra copy for yourself. You'll use it one of these days."

It became a contest, then, among the apprentices, to see who could first cast a spell from one of the Great Books. The Masters took no apparent notice, though, as Adri-nes acidly observed, one of them always seemed to be around when one of the apprentices drew a focus-circle. Rayd ended up under Demachee's direct supervision when he took the backlash of a spell directly upon himself one night; the news that he'd been blinded as a result of his own efforts dampened their eagerness for a while. Rizard used the incident as an object lesson; concentration on exercises increased substantially. Still, by the time the trees in the front garden had put forth leaves, each of the apprentices had his or her own spell chosen.

Competition was not their only occupation; this spring day, Alissa had received a visit from her mother. Alissa's mother was an older image of her daughter, of the same height but ten pounds heavier, her hair whiter. The three young men stood about the fountain in the courtyard, trying to be inconspicuous as Alissa greeted her mother with exuberant cries and extravagant hugs. The fountain water had turned and cleared again before Alissa came to the point of taking her mother by the arm and half-dragging her over to introduce her.

Worse still, the woman knew Adri-nes' family, and spent no little time gushing about how well dear Lady Elise looked. Adri-nes stood there smiling, holding her hand, as if he had seen his parents within the last three years or so.

Jazen suffered through the formal greetings, ducking his head and mumbling, "I, uh, I don't know," to all the woman's questions. He had no idea what he was answering, only that he wanted to be away from the woman's bright knowing eyes that probed him, as if looking for his antecedents in the arrangement of his features, in the length of his bones, the size of his hands.

Alissa was too excited to stand with them long; after a few

minutes she pulled her mother away, promising to bring her back after giving her the full tour of the Guildhouse.

Adri-nes, Meleas, and Jazen looked at each other. "Shall we wait?" Meleas drawled.

"I promised a lady I'd visit her," Adri-nes murmured, making a patently false show of regret.

"Good. Then you won't be around to tell her I've gone to soak a horse's leg in liniment." Meleas smiled. "I should be finished by dinnertime."

"I won't," Adri-nes said, smirking. "Jazen?"

"I have something I need to do," Jazen said hastily. "In the city."

They went their separate ways, and Jazen slipped out the front gate to go back into Mirlacca.

It had been long since he had gone anywhere in the city alone; usually several of them went out together. He walked quickly down the Guildhouse way, past the intersection with the jeweler's lane, before the fact of being alone reminded him of where he had gone the last time.

He had no idea whether Gilé would remember him or not, but he still carried the half-made knife with him, and a long afternoon's work would just about finish it. He headed for the southwest, through the twisting ways of the city, considerably more sure of himself now than he had been the autumn before.

The street had not changed so much; it still rang with the music of hammers and anvils, light chimes rather than the heavy bells of the great work, still stank of coal and burned leather, still gleamed with the dust of precious metals. The shop Gilé kept still displayed good wares, eating-knives and double-pronged items for spearing food. Jazen picked one up, examining it curiously; one prong was flattened, but the metal was too soft to take a good edge.

"A gift for a lady," Gilé said. "The latest thing at court, and we have a clever sheath for them, by agreement with the leatherworkers."

Jazen set the implement carefully back in its place and looked up to meet the shopkeeper's eyes. "Branching out, then?"

"Ah, the Smith of Unfinishing!" Gilé laughed. "And where have you been? Still living on the high side of the hill?"

"Ah, no." Jazen was reluctant, suddenly, to tell the man where he lived. When he walked this street, he was a smith, not an apprentice exorcist. "How are you, Gilé?"

"Well enough, well enough. You have changed, boy. Grown up—I almost didn't know you. Got some more muscle on you. Come back behind. Did you ever finish that knife you were working on?"

Laughing awkwardly, Jazen pulled the half-made weapon from his belt pouch and showed it to the other man. Gilé lifted the barrier between shop and street, and Jazen stepped through, back into a place at once familiar and strange.

By the time the sun slipped down, he had heard all about Gilé's wedding, the politics of the Guild of Smiths, the price and hardness of the newest steel ingots, the profit of selling a custom sheath with a knife. Gilé did not expect him to stand idle and listen; the fire was hot, and he had a hammer shoved into his hands as soon as he stepped behind the screen. He worked as Gilé talked, listening with half his mind and putting the finish on the blade with the other, from the fire to the polish wheel, from the honing strap to the soft leather buffer. Gilé watched and talked, offering light criticism, suggestions, anecdotes.

Finally he held the blade up to the last rays of the sun, watching the light glistening in the shimmering wave pattern in the steel and reflecting off the polished guards, and wire wrapped tight around the grip. The only shadow lay in the narrow groove running down the length of the blade for lightness. It was work such as Belzec, back in Smattac, had never seen; Gilé, watching, was impressed. "And does it have an edge?" he asked, half-joking.

Jazen arched his eyebrows and held out his arm, looking at the dark hair. "Well, we shall see—"

He set the blade on the back of his arm, pulled it lightly toward him, and blew gently.

A patch of dark hair danced into the air.

"Now you have to sharpen it again," Gilé said, ever practical. Jazen smiled.

When he left the smith's house late that evening, he carried at his hip a new sheath, a new knife hilted in metal and leather. It rode there as if it were a part of him.

He no longer felt alone.

Chapter 15

By the time the leaves of the courtyard trees fell into the pool of the fountain, Jazen was almost used to going with Vettazen to the palace. Sometimes he and Meleas played escort, sometimes he went alone. Once in a very long while Adri-nes came too, and then they took the long way around, to avoid Adri's oldest brother, or any other members of his family. No one wanted a repetition of the confrontation at the Presentation.

Back at the Guildhouse, some of the other apprentices, particularly Mikal, at first resented the fact that when Vettazen chose to have an escort, Jazen was always included, no matter who else went along. After a while they took it for granted. The rest of them worked magic, they reasoned; Jazen was a bodyguard. After a while he thought of it that way too.

He was no longer uncomfortable walking on mosaic floors, exchanging small talk with courtiers as they waited for Lasvennat's pleasure or that of some other lord. They spent hours, sometimes, waiting. Occasionally several of the lesser nobles would summon them, as if they were performers in a street fair juggling demons for their pleasure.

It was always Vettazen, never Firaloy, never Rizard or any of the other Masters. She would not perform for the nobles, save for a moment or two—enough to make them suspect the possibility of the power she possessed, not enough to make them fear. Her dignity, and the scraps she threw them, made them hunger for her the more.

"What did you see tonight?" Vettazen asked Jazen one cool

evening, as they threaded their way through a maze of alleys behind the palace, heading home.

Jazen knit his brows. "What do you mean? We saw Lord Lasvennat, and Lady Ritash. And the Heir. He doesn't look any better."

"Listen to the question, Jazen. What did you see tonight?"

So it was another lesson. He drew a deep breath. "I saw nobles, and their servants. They hovered around His Highness, and they flattered you."

"And?" They had to walk single file through the alley, kicking garbage out of their way; the houses leaned in to one another, almost touching at the rooftops. Jazen could hear Vettazen's footsteps behind him, but it was too dark to see. The street itself was quiet; dozens of people might be behind the thick walls his shoulder brushed against, but no sound would penetrate.

He thought about the question. She was looking for something. Not people. Feeling his way along the wall, he turned the corner into a wider street, glanced back to make sure she was still there.

"How did they seem?" she prompted.

"They seemed . . ." He paused, considering the looks that passed between those who did not know themselves observed, the brittle laughter, the sharp movements. All those things were typical of the nobles. But there was, perhaps, something more—something in the way Lasvennat moved toward them as they were taking their leave—

"There's something specific Lasvennat wants," he said, sure of it. "He wants something, but he doesn't want to ask you in front of the others. And when the Heir started coughing, he looked—I don't know. He was expecting something, I thought."

"Very good." Vettazen was smiling; he could hear it in her voice. "And what might that be?"

"I don't know."

She moved up to walk beside him, down the middle of the street. The wider streets in Mirlacca, in the newest or richest quarters, were relatively clean, and graveled to help the carriages of the wealthy travel smoothly. The rocks crunched under their feet. Here, too, slow-burning torches marked the intersections, providing the illusion of light to walk by.

"Well," she said at last, "at least you admit it when you don't know something."

He shrugged. "There's so much I don't know, one more thing is no shame."

She laughed. "Would that more of us knew so much. Well, then—with regard to our evening, and that which the good Lord Lasvennat wishes to know: I don't know either."

"How could *I* know, then?"

Vettazen smiled at him. "I thought you might have an intuition. People do, sometimes. And you do have a good sense about people, Jazen."

"Do I?"

She nodded. "Of course you do. That's why you're here, isn't it? Because you thought you could trust us, Firaloy and Adri-nes and Meleas and me? You knew that."

He shrugged again. "I was lucky."

"And luck was all it was, of course. As you wish. But if some idea should occur to you, what Lord Lasvennat wants so badly, even some wisp of an idea, you come to me and tell me. All right?"

They turned the last quarter, headed up the hill toward the Guildhouse gates.

"How am I to know," Jazen said consideringly, "whether the wisp of an idea is a good idea, or just something to tell you?"

Vettazen laughed again, a gentle, silvery laugh. "Oh, Jazen, if you only knew how wise you are. Don't worry about it. Just promise me you'll come to me, and let me worry about whether it's truth or not."

"As you say," Jazen said doubtfully. They were standing at the gate now, and he pounded on it with the flat of his hand. "Why," he went on, "can't we find a spell to let us know who stands at the door?"

"Because then we'd have no reason to keep you up all night standing watch," she said sweetly, as the gate opened wide before them. "And it's your turn tonight, isn't it? Thank you, Alissa; Jazen will take over now."

Alissa nodded, stuffing a fist in her mouth in a futile effort to swallow a yawn. "Everybody's in," she said, preparing to follow Vettazen inside. "Should be quiet."

With that she was gone too, and Jazen was alone in the chill of the deep night. There was no point in standing around in the courtyard, watching the water in the fountain pool ice over; the apprentices on door duty stayed in the tack room. The animals in their stalls snuffled greetings, or merely looked over the half-doors of their stalls to see who was there and then ignored him.

He rather liked the peace and quiet of door duty; he could practice his reading and writing in the light of the carefully shielded torches. Tonight, though, he was still wondering about what he was supposed to have seen in the palace. He was flattered, and rather taken aback, at Vettazen's remark that he had a good sense about people; was that, perhaps, his particular gift? Or was it only the ability to watch, developed out of the need to know when a blow would come his way if he were not careful?

He sighed. Since that day when he had tried to call his knife, he had not felt anything he could call power. Others claimed to have it; Mikal was particularly loud in that respect. One of the reasons he was so close to Adri-nes and Meleas, Jazen thought, was that neither of them made any particular claim to spectacular gifts. Adri could not work the spells he wrote at all; Meleas could hold a maddened horse with a touch, or coax a terrified kitten into his arms, but he could not cast spells. The Masters debated about it. Rumors floated that some considered Meleas' ability to be demon-born because his mother had been possessed; Firaloy declared the idea nonsense and threatened to throw out anyone who suggested such a thing again in his hearing. Meanwhile Meleas studied with the rest, broadening his knowledge, talking to the animals and listening to what they had to say. Mostly, he reported, they talked about food. And even though twelve-year-old Alissa was beginning to find some success with a specialized branch of herb magic, there didn't seem to be much demand for a gift of making saffron turn blue. She was a friend, too. Jazen felt he fit in with her, Adri, and Meleas, better than with the others who could create more impressive illusions.

He pulled his knife out of its sheath, turning it over and over in his hands. It was his best work, far better than any magic he'd ever done. Perhaps he should stick to metalwork after all.

"Jazen?" Alissa stuck her head around the corner. "Did you see my book?"

He looked up, startled. "There's no book here. What are you doing still awake?"

"I was thinking about something and couldn't sleep. I thought I left my book here. It has to be—there it is." The book in question was made of thin shingles of wood looped together at one end to protect the rough paper pages between. "I hate it when I lose things."

"You must hate it a lot, then." Jazen smiled. "You lose everything you put a hand to." His glance fell on the knife in his hands, and an idea suddenly occurred to him. The last time, the knife had not been complete—

"Alissa, help me."

"What?" She was yawning again. "I only came down for this. What do you want? It's cold."

"I want to try something." He held out the knife to her, hilt first. "I want you to take this and hide it somewhere."

"Have you been getting into the wine?" the little girl said, looking doubtfully from blade to man and back again.

"No, really. I want to see if I can make it come back to me."

From the expression on her face, he could tell she wasn't sanguine about his chances of success. Still, she took the knife, carefully. "How long are you going to try?"

"Just tonight. Really." He hesitated. "Don't hide it too well, please. If this doesn't work, I want to find it again in the morning."

She stuck out her tongue at him, tucked the blade in her belt, and went away.

Then he had to wait, to give her enough time to put the knife somewhere. The masters all recommended meditation, to gather one's concentration, to focus one's powers. Jazen, who was not at all sure he had any such power anyway, paced, up

THE FOUNTAINS OF MIRLACCA

and down the aisle beside the stall doors until the roan mule reached over and snapped at him.

He laughed. "Would Meleas say you were telling me to let you sleep in peace, brother?"

The mule eyed him, waiting for another chance. Jazen slapped lightly at his muzzle, ducking as the animal threw up its head, and went back to the tack room.

Now he could remain still. Spells were a way to focus the will.... He sat down cross-legged on the cold, straw-strewn earth, got up again hastily to look for a spare blanket, spent some time creating a comfortable place to establish himself.

Finally he had a small nest set up on the ground, and was certain Alissa had not only had time to hide the knife but was probably already fast asleep. Sitting down again, he took a deep breath and closed his eyes.

He wasn't sure how one spoke to an inanimate object. He tried first to create the image of the knife in his mind: the double-edged blade half again longer than his own hand; the double-shouldered guard; the wire-bound hilt; the knob on the end, not too small, not too large. It was a good knife, serviceable, without flaws; the blade shimmered with its melded metals, but you had to know what you were seeing. Otherwise it was quite plain and unprepossessing. His best work.

He called up the memory of that hilt in his hand, of how well it fit; of how the wrapped wire gave him something to hold on to. It was proportioned properly, too. He could balance it on a fingertip.

His breathing slowed. It was *his* knife; his strength and sweat and some drops of his blood, too, when he'd cut himself on a ragged bit of metal, had gone into the making of it. He had watched the imps dancing on its edge, out of the corner of his eye. It was part of him, made part of him as nothing had ever been before, and he wanted it *back* from wherever it was, wanted to *know* where it was—

In the same moment, he saw very clearly an image of the knife, stuck deep in a pile of straw around the fountain, and the sheath at his hip burst into flames.

Chapter
16

He yelped in shock, clawed at the strings to rip away his belt and fling it, sheath and all, across the room. The flames had caught at his shirt, too, and an insanely giggling, red and golden imp was climbing up his tunic lacings. Screaming, he beat at the thing. It snarled at him, its face all beak and narrow eyes, its claws digging through leather and cloth to ribs, leaving welts and blisters as it advanced, licking at him and spreading wings of sparks and ash that smoldered, flared, and popped new implings into being. They in turn dug into his skin and clothing, tore at him.

Frantic, he dropped, rolled, crushing the flames into the straw. The imp shrieked in rage and was smothered out of existence.

Across the room, the sheath, resting point-first in a loose bale of straw, was enveloped in flames. Billows of smoke rose and hung in the air. The animals in the stalls next door kicked at the walls and called out at the smell of smoke.

It was only a small fire, as yet. He staggered out into the courtyard, fumbling for a bucket.

The cold night air slapped him. Gasping, he stumbled to the fountain and dashed the bucket in it, filling it halfway and turning back to the stable.

The back wall of the room was a solid mass of flames. As he watched, the halters and ropes hung neatly on the wall turned red, brightened, and crumbled to the floor. The horses screamed. The door to the roan mule's stall burst outward from the bottom, and the mule brayed and burst out, thundering past him. The fire roared, probed the walls, sent tongues of flame probing into the rafters and beams of the roof.

Those beams were the floor to Meleas' rooms. Jazen plunged back into the tack room, calling for him, yelling to wake him up and get him out of the stable, away from the smoke, the fire.

For all the brightness of the flames, it was chokingly dark inside the stable; smoke hung in drapes from the ceiling. He could see nothing, nothing at all. He could tell the bucket in his hand was empty only from the lightness of it; he needed to get more water, put the water on the fire, put out the fire. The roaring of the fire was a buzzing in his ears. He couldn't see.

The smoke was thick in his lungs, spreading itself across his face, his mouth, sucking the air out and devouring it. Fear shot through his veins and he spun around, trying to find the door back to the courtyard. The bucket hit something solid and knocked him off balance, sending him to both hands and one knee, then to both knees. He could hear shouting now, far away, on the other side of the blackness. He could hear the laughter of the imps in the flames, dancing free in a fire larger than any he had seen before. He had always thought he would die in the heat of the forge. . . . There were lights flickering before his eyes, not the colors of fire but of silks, blue and green and red and yellow, and he was sinking to the ground, his fingers scrabbling at the earth.

Someone, or more than one, was dragging him by his feet, the straw rolling up past his chin, his cheek, his eye, over the lintel of the stable, across the flat stones. Dropping his feet, they threw him over on his back. The smoke melted away from his skin, taking the heat with it. Fingers pressed roughly under his jaw, seeking a pulse. His head was jerked back, leaving his jaw gaping, and his nostrils pinched shut. A mouth closed over his and pushed breath into his lungs, came away again as hands pushed at his rib cage and forced the air out. And again. And again. He couldn't move, couldn't even open his eyes; could only lie there, with the roaring of the fire and the screaming of living things in his ears, feeling the spatter of gravel as people ran past, the scrambling of effort to quench the fire.

Someone took him by the shoulders and shook him, and his lungs were working again, rising and falling like the great bellows, gulping in clean air, untainted by smoke. His eyes opened, and his head rolled to one side, as if of its own volition; he could not move, could barely breathe. There wasn't enough air in the air.

He was lying halfway across the courtyard, his vision blocked by the fountain. Horses milled, fighting their tethers to get back into the treacherous safety of their stalls. Shadowy figures raced back and forth. Flames fingered the sky. Masters and apprentices alike, supplemented by people Jazen barely recognized from having seen them in the street, passed buckets along a human chain. Fire outside of its appointed place was the enemy. . . . Belzec had said that.

Jazen fainted.

Demachee the Healer had a large room to herself in the east wing of the house. The early sun came through the tall windows, a cold, watery light striping the benches and shelves crowded with pots and jars and mortars with pestles thrust askew, and crept up the side of the cot set up against the wall. The unbleached sheets were pulled up to Jazen's chin. He coughed, experimentally, and it triggered a fit of real coughing, tearing at his throat. He propped himself up on one arm, and the sheet slipped down. He snatched at it as Alissa came in and shut the door behind her.

"Oh, you're awake." She had her hands on her hips again. "I hope you're proud of yourself."

He tried to say something, but his throat was as raw as if he had swallowed cracked glass.

"Oh, be still. I can fix something for you—"

"Meleas—" he forced himself to say.

"Oh. Meleas?" She was talking over her shoulder now, busying herself with a heating dish, a pot of honey, a bottle of wine. "He's fine. And a good thing for you it is, too, that he got all the animals out; he'd fair to kill you if they'd got hurt. What did you *do* last night?"

THE FOUNTAINS OF MIRLACCA

He shook his head, flopped back on the cot dizzy with relief. Alissa was not disturbed by his lack of response. "You're in a lot of trouble anyway. Half the stable's gone. All the harness is burned up. Gods alone know how we'll replace it; Rache says that her friends are laughing at us. Ill luck isn't supposed to find sorcerers, they say." Turning to him with a deep cup, she asked, "Can you sit up again, or shall I call Mikal in to help?"

Grimacing, he found the strength to sit up, wedging himself against the wall, and the youngest apprentice sat on the edge of the cot and held the cup to his lips. The liquid was smooth and harsh at once, sweet from the honey, cutting the phlegm. He swallowed wrong, and Alissa pulled the drink back and held a cloth of soft cotton to his mouth as he hacked and choked. The cloth came away black.

"Soot inside you," she said critically. "You're lucky you weren't in there long; there was oil in the straw, gods know why. Demachee says you'll be all right with just rest, and some things she'll make up to help you cough."

"I don't need help coughing," he muttered rebelliously. It started another fit, and he gagged up more black mucus. After, he lay back down and tried not to breathe at all.

"So did it work?" she asked, taking the cloth away and bringing him a new one.

"What?" he whispered.

"The spell you were trying. To find the knife. That's why you had me hide it, wasn't it?"

The spell. He had nearly forgotten. "It was by the fountain. In the straw." His hand brushed across his face, his hair. "What . . . ?"

"We had to cut some of your hair. It got burned. And, well, it was too long anyway, so I trimmed it."

It was almost funny. He had kept his hair cut short for so long for just that reason while he worked at the forge. Letting it grow long had been a way of telling himself he was free of all that, but fire reached out for him anyway.

"I suppose they're angry. The Masters, I mean."

"Well, I should think so." Alissa was back at the table, mixing up another potion. "The stables will have to be rebuilt. They wanted to know what happened."

"Who told them?"

"No one has, yet," Vettazen said, striding into the room with an air of vast irritation. "Alissa told us you asked her to hide your knife, and the next thing we know the whole compound nearly goes up in flames. What happened in there? You of all people know better than to play games with fire."

He lay back and tried to look pathetic. "I was—practicing." He coughed experimentally. The bid for sympathy turned into another full-fledged choking upheaval.

Vettazen let Alissa duck past her and tend to her patient. She waited until Jazen was lying down again, and then asked, inexorably, "Practicing what, exactly?"

Closing his eyes, Jazen gave up. "A finding spell. For my knife. It worked, too; I found it. But my sheath caught fire—" *Caught fire* was putting it mildly; resin-soaked logs exploded that way, but nothing else he could think of.

"You have heard us mention backspells, from time to time?" Vettazen inquired, her voice deceptively mild. "It did not occur to you that a backlash might be associated with your finding spell?"

It hadn't, in fact, but Jazen was unwilling to admit that. Now, too late, he remembered what had happened the first time he had drawn the circle and tried the spell. Opening one eye, he looked for some support from Alissa, but she had her back to him. Vettazen, on the other hand, was standing over him, glaring down at him. "No, mistress."

"I see." Vettazen continued to glare. "It did not occur to you that perhaps this might be a greater spell than you were equipped to handle?"

"No, mistress." He could barely whisper the words. Vettazen was angrier than he'd ever seen her. The anger didn't bother him nearly as much as the sound of disappointment in her voice. No one had ever had expectations for him before.

"I see." She exhaled heavily. "Alissa, when will he be able to leave here?"

"Mistress Demachee says breathing smoke can cause great trouble, mistress." Alissa was being unwontedly formal. "She

THE FOUNTAINS OF MIRLACCA

wants to keep Jazen here for at least two days, to make sure he got out in time."

"Very well." Vettazen wiped her hands down the sides of her skirt. "As soon as Mistress Demachee is satisfied that it is appropriate, you are to move back to your room, Jazen, and stay there until the Masters of your guild summon you."

He had been out of the infirmary for three days before the knock on the door finally came. It was Mikal, looking grim and condemnatory and quite pleased with his task as message-bearer: Jazen was ordered to present himself immediately to a gathering of all the masters, and to bring the iyiza knife with him.

"What are they going to do?" he asked, before he could stop himself.

Mikal shrugged. "I don't know. They're *very* angry. Maybe they'll throw you out . . . Maybe they'll just flog you." He left Jazen standing staring at his back as he nearly ran down the hall, as if afraid that being near the culprit might cause him to be accused too.

The gallery on the second floor of the Guildhouse ran the length of the front of the building. The windows overlooking the courtyard below were set deeply enough that one could sit on the benches and read, or merely look out the window and think, hiding oneself if necessary behind the long curtains that provided insulation against the winter cold. No one was sitting there now.

At one end of the gallery, a long table was set up, and the eight Masters of the Guildhouse sat at it, waiting for Jazen. Entering from the other end, he had to walk the length of the building toward them, feeling their eyes upon him, looking desperately for some sign of what they were thinking. Firaloy held center position, tapping a stylus point against the surface before him, the skin around his eyes wrinkled as he strained to focus. On his right sat Demachee, the healer, a thin, nervous woman with a tic; to his left was the elegant, bejeweled Rizard, his face unreadable as always. A lord, Meleas thought Rizard was; the man looked it now, remote and uninvolved.

To Rizard's left sat Tiris, Rayd's master, then Vettazen at

the end of the table, her gray eyes sad. On the other side of Demachee was Chezayot of desert Elzael, bundled up in several layers of clothing and cloak, always complaining about the cold; Dalzen, Mikal's master, as supercilious as his student; and the last master of the guild, Erriziachet, a fat blond woman who always carried a deck of fortunetelling cards. When Jazen was four strides away from the table, Firaloy raised his hand, and Jazen stopped, taking whatever comfort there might be in the fact that none of the other apprentices was invited to this particular gathering.

No stool was available, and Jazen wasn't sure he would have used it if there were. The eight masters of the Guild of Exorcists stared at him, and he didn't need the silent hum of magic in the air to tell him of their power. Only once before, when Firaloy had made his first speech to the apprentices assembled, had he seen all eight of them together this way.

Vettazen, it seemed, was speaking for the Masters as a body on this occasion, though Jazen could tell that Rizard wanted very much to supplement her words with some acid comments of his own. She summarized the events of the night before in the stable in a succinct fashion. None of it appeared to be new to any of them.

He had thought that this further experimentation with his knife was innocent. Apparently, the masters did not share that opinion. Clearly, they were less than pleased about the unauthorized experimentation. They passed the knife among them, with much whispering and pursing of lips and shaking of heads. Jazen gathered that they thought the knife had been enspelled in one single session; he didn't tell them about the forging at Gilé's. Nor did he tell them about the imps in the forgeflames. They hardly seemed important any more, anyway.

The masters examined the pattern of the spell he used, and found that it could be modified, to a limited extent, to find other things associated with the spellcaster. That, they told him, meant it was magic, and not simply a peculiar gift of his own.

"Jazen sr'Yat," Vettazen said finally, from her place at the end of the table, "surely you recognized the danger in attempting magic under uncontrolled conditions?"

He tried not to flinch at the surname he hadn't heard in so long; he hadn't known Vettazen even remembered it. A dozen answers came to mind. They all sounded too much like excuses for his comfort. He tossed his head to get a stray lock of hair out of his eyes, and lowered his gaze to the broad planks and straw of the floor. The shiver that crawled up his spine, he told himself, was from the draft that came through the curtained, open windows.

"Jazen," Vettazen said impatiently, "we have not found so many people who can find magic, either within themselves or outside, to be able to send you away. And we are still protected, in large part, by the fact that it is fashionable in most circles to declare that magic no longer exists.

"But that fashion can change in an instant—it *is* changing—and the change must be in our favor. I will not have apprentices of this guild casting spells at random in the marketplace to terrorize the horses and getting us all accused of being Yaan Maat ourselves. Perhaps you haven't seen what happens to a human being accused of being a demon."

All eight masters were staring at him. Some of them, rumor said, had been accused at some time or another; the skin of Tiris' hands, for example, was thick and tight and white. Jazen had long since recognized scarring from fire; it occurred to him suddenly that perhaps Tiris hadn't obtained those scars, as Jazen himself had obtained similar, far less extensive, scars, through carelessness at a forge. Jazen knew the pain that flames could bring. He could not, suddenly, stop looking at those hands. Tiris looked back at him, hazel eyes as grim as stone.

Demonspawn . . .

He parted his lips to take a steadying breath. Vettazen, thinking he was about to speak, forestalled him.

"Our purpose is not to play at magic, but to destroy Yaan Maat. In order to do so we must study *under controlled conditions*—" Here she glared at him. He dropped his gaze again. "But we will not put our colleagues in peril so that you can perform experiments. That peril is real. Look about you if you doubt it. Do we make ourselves clear?"

He nodded dumbly. They were going to cast him out; he knew it.

"You are most fortunate that whatever damage was done remained within the walls of this house. Had it occurred outside, you would have been subject to whatever censure the authorities, or the public, would have been pleased to make. We as a guild are not yet strong enough to claim the right to discipline our own apprentices.

"But we established this guild, in part, so that young persons with gifts such as yours could learn to control those gifts without the risk of losing their lives as a result of that censure. We have set ourselves a great task, and we believe that we need every gifted person we can train to meet the challenge we fear may one day face us.

"Therefore, in penance for your lack of proper discipline and deliberate disobedience to the direction of the masters of your guild, you are confined to the Guildhouse until further notice. You are required to assist in repairing the damage you caused to the stable. You are forbidden to attempt any more workings except under the direct supervision of one of the Masters of the Guild. You are hereby assigned to the most menial duties of the house in service to your brother and sister apprentices, and in addition to your regular studies—" At this point Tiris leaned over and whispered something in her ear. She checked herself, nodded, and went on, "In addition to your regular studies you will report to me to perform such tasks as I require."

He was so dazed by the lightness of the sentence that he nearly forgot to bow to them as he left. Instead of a punishment, it was a triumph, or at least a relief.

"I've *tried* burning rose petals," Mikal was telling Alissa, his voice petulant, as Jazen came down into the refectory for the midday meal, the next day. "They make me sneeze. Isn't there something else I can try?"

There was a small silence as the apprentices looked up, registering Jazen's entrance, and then away again, conspicuously returning to their interrupted conversations. Adri-nes shifted over to make space for him on the bench, and he took it, gratefully. Rache put an empty bowl in front of him, complaining as usual, and he filled it from the large pot in the middle of the table, grabbed one of the pile of spoons, and dug in. He hadn't realized he was so hungry. Sitting there, sharing the bowl of salt and passing the pitcher of ale, he felt as if, disciplined or not, he belonged with the rest of the apprentices. He was one of those few—Vettazen had said it herself, he had the evidence—who could use magic.

He could listen, now, to the work that the others were doing, and not feel inadequate or out of place. Granted, they had been working spells under the supervision of the masters all along, while he had had no such tutoring; still, he had it now, and he was one of them, even if he was condemned to emptying their chamber pots forever.

"The scroll says rose petals," Alissa insisted. "I can't help that." She watched Mikal walk away, and snickered to the men on either side of her. "Serves him right for wanting an aphrodisiac. He's allergic to roses."

"And all *your* spells involve roses, don't they." Meleas wasn't asking a question.

Alissa smiled sweetly. "All the aphrodisiac spells, at any rate."

"What are you all working on?" Adri-nes asked, spearing a chunk of carrot and dipping it into the white sauce. "Anything of mine?"

"Who would want to?" said Prex, curling an elegant lip. "The last one of your spells *I* tried . . ."

The rest of them laughed. Adri-nes had a crush on Prex, at least this week. His suit was not furthered by the effect the last spell he had created, just for her, had had on her hands. That effect, the masters decreed, had to be reversed by the apprentices or not at all. So far, no one had succeeded in getting rid of the last wart.

"I have to do something with air," Alissa said. "What am I supposed to do with *air*? Blow all the leaves off the trees? What good is that?"

"You can push clouds around," Jazen reminded her. "Clouds bring rain, and rain helps your plants grow."

Alissa brightened. "That's right, isn't it? I like that. Don't tell Demachee," she added, lowering her voice dramatically. "I think she thinks she's found something impossible for me to do."

"What about you, Jazen?" Prex smiled at him. "What will Vettazen set you to doing, do you think?"

He blushed and ducked his head, hoping Adri-nes could see that the girl was simply teasing him. "I don't know. Perhaps an illusion." A mouthful of meat saved him from having to go into any more detail. They wondered in his hearing what had gone on in his meeting with the Masters; Mikal, at least, had been greatly surprised that he was even permitted to stay. Jazen chose to tell them only that the masters had assigned him to work with Vettazen. He'd explain his permanent assignment to scutwork only if they actually asked him about it. It wasn't that different from the work he had always done, helping Rache. And helping repair the stable was only logical.

And while he was at it, he and Meleas could set up a small firepit outside the stable for minor metal repairs and farrier work. He thought fleetingly of Gilé's forks, wondering if he could duplicate them. Being confined to the Guildhouse was not that much of a hardship, all in all.

"Illusion?" It was Mikal, back again with a new pitcher of ale. "That's *my* area. What illusion are you working on?" He behaved as if he thought he owned the entire aspect of illusion.

Jazen swallowed. "Something to make people think other people listen to them," he snapped. The others around the table chuckled. Mikal looked bewildered, then suspicious.

"Don't try any of my illusions," he warned. "They're far too advanced for you."

"I wouldn't dream of it," Jazen said sourly. He was beginning to think that perhaps he *ought* to find something to work on, whether Vettazen tutored him on a specific spell or not, if only to shut Mikal up. Mikal refused to accept the burning of the stable as a major working within the meaning of the bet; Jazen thought that he wouldn't have to actually *work* a spell, not when he'd been forbidden, but he could at least *find* one he could do—now that he knew he could.

"My family has always had a gift for illusions," Mikal went on, as if Jazen had said nothing. "My father's kin, particularly. My uncle would have come here, but . . ."

". . . he had to clean out the pigsty." Meleas completed the sentence.

From Meleas, it might have been a compliment; Mikal could not decide. He returned to addressing Jazen. "Is your family gifted?"

Adri-nes, sitting beside Jazen, inhaled sharply. Jazen lifted his head and stared directly into Mikal's eyes. "In my country," he said deliberately, "it is considered quite rude to ask personal questions about a stranger's family."

Mikal blustered, sputtered. "I meant no offense—"

"Then give none," Jazen advised, his voice very quiet.

Prex broke the moment by standing up and deliberately spilling the last of the gravy in her trencher over Alissa's new tunic. Alissa reacted with predictable fury. By the time apologies were made and reluctantly accepted, the others had risen from the table to go to their various afternoon assignments.

Which, in Jazen's case, meant back to Vettazen. Standing before the door to her workroom, he took a deep breath and lifted his hand to knock.

The door opened before his knuckles touched it. Vettazen was sitting at her table across the room. There was no one at the door.

"Don't just stand there," she said irritably. "Get in here."

He stepped inside. The door swung silently shut, again under its own power.

He wasn't sure what to do next; the scrolls he had laboriously copied out were neatly rolled and tucked back into their protective leather cylinders and placed back on the shelves. Their identifying tags hung over the shelf edges like so much fringe.

Vettazen noticed him still standing, and shook her head. "I don't know what I'm supposed to do with you," she muttered. "Do you realize that mess yesterday delayed Firaloy's departure? He's going to have to camp on the road tonight, and it's all your fault."

"I'm sorry." Jazen couldn't think of anything else to say.

"I imagine you are, but not as sorry as you could be. *Flames,*" she added under her breath. "I have work to do here. Go—" she waved her hand in the direction of the cabinets in the back of the room—"go put those in order until I can think of something else for you to do. Make me some spell pouches for the work in the green book, and then I suppose you can clean the place up."

"Yes, mistress." Formality seemed to be politic for the time being. He moved to the back of the room and realized he had just been given a free hand to explore to his heart's content. It was odd how very light this punishment was turning out to be.

The cabinets were jumbled with a number of things he had no way of identifying, as well as others he recognized: bunches of herbs, tied together; bits of string and twisted metal; wooden shingles with symbols scratched or marked upon them; wax tablets; styli; little boxes and jars filled with solids and liquids; even a tall stack of clean, unmarked paper. The easiest way to tackle the task, he decided, was to put everything on the floor and then sort it out. Mindful of stories he had heard from Alissa and Demachee, he kept the herbs separate from each other unless he was absolutely sure they were innocuous. He had no idea of the other things and how they might interact; shortly he was surrounded by individual small piles of things, and the cabinet was nearly empty.

Nearly, except for a box at the back, with an iron key lying beside it. The box was locked.

The key fit the lock.

The key turned.

He tilted it to the light, trying to see inside. It was difficult, as if the last ray of the sun coming through the high window deliberately dodged out of the way.

"Do you want to see?" Vettazen said, from directly behind him. He jumped.

"Ah, I was—was . . ."

"You were trying to find out what was inside a locked box which belongs to someone else. Let's not lose sight of that.

Ah, you're a troublemaker, Jazen sr'Yat." Taking the box from his hands, Vettazen murmured something, and opened it, using both hands to break it apart. The hinged top folded back to reveal a lining of dark blue velvet. It contained only a single object.

Vettazen reached inside, held the object out to him. "As for this particular box, it holds a mataal. A demon's soul. See?"

It looked like a thin, oval piece of ivory, not even large enough to cover the palm of her hand. The edge was milled, as coins were to keep the metal from being shaved. He had seen broken mataals many times by now, beginning with the debris on the ground in Heza; they all looked dull, lifeless, plain, like worn-out counters from a gambler's game. This one was different. It was nearly whole, missing only the smallest chip out of one edge.

On the glowing, pearlescent surface of this mataal, designs were etched: summerflowers in half-bloom, the petals not yet fully extended. Whoever had done this had used the color of the material well; the flowers' deepest color was at their heart, and the lines followed the barely discernible tints of pink and blue and gray.

It was beautiful. The surface seemed to glow, as if it were soft light made solid. Jazen's hand lifted, and he watched, fascinated and wholly unable to stop, as his fingers reached out to stroke the object resting in the palm of Vettazen's hand.

"Ah, no." Strong, wrinkled fingers closed over the glowing oval, and the attraction abruptly vanished. "This you do not want to touch without the proper protections, I promise you. This is not something for a childish prank, or even a serious effort, without study and preparation. You need to know what this thing looks like, so that you can close your eyes to it immediately.

"And so that you'll not go snooping in locked boxes again," she added, dropping the thing back into the box and turning the key with a decisive *click*. "You had the sense to note, I hope, that this thing was neither burned nor broken?"

Jazen blinked. "It was—alive?"

Vettazen laughed, a short, sharp bark without amusement.

"I truly hope not, boy. Were it so, you and I both would be taken by now. Or so I think."

"You're not sure?"

She shook her head. "No, I'm not sure. Nor am I sure how much protection the locked box truly gives me. Perhaps there's nothing there, after all. But I work no magic at all while this box is open. Just in case. And I don't want you taking it in your head to do so either, do you understand?"

"But it glowed," Jazen protested, as she turned and tucked the box into the farthest recesses of the cabinet. "It had power."

"Did it?" she said, looking at him curiously. "What did it look like, then?" The cabinet door clicked shut, and she turned the key in the lock and slipped it in her pocket.

"Couldn't you see?"

"I could see you wanted to touch it, and not entirely of your own will. I saw no glow. What did it look like?"

Describing the shimmer of the mataal wasn't as easy as he thought. He opened his mouth and shut it again several times, discarding analogies.

"You look like a fish," Vettazen snapped at last. "Put your body to use, even if your mind is useless; clean up this mess on the floor. And if you find any more locked boxes, boy, ask someone before you try their keys." She swept back to her table and pulled out another book.

"Wasn't it dangerous to leave it there with the key beside it?" he asked, dumping the bits of string into one empty box and the metal into another.

"Locks are for honest men," she said stingingly. "For the most part, a thief would receive the appropriate consequences."

"I'm not a thief!"

His tone brought her head up to look over at him.

"No, you are not," she agreed at last. "But you're curious, boy, and that curiosity will one day be the saving or the breaking of you. I had forgotten the box was there when I told you to clean. If something had happened to you, it would be as much my fault as yours—*this* time."

Chapter 17

While the rest of the apprentices, particularly the obnoxious Mikal, boasted of the magic they were learning, Jazen rose in the morning, swept, scrubbed, ate breakfast, carried scraps to the pig ensconced in the far corner of the stableyard, scrubbed again, reported to Vettazen, and cleaned, sorted, dusted, yet more. He avoided the cabinet in her workroom.

And when there was no more to clean in Vettazen's workroom, she set him to copying again, while she remained at her table, comparing scrolls, muttering to herself, making notes. She made two more trips to the palace, traveling alone now; evidently his confinement to the Guildhouse was quite serious, and she did not bother with any of the others. As winter set in, she was ever more deeply involved in her books and scrolls and notes. Some few times she would leave to go to another of the masters' workrooms, come stomping back muttering to herself about the Heir, about the machinations of the great ones at court. Some few times other masters would come and visit her, and they would put their heads together in soft, whispered debates. Jazen strained to hear, without success; after a time, he thought they must have a spell for blurring their conversations against eavesdroppers, and he began looking for such things in Vettazen's records.

He was supposed to learn, after all, and it didn't seem to make much difference what he copied, as long as he did so in a clean hand and completely. If nothing else, between the rotework and his own interest, his ability to read and write finally became polished. It allowed him to pick and choose through the manuscripts.

Until, of course, there were the manuscripts he couldn't read at all.

"What's this?" he said, feeling rather indignant. "This makes no sense." He was looking through an oddly bound book, with boards of leather instead of solid wood, filled with small, tight marks in curves and angles he didn't recognize.

Vettazen looked over, sighed, got up to stretch and come look over his shoulder. "Elzaeli. Chezayot is from Elzael. Don't look so affronted, boy, it's a different language, uses a different script from ours. You'll learn it, too, in due time."

"A different language? But why do they need a different way of writing it?" For some reason, he had never thought about that before—that all the different languages he had heard in the squares and the marketplaces each had their own way of writing, too. It left him feeling mightily discouraged.

Vettazen was trying not to laugh at him, he could tell. "There are a hundred hundred different languages in the world, boy, and some of them—not all—are written very differently than ours. Not every land has our history. Why, are you finding your world stretching a bit around the edges, then?"

"But why do they *need*—"

Vettazen gave up the struggle, laughed and shook her head. "They'd say the same about you, you know. They're different nations. Some of them don't even acknowledge the Emperor. They have their own lords."

That much at least he knew, having heard it before from Adri-nes, but the different alphabets still made no sense. He shrugged and set the book aside. He would look at it later, try to reproduce the pages; perhaps he could get Chezayot to tell him what the marks meant. He wondered what Elzaeli sounded like.

"I've got an appointment," Vettazen said abruptly, reaching for a thick shawl. "Finish one more; we'll talk later about what else I'll have you do."

The room seemed very empty when she left. Wandering over by the window, Jazen pulled up a chair and stepped up on it to look out the window. In the courtyard below he could see Meleas checking the leg of the roan mule; the animal was pulling away from him, trying to get to the fountain, as if water had been deliberately withheld from him for a month. Jazen glanced up to check the angle of the sun, and understood why Meleas was holding the beast away.

The mule whipped its head around and went up; Meleas dropped the rope to keep from being hauled into the air with it; the mule lunged toward the fountain—

—as the water began to thicken, redden, and stink.

The mule brayed with outrage and bolted away, limping badly.

Meleas cursed and went after the animal. Vettazen, watching from the doorway, crossed the courtyard to the fountain and stood there, watching, for the long minutes until the liquid changed, clearing, becoming water again. She reached down, cupping a handful, and tasted it, as if to make sure.

It was cold, standing in the window. Jazen stepped down again, pulling the curtain across, angled the torch reflector. The rim of light caught the mass of papers on the table in the corner.

He was fairly certain, from watching Vettazen for so many days, that there were no nasty surprises in the boxes on the table. Only manuscripts, just like the ones that he was copying at his own, smaller table on the other side of the room—

If there were a hundred hundred languages in the world, perhaps some more of them could be found in the books and scrolls and papers on Vettazen's desk. *". . . you're curious, boy, and that curiosity will one day be the saving or the breaking of you. . . ."*

He didn't think she would mind *very* much if he only looked.

He brushed at the top page with his fingertips. She'd made no effort to cover anything, after all. So it must be all right, just to look.

The top page contained notes about distances, mentioning several places he vaguely remembered. Nothing very interesting there.

The pages underneath contained some remarks about wasting illnesses—the Heir again, he thought, though Vettazen was not fool enough to write that down—and the other interests of members of the court circle, gleaned from recent visits, scrawled in Vettazen's harsh, spiky writing. The comments next to some of them were less than respectful of their subjects' noble estate.

Some of the books and scrolls were histories of Mirlacca, some dating from before the Demon Wars. He glanced at them without much interest; next to Vettazen's trenchant observations, dry history of the past three hundred years failed to command his attention.

And then the notes took a more serious turn. Vettazen, apparently, had found the histories rather more engaging. She was studying the phenomenon of the fountains of Mirlacca—when the waters had begun turning to blood, which fountains were involved, how far beyond the city the waters turned.

Another page was a list of names.

Another looked like a summary of various healing spells, with notes about backspells scrawled across the lines of writing. In the margins, in cramped writing, appeared the name of Lasvennat. Vettazen associated Lasvennat with serious spells like these? Jazen laughed to himself, trying to imagine the great lord involved in grinding herbs or making his own wax tapers. But the name kept recurring.

"Not likely," Meleas said decisively, narrowing his eyes at the roan mule, now standing docile in his stall, eating his evening ration of hay. "Lasvennat? He's as much a pig as you are."

It took Jazen a moment to realize that the last remark had been directed at the mule, not at him.

"Maybe she was going to sell him one of the spells for the Heir," Meleas went on. He was braiding a rope and still glaring at the mule. "Or maybe she just thought of him and was making a note."

"On good vellum? I don't think so. And these were high magic. I didn't even want to touch the hides they were written on."

Meleas shrugged. "I don't know, then. She looks at all kinds of spells. She's a Master; it's what she does."

"I think she's trying to find out what causes the fountains to turn."

That, at least, got Meleas' attention. "The fountains? What for? They've been turning for centuries. Who cares?"

"Vettazen does."

"And more power to her. As if she needed it. Watch it, the beast's going to . . ."

But the mule had already stretched his neck impossibly far over the bottom half of his stall door and snapped at Jazen's head. Jazen yelped. The animal got away with a scant dozen hairs.

Vettazen returned very late that night, long after the moon had set. She entered her workroom as if returning to a refuge, tossing her cloak onto a chair and leaning back, stretching, as if she had spent too long hunched over. "And what are you expecting, boy?" She didn't turn around. "Why are you up so late?"

"I was curious," he said.

She laughed, reaching for a pitcher of ale and pouring a cupful. After a moment she filled a second cup and carried it over to the smaller table, setting it in front of Jazen. "You're always curious," she said.

She looked very tired, the lines around the eyes deep. The cup in her hand trembled. She took a deep draught and set it carefully on the table, wiping a scrap of foam from her lip with her other hand. "What are you curious about this time?"

Jazen wrapped his fingers around the rough clay surface of his own cup, stared into the brown circle surrounded by white foam. "I looked at your papers," he admitted. "I saw about the fountains. Are you trying to find out why the fountains turn?"

Vettazen squeezed her eyes shut. "Yes. Among other things, of course."

"Is Lord Lasvennat . . . ?" He didn't know how to phrase the question. It sounded silly, even to him.

"Is Lasvennat involved with the fountains turning?" Vettazen rubbed her eyes. "I don't see how. It's been going on for centuries, since before the war. Ah, I'm too old for this."

"Then why do you have his name in your notes?"

"You did read them all, didn't you." She chuckled again. "I have his name there because I cannot decide whether Lord Lasvennat is very strong, or merely a fool. He's not the only one at court who dabbles in magic. But he's one of the loudest of those who decry it, while at the same time he sponsors us. And he seeks power, particularly now that the Heir is ill again. I want to make sure we don't become the source of it. I don't like the man."

This was no particular news. Jazen was tired, too, and the liquor was relaxing him to sleep. "What does the Emperor think of us?" he asked, fighting a yawn.

Vettazen finished her drink and put the cup down quietly. "Where's your knife, Jazen?"

Without thinking, he called the image to mind. It was hard to see, as if—"Someplace dark. Inside something."

She yawned, too, widely, and covered her mouth to keep her breath from escaping entirely. "Ah, come now. Pull back. Where is it?"

He was struggling to keep from laying his head down on the table and taking a quick nap. At his side, the empty scabbard heated; absentmindedly he thought the rivets ought to be cooler. After a moment, they were. "Cabinet. In the cabinet over there."

Vettazen smiled sleepily. "I thought so. You try too hard sometimes, Jazen. You have a starving mind."

"What does that mean?" he mumbled. It was much easier to talk with his eyes shut. When she didn't answer, he added, "You didn't say. What the Emperor thinks of us."

She was still silent. With an effort, he opened his eyes, only to see her sitting across from him fast asleep. She looked younger in her sleep, he thought fuzzily. She looked as if she didn't have so many things to worry about.

He considered getting up, getting *her* up, helping her get to her sleeping room, but it was all far too much effort, and much easier just to remain still.

Vettazen slid gracefully forward to rest her face on the

table. It looked like an uncomfortable position. Frowning, he snagged his own cloak from the peg in the wall and wadded it up on the table, picked up the master's unresisting head and put it down again on the folds of wool, took a corner and the hood for his own pillow, and slipped off peacefully to sleep.

Chapter
18

Two days later, Vettazen disappeared.

She left in midafternoon, having sent Jazen out on errands. When he came back, her workroom was empty, the clutter on the table neatly put away.

It didn't feel right. The table looked naked, with the stack of papers in one corner, and all the dull wood showing. But the comings and goings of the masters were none of his concern, Vettazen had made that much clear; she had found several more books of spells she directed him to study and assemble pouches for, scribing each one with the proper date so that whoever used it would know if the ingredients were fresh.

Adri-nes looked in on him, surprising him into jabbing his thumb with the leather needle. Waving the other man in, he sucked at the welling blood.

"Where's Vettazen?" Adri-nes said. "Demachee is looking for her. She's wanted at the palace; they say the Heir is worse."

Jazen shook his head. "She was here earlier. I was looking for some candles, and when I got back she'd gone out."

"Where to?"

"Don't know." The bleeding had slowed enough that he could wipe the remaining streak against his tunic. "Haven't seen her."

"Well, what am I supposed to tell Demachee?" Adri-nes sprawled on an extra chair, in no apparent hurry to leave.

Jazen shrugged, picking up the needle again. "That she went somewhere."

"And she'll be back when she comes back. I'll bet she's already at the palace—Demachee will be furious. She doesn't like going there without Vettazen to hold her hand, and she doesn't like Vettazen giving out her cures either," Adri-nes mused. "Well enough. Tiris is gone too, but at least he left a note. Someone claims there's a demon loose in some little town north of Ehrlit's Pass, so he went galloping off to see about it."

"Well," Jazen muttered, jabbing the needle through a particularly tough bit of leather, "isn't that what we're all supposed to do, one day?"

"I wouldn't worry about it," Adri said, swinging his boots off the table. "I have a new set of spells the masters want to try—Rizard says they can't possibly work." He smirked. "The last time he said that, the backspell made glass almost good enough for a window."

"And what was the original spell supposed to do?" Jazen inquired disingenuously.

Adri-nes had the grace to look embarrassed. "It was a scrying spell, actually."

"And did it work?" Jazen didn't dare look up for fear of laughing. He had heard other versions of this story before.

"Well, there are still some difficulties," Adri-nes admitted. "But it almost worked. Really."

"Well, perhaps if you get it to work properly we'll have fine windows too, as good as those in the palace. Not bad at all." He jabbed his thumb again, lightly.

"Oh, go ahead and laugh," Adri-nes snapped. "Better than getting blood on the pouch. Gods only know how *that* would burn things."

Jazen looked at the redness welling on the fleshy pad, then at the leather bag meant to hold the pure ingredients necessary for a spell. Flames knew what contaminating effect human blood might have. "You have a point."

"Use a thimble," Adri-nes advised. "I'll go tell Demachee that Vettazen's off somewhere. Maybe ask some of the other masters if they've seen her. Though they're all working tonight on one thing or another. Probably won't be able to get them to answer their doors."

Jazen lifted a hand in farewell, and Adri-nes left. Jazen set the spell pouch aside and wandered over to the window, pulling aside the curtain to look down three stories into the courtyard. Prex was flirting with Meleas; Alissa lurked in a corner, glaring. Jazen raised an eyebrow. He'd had no idea little Alissa was jealous of his friend, but it certainly looked like it.

He wandered around the room, picking up books and putting them back without looking at them, studying a rack of knives. The knives reminded him, suddenly, of the conversation he had had with Vettazen two days before, over the cups of ale that had so unaccountably put them both to sleep. He hadn't asked her about it the next day, and Vettazen had never raised the subject. He suspected the ale had been drugged with something Vettazen used to help her sleep.

But she'd asked him to find his own knife. And he'd seen it—and while the sheath had warmed perceptibly, it hadn't done more than that. It was, he thought, a subtle lesson. Though perhaps he ought to find whatever it was she used, and try it again.

Vettazen did not return by suppertime, eaten in midafternoon at this time of year. Jazen got a bowl of rice and vegetables and sat stirring them in the sauce, listening to the chatter at the table. Netchame was arguing heatedly with Leiad, another of the apprentices; Adri-nes was listening to Meleas explain the finer points of hay selection from the point of view of a goat. At the upper table, Erriziachet, Dalzen, and Firaloy ate quietly, each occupied with private thoughts.

"And I don't think there *is* a difference," Alissa was saying. "Jazen, are you listening?"

"No," he answered honestly.

"Well, why didn't you say something?" she demanded. "Really, you can be so annoying."

He smiled apologetically at her, shoved the bowl of food aside. "Whose turn is it to help Rache?"

"Yours," Meleas said, without missing a beat. "No one has said any different."

"Flames." But the curse was without rancor, and Jazen got up and started collecting empty dishes and trenchers.

Cleaning up consisted of washing the dishes and taking the

THE FOUNTAINS OF MIRLACCA

trenchers and scraps out to the pig; he would have to wait until the common room was empty before wiping down the tables. The occupants wouldn't leave for hours yet; normally he would stay with them, trading stories, talking about their studies.

Not this night. Restless, he climbed the steps to the observation tower, stepped out on the little platform, and looked out over the roofs of Mirlacca.

The sun was setting. The gilded dome of the palace shone; the lesser towers within the palace walls, surrounding the imperial residence, took on a glow as well. And around the walls, like progressively more soiled lacework, the rest of the city spread out, falling more and more into the shadows. Lines of smoke threaded up from chimneys, dark lines against the deepening blue of the sky.

If he closed his eyes and concentrated, he could hear a soft, unending buzz of noise from the city, a buzz punctuated by a faint shout, a scream, the cry of an animal in pain. He could smell the city—dirt and living creatures crowded too closely together, the unending flavor of smoke in the air, the scent of fruit trees and flowers. Mirlacca was well known for its flowers. Alissa had said once she thought it was something in the water that made them grow so richly and well.

The dark stripe that was the Street of the Forge, far on the other side of the city, was rapidly disappearing in the gathering dusk. The torches at street corners began appearing, pinpoints of sharp brightness against the soft blanket of darkness.

He'd been in this city for more than two years now.

It was not yet home; it was too large to be home. But he couldn't imagine going back to Smattac.

For a moment he felt lost, homesick, floating between the two, as if he existed on a plane that was part of, yet not identical with, both—great city and small village.

And Vettazen was off somewhere, doing whatever she was doing. Off speaking to the powerful—men and women so powerful they had no real meaning to the likes of Jazen sr'Yat, man of no clan, no family, no name, an uncertain skill. What had meaning to him were the occupants of this Guildhouse. Its masters were still struggling to lay down its rules; its reason for existence was scarcely accepted as legitimate. Even he himself wasn't sure it was legitimate; he'd never seen a demon, unless one looked back at him from a mirror. And perhaps one did. Eri Weaver's-daughter had thought so. *Demonspawn,* she'd called him.

He had heard of the Yaan Maat daily over the past two years. He had seen a mataal glowing as if alive, but he had seen mold on ponds glowing, too. It might not be magic, not really.

A part of his mind laughed at himself. After all this time, all he had seen and done, surely he accepted that demons were real, not just stories from history. But he resisted it, nonetheless; another part of him still felt that if he accepted it, perhaps Eri's accusation, still echoing in his memory, was true. No one knew where he came from, who his parents and kin were. He was a bastard, after all.

What he knew was real was the magic he had worked in the making, in the finding of his knife. He could close his eyes and see the knife, feel the backspell. He could watch the masters and apprentices work magic, too, and doubtless they felt as he had when filled with the passionate, seductive, glorious power of the focused will. If magic was the legacy of demons, then perhaps the demons hadn't been so bad after all.

He closed his eyes, seeking.

The answer came immediately, without very much heat at all. The knife was still there, in the cabinet.

He left the observation platform and went back downstairs, to Vettazen's workroom, to the cabinet, and opened the door, reached in, and took the wrapped package out of the back and opened it. There, as he had seen, lay the knife.

It was a good piece of work, and it was his. Balancing it in his hand, he considered; surely, if Vettazen told him to seek the thing, it was all right to take it back again, wasn't it? It was *his,* after all, and more so than any knife purchased in a market. He had *made* it from the raw metal.

He slipped it back into the still-warm scabbard and took a deep breath. He couldn't shake the feeling that there was something wrong. If he could modify the knife-finding spell and use it to find Vettazen, he would feel considerably more comfortable about matters.

Closing his eyes, he tried. He saw nothing but the darkness of his own eyelids. There was no surge of power. The spell for the knife evidently meant nothing for finding people.

It was one more project for Adri-nes, he thought sourly. Wandering over to Vettazen's table, he looked at the unlikely neatness of the stack of papers on the side. Vettazen would never have done such a thing without expecting him to go through them—and she hadn't told him not to.

Sitting down, he pulled the pile of papers over and began to page through them, looking.

More information about the fountains—when they were built, by whom. When the waters first started to turn. One piece of vellum had odd marks on it, squares and stripes and patches of green and blue; he puzzled over it for a candlemark, suddenly realizing it was a map, a map of Mirlacca, and the blue patches were the fountains—the large ones the Great Fountains by the Compass Gates, the little ones scattered all over the city, even the fountains within the palace walls. For amusement, he began matching the dates of the first appearances of blood in the fountains with their locations on the map.

Two hundred years ago just before the ending of the Demon Wars, the waters had begun to run red, consistently, once a day at noon. He remembered reading the record of the first discovery in a diary someone had saved from so long ago—

. . . not only doe they Slaye us but they have even now turnd our Waters foul each daye. . . .

The contamination had spread first in the northeast corner of the city. Then, Vettazen had noted, the phenomenon had ceased. He read the notes with interest; this was the first time he had ever heard that the fountains of Mirlacca had run pure at any time since the defeat of the Yaan Maat. But the surcease had not lasted long, only a handful of years, and had begun again in the fountains of the palace itself, spreading out from there like ripples.

In the palace? Was that, perhaps, why Vettazen kept returning there, and not for the uncertain favor of Lord Lasvennat and his ilk?

The workroom was very quiet. As quiet as it had been a few nights before, when Vettazen's potion had nearly put him to sleep. He had felt very calm then, very rested, and she had asked him to find the knife and there had been hardly any backspell at all, only a little nudge to remind himself that he really was working magic.

He closed his eyes and breathed deep, trying to focus himself, trying to re-create the sensation associated with magic. After a while he slipped into a warm, peaceful state, cradled in calmness, one mote in a universe of unthreatening possibilities. He breathed deeply, feeling quiet. Calm. Assured. Remote.

There was his seeking spell—difficult to pull one's attention away from the knife it was locked to—but surely the principle was the same—and there—

There was Vettazen. Poor Vettazen, she looked so uncomfortable. So angry, and frustrated, as if she wanted very much to do something and was unable to—as if such a feeling was new and unfamiliar. And she was afraid—that was interesting; he had never imagined Vettazen afraid before.

The image floated by. He followed it, mildly interested, but the more intent upon it he became, the more obscured it was. Finally, with the image blurred almost beyond recognition, he shifted his attention casually away. As he did so, he caught a glimpse of an inkwell and a jeweled bell. Then all of it was gone.

He drifted a while longer in the darkness, sometimes looking around at other motes floating by, sometimes not. After a time he became aware that he was cold.

He came out of the trance abruptly, gasping, as if he had forgotten to breathe. He was sitting at the little table in the workroom still; the curtain at the window was flapping wildly, the torches and the fire had gone out, and only Vettazen's precious glass lamp provided any light at all. Breathing hard, he considered.

The inkwell and bell were in Lord Lazvennat's quarters; he had seen them there the first time, and every visit thereafter. So, if the seeking was right, Vettazen was there, in Lasvenhat's rooms. And she did not *want* to be there; now that Jazen was out from under the effects of his own spell he could recall vividly the sensation of fear in the woman.

The memory made him angry, very angry, very suddenly, and he had nowhere to put his anger. The smoldering logs in the fireplace exploded abruptly into flames, and he jumped. The fire roared up the chimney. Appalled, he got up and went over to look at the logs, poking cautiously at them with a fire iron; the flames died down again, but not before he saw the cursing face of an imp, who shook its tiny fist at him before dancing upward on a tongue of fire to disappear up the chimney in a shower of sparks.

At that moment he felt Vettazen scream.

Panicked, he ran, down the steps through a darkened and still disorderly common room. Mikal was slumped at the table, his precious necklace of charms in pieces around him; across from him, Alissa had slipped to the stone floor and was lying senseless, her mouth barely open. Not far away, Adri-nes and Rizard sagged against each other in an elegant heap, a discarded scroll lying between their feet. Five slumped bodies near the fire proved to be Rache, Demachee, Netchame, Erriziachet, and Leiad, sleeping as if drugged. He ran from one to another, shaking them, shouting at them, but there was no response. Frustrated, he ran out into the courtyard past the merrily splattering fountain, to the courtyard gate, where he found Meleas in a deep, unshakable sleep as well.

It was the backspell—the price of finding Vettazen in his waking trance was to entrance everyone else in her home—and realizing it, he cursed and wrestled open the gate to the Guildhouse and ran out into the street, into the city, toward the palace, alone.

Chapter 19

He came to the side gate of the palace and beat on the door, sagging against the plain wood to catch his breath. The door swung inward and he nearly staggered into the arms of the guardsman standing there. Seeing the condition Jazen was in, and seeing no one with him, the man slammed him up against the wall of the guardroom. "Who are ye, and what d'ye want?"

Jazen shook his head, still gasping. As he opened his mouth it occurred to him that accusing one of the Emperor's own friends of kidnapping was probably not the best way to find Vettazen. He shut his mouth again, swallowed. "Vettazen sr'Islit," he croaked. "Message. Important. She came here—"

The guard was one he had seen before, and more importantly, one who now remembered him. "One of the wizard brats, are ye?" the man growled, clearly not impressed. "What message?"

"Can't—I have to—give it to her directly." He was recovering somewhat, but if the guard wanted to think he was still breathless with exhaustion, so much the better. "With—Lord Lasvennat—"

Far away, he heard Vettazen scream again, this time in more pain than fury.

"I have to see her!" he yelled. He could not believe the man had not heard.

The guard stared at him as if he were mad, or possessed, and stepped back. "Aye, then—"

Jazen dodged past, pulled open the inner door, and was out in the tiled corridor, running for all he was worth, with the

THE FOUNTAINS OF MIRLACCA 181

guard shouting after him. For a few heady moments he thought there would be no pursuit; the guard could not leave his post; he could go down the hallway, all the way to the door that led to the stairs, to the upper floors, to the room with the table he had seen—

But the guard was shouting, and the people in the corridor, few enough at this late hour, could connect a running stranger in journeyman's clothing with the outraged bellows. Another man wearing guard's badges snatched at him as he went by, and another, until he was trailing a small horde of pursuers all shouting to alert those ahead. Pelting for all he was worth down the hall of banners, he lost count, realizing suddenly that the door he should have gone through was behind him now, and worse, behind his followers. Skidding to a halt, he tried to go back, and fell directly into their ungentle hands.

The last thing he knew, as they beat him into unconsciousness, was the feeling of someone snatching away the iyiza knife, and the sound of Vettazen screaming.

He woke to see a blue- and gold-clad servant, upper-level by the curl of his lip, leaning over him, inspecting him by the glare of a torch, and he recognized the rabbity face of Lasvennat's chamberlain. As he squinted against the brightness, the torch drew back, and he could see shadows of other guards standing behind the servant. He was in a large room then, not one of the small cells rumored to be in the lowest levels of the palace.

"Aye, the wizard's brat," the man said. Jazen lifted the back of one hand to wipe blood away from the corner of his mouth. "And he was armed? Give me the weapon. I'll tell my lord."

"I came with a message," Jazen said thickly. "For Vettazen. Where is she?"

The man paused and looked him over, without sympathy. "Not here, boy. She's never been here. And it's a poor cover for a thief."

"Thief—I'm not a thief! I'm looking for the lady Vettazen of the Guild of Exorcists. She's in your master's rooms—"

The servant laughed harshly. "My lord may well have a lady in his rooms, boy, but she'll be younger and prettier than any false wizard." He turned away, toward the massive cell door. The guards turned with him, their keys clanking.

"I know she's there! I saw her!"

"Deluded," the chamberlain remarked. "They all claim to be able to see things."

"So do I, when I drink enough," one of the guards said, and the rest of them laughed as the door swung shut behind them.

Jazen sat up, unsteadily, and took stock of himself. His head was still ringing from the blow that had knocked him out, and he fought the urge to throw up whatever remained of his last meal. After a long time the dizziness faded to the point that he could, so long as he used the wall to support himself, get to his feet. Swallowing two or three times, he breathed deeply.

He had some sore, maybe broken, ribs, he thought, but his arms and legs and hands and feet, while bruised, seemed intact. His belt was gone, knife and scabbard and all. They had left him his shirt and tunic, hose and shoes, though, and the straw he had been lying upon was fairly clean, so the visit of the chamberlain had been expected. He had no idea if he would be left here or not. He rather expected not; even taking into account the rustling of a rat in the far corner of the room, this place was far too good for an ordinary prisoner. It looked more like the kind of dungeon Adri-nes delighted in describing, the kind of place one of the lesser nobility might be kept in. Adri-nes said that jailers could often be bribed to provide extra amenities in a prison like this—of course, Adri-nes never said how, exactly, he knew such things, and he was back at the Guildhouse, probably still asleep, and not available for either advice or a loan.

It was certainly not a place for the likes of Jazen sr'Yat. Now that he'd been dismissed as being of no importance— merely an apprentice—they'd either move him into a less agreeable part of the dungeons, or throw him out into the streets.

And somehow he doubted that last. Why would the chamberlain lie about Vettazen having been there? Surely enough people had seen her come, often enough, that such a statement would be as transparent as Lasvennat's glass doors. Yet he had done so with only a flicker of hesitation, which meant the man

THE FOUNTAINS OF MIRLACCA

did not expect his statement to be refuted—and certainly not by one of Vettazen's own apprentices, who would carry word back to the Guildhouse, causing all of them to inquire as well.

He wondered if anyone at the Guildhouse were awake yet.

He wondered how long he himself had been unconscious.

He was feeling well enough now to go over to the door and look through the small grate at the top. He could see nothing but an identical door, with an identical grate, six feet away on the other side of the hallway, set into a foot-deep recess in the wall. At least, he hoped it was identical; it wasn't barred, and the lock was built in.

Gilé had shown him the making of such locks. Gross, clumsy things they were; it needed only the right tools to lift the latching mechanism, pull the tongue back. Of course, he had no such tools on his person, but they were simple enough. Surely somewhere in a room so large he could find a couple of pieces of metal, bent just so—

He could not, of course. He did surprise the rat, feasting on the remains of what appeared to have been a prisoner's meal; the animal chittered angrily at him and disappeared into a crack in the wall, the tip of its bare pink tail whipping out of sight in an instant.

There was a bed in one corner, bolted to the floor; apparently he didn't rate quite highly enough to have been thrown on it, though from the looks of the mattress, thin, old, and probably crawling with lice, he was grateful. It was distasteful enough to have to touch the woven straw to shift it aside and examine the frame. It looked like a discard from someone's home, perhaps someone like the arrogant chamberlain. The frame was solidly constructed, with glue and wooden pegs; the only signs of damage were in the fan of the headboard, in the cracked hardwood dowels. One sharp point, canted out at an angle, was covered with a suspicious-looking stain.

Jazen was not inclined to use the dowel either for a weapon or a means of suicide, if that was, in fact, what the stain indicated. He wrenched at the wood, putting his back into it, the memory of Belzec's jeers about his slight stature and lack of muscle, his inability to swing the great hammer drowning out the pain from his side, and it was with a loud crack and no particular surprise that he found himself sitting on his rump halfway across the room, a slender, sharp stick in his hand.

Picking himself up, he looked at the stick, then at the keyhole. The keyhole was large enough to see through, large enough to accept the stick and a little over— Placing one end on the ground, he leaned into it, wincing. With another loud crack, the shaft splintered.

Nobility rarely built locks, more rarely understood their mechanisms. Prisons for the rich did not, therefore, require complex locks, merely sturdy ones, in order to keep their prisoners secure.

On the other hand, a bastard smith's boy knew all about locks and their workings, and how two slender sticks, seasoned almost as hard as iron itself, could probe the mechanism and lift it open. It occurred to Jazen, as he tucked the sticks into the top of his boot before venturing out into the hall, that he could always make a living as a sneak thief if the Guildhouse abandoned him.

He had no idea what time it was, or even if it was the same day. The passage was empty; the torch in its sconce was guttering low. He paused for a split second to try to work the locating spell again, trying to summon the sense of peace, of power— He might as well have been exercising his imagination for all the good it did him.

He had no idea where he was in the palace, no idea where he was in relation to Lasvennat's rooms, no idea if Vettazen was even still there. The only thing he knew for certain was that she wasn't *here*. Picking a direction at random, he started down the hallway at a stiff trot.

He found a stone stairway leading upward, just as a pair of guards appeared at the top; he ducked around behind the stairs, pressed himself into the corner where the stairs joined the wall, and tried very hard to think of himself as invisible. It seemed to work; at least the guards clattered past without appearing to see him. He scrambled up the stairs to find himself on yet another floor he had never seen before. At least this one had windows; he spared a glance to see that it was after sunset. Whether it was the same night or not he had no idea.

There were even more people on the ground floor of the palace, servants mostly. He didn't seem so very much out of place, though one or two looked at him oddly. He followed one young man wearing a blue and gold badge to the kitchens, realized he was starving, and filched a meat roll from a tray while he tried to figure out what to do next. Trying the location spell again only worsened his headache. The man wearing the Lasvennat badge spoke intently to someone who had an air of authority and a large wooden spoon. When he left, Jazen followed, taking another meat roll to see him on his way.

The badged man did not, as hoped, lead him directly back to the Lasvennat rooms. He did, however, lead Jazen to a section of corridors with a mosaic floor pattern that at least looked familiar, with banners and anterooms. Jazen was trying to identify the sequence of banners when the man suddenly turned, snatched him, and slammed him into the wall.

"Who are you, boy, and why are you following me?" he said, his fists wrapped up in Jazen's shirt.

It left Jazen's knee free, and he put it to good use. Apparently a cry of anguish was not so unusual in the mosaic halls of the imperial palace.

He didn't quite have the nerve to strip the man and wear his blue and gold jacket, but he took the riband from the sleeve, hoping it would give him some credibility, fumbling it into place around his upper arm. He couldn't tell whether it made the slightest difference; all the badged servants he met looked down their noses at him with exactly the same expressions they had used on his very first visit, so long ago.

He found the spiral stairs leading upward, and took them three at a time. There were fewer people at this level, and the windows he passed now showed utter darkness outside. Now he was in an area he knew; he had gone this way before, many times. He set his shoulders and moved quickly, not hurriedly, up into the section of the palace reserved for the noble, the royal intimates, as if he belonged to someone who had business there.

Until at last he came to the blue and gold door carved with flowers. Vettazen had always knocked. He ran his fingers over the carving, looking for a handle, some way to open the door.

There was nothing. He took a deep breath, leaning his forehead against the painted blue and gold, trying to find the darkness, trying to find Vettazen. He couldn't find anything except the darkness of his own eyelids.

Somehow he must have brushed some hidden latch; the door swung ajar. At the same time, he heard someone coming up the last flight of steps. He slipped inside the room, his breath coming short, expecting to be discovered, beaten again or worse.

The room was empty. He pulled the door shut behind him and looked around. There was the table, with the inkwell and quill and jeweled bell; the tapestries; the doors of glass, standing open just enough to let in a breeze, making the tapestries move gently.

A soft knocking came from the door. Panicking again, he looked around wildly for a hiding place, ducked out the glass doors and into the rooftop garden as the door to the inner room opened and the chamberlain came out, crossed the room without glancing his way. A bird rose up, shrieking, as Jazen hid as best he could behind a tree. The chamberlain looked around at the sound without seeing him and then turned back to the door, conferred briefly with someone, took a tray with a message, closed the door, and went back into the inner room.

Jazen sagged against the tree in relief, clutching at the rough bark under his fingers. His mouth was dry. Now that he was here, he had no idea what to do next. Vettazen had been here; she was not here now. And even if he found her, what could he do, an apprentice, a nobody, unarmed?

Within the anteroom, a clock chimed, the Opposite Hour of darkest night. It told him, at least, what time it was. Keeping a wary eye on the room, he slipped over to the little fountain, scooping up a handful of liquid and bringing it to his lips.

The smell warned him, a split second before he tasted not water, but something warm, thick, coppery. He gagged violently.

The fountains of Mirlacca ran with human blood, every day at noon; and now, it seemed, at midnight as well.

Chapter 20

He was choking so badly he barely noticed the chamberlain bursting through the inner door, calling for guards. They surrounded him, pushed him back against the lip of the fountain. He was still retching, wiping frantically, uselessly, at his mouth and tongue, when Lord Lasvennat came out to view him, as he remained captive between two tall manservants. Behind Lasvennat, Cadan stood, watching, silent.

"And who is this?" the noble murmured, using a carved cane to tug lightly at the ribbon around Jazen's upper arm. He was dressed in an embroidered coat, with a silk undershirt dyed the same blue as the powder on his hair, and white breeches, sullied by a red-brown stain on the upper thigh. The light of the torches glittered in the powder, as if it were ground sapphires. There were no rings on his hands, which were pale, small. "A thief? Oh, do stop, boy. It's only blood. One can develop a taste for it, with patience."

"I'm no thief," Jazen said furiously, forgetting for the moment his consideration of other possible futures. "Don't call me that."

The finely plucked brows arched. "It does speak. How amusing."

"Where is Vettazen?"

"Vettazen?" The noble affected surprise. "Oh, yes. The wizard woman. You've come with her, haven't you? Are you one of her little wizardlings?"

"Exorcist," Jazen said. It seemed important, for some reason. He couldn't move, pinned between the two men.

Lasvennat chuckled. "Oh, yes. Of course. Exorcist. Well, the hour has passed, but it will come again, and you'll be useful too." He waved the cane negligently at the two servants.

They half-carried, half-dragged him into the inner room, through it and into yet another, dropping him on the floor like so much luggage. He could not help crying out as the fall jarred his side, but as soon as they were gone he picked himself up to look around. The room was lit by a single glass lamp on a long table. It cast long shadows in the corners, made strange things seem familiar, familiar things seem odd.

And in the corner, in the shadows, lay a darker shadow, and it made a sound. He took the lamp in his hand and went over to investigate. The shadow took on the form of a large, ragged roll of cloth. As he held the lamp closer, it took the form of a human being.

"Vettazen?"

She moaned again.

He touched her nervously, plucking up her cloak and his courage with the same gesture, and moved a stiff fold of cloth away from her face.

She moaned again.

He couldn't see any marks. He couldn't see very much at all, in fact. Setting the lamp down on the edge of the table, he went back to his teacher and slipped an arm under her shoulders. As he raised her, the cloth fell away from her upper body, and he gasped.

Vettazen's tunic barely remained substantial enough to preserve modesty. It was slit in dozens of places, and each slice was matched in her flesh. The sleeves had been cut completely away from her arms, and her arms themselves were crisscrossed with cuts, some shallow, some deeper. They still oozed blood, made her slippery to hold on to.

He started to lay her down again, but she caught at his shoulder. "Jazen?" The word was only a breath.

"Yes, mistress. I'm here. Let me—"

"No."

She still had the habit of command. He stopped, watched as her tongue crept out, licked futilely at the corners of her mouth. "Sit up. Water."

THE FOUNTAINS OF MIRLACCA

Unable to hold her up and still look for water, he had to prop her against the wall while he went to look. If he had to, he would call for the guards who must surely be there, but he had no particular illusions about how a request for water would be received.

The room was nearly empty, save for the two of them and the table. It looked almost like a workman's bench, waist-high and three times as long as it was wide; besides the lamp it held a casket, a broad pearl-encrusted box with a domed lid. It held, too, a shallow plate, a gore-encrusted knife, and an ewer of water. He snatched the ewer up and brought it over to Vettazen, only to find her eyeing it with an odd smile on her face. She drank, one swallow at a time, and when he would have pulled the pitcher away she held it in place, as if the sensation alone of the liquid against her lips helped to refresh her.

After long minutes she let him lower the ewer to the floor. She had the strength to lift her hand and wipe away the remaining drops; then her hand fell back. Jazen caught at it.

"What did he do to you?" he whispered. There was no one there, but he couldn't bring himself to speak normally. "What happened here? Why is he doing this?"

Vettazen swallowed. "Where are the others?"

Jazen shook his head. "They're—I'm the only one. I was trying to find you, and they all fell asleep—"

The woman rolled her eyes, and for a moment Jazen was afraid she was going to pass out. But then she brought him back into focus, and said, "You have to get out of here, boy. Tell them Lasvennat has—" She swallowed again, convulsively. "Tell them the House of Lasvennat has let a demon loose in the world."

It rocked him back physically as well as mentally. He sat and stared at her open-mouthed, certain she had gone mad from the pain. Her wounds were weeping blood again. Paradoxically, as she bled her voice gained strength.

"Lasvennat has a mataal. It's been in his family for generations. Long ago they found a way to feed the thing, and in turn it allows them to influence the Emperor and the Heir." She paused, closed her eyes. After a moment they popped open again. "The present lord has been using magic, too, dribs and drabs of it. But now that the Heir is expected to die, he's trying to get himself named to succeed. Heir-presumptive. He's been working greater spells—feeding the demon.

"The thing is, it's getting strong. I don't think he really can control it. It's sitting there, in the mataal, and it's going to get loose— They've been feeding it blood every day now for more than two hundred years, as best I can tell. Keeping his family in power. And now—he needs more power as the boy dies."

He tried to quiet her, make her preserve her strength. She held up her hand. "Wizard's blood is said to be very effective. . . . Show Rizard the records—tell him what I said. He'll be able to figure it out."

"I can't leave you here," he protested.

"Did you hear me, boy?" But her voice had faded again to a raspy whisper, and it was a minute or two before she could go on. "You've got to tell them. It mustn't get out. We don't know how to kill it—"

"Dalzen did an exorcism," he whispered, frantic.

She shook her head. "Flames, boy, so did I once. Casts them out. Doesn't kill them—we think. Not sure. Don't know for sure what kills them—if anything will. Don't know enough. Not enough."

She coughed, hollowly, and Jazen flinched. Helping her to sit up again, he gave her another drink.

"I can't leave you here," he said at last. "Maybe I can cast a spell to break the mataal. Maybe that would do it. If you could help me—"

"No! No spells. No magic." Vettazen's voice wavered. "Didn't you listen, boy? It's been feeding for two hundred years. Use magic around that mataal, you'd let what's in it loose." She shook her head. "No magic."

"Can I just *break* the thing?" he asked, frustrated. "Just smash it?"

Vettazen stared into space, her gaze going in and out of focus. "Don't know," she said at last. "Don't know.

"But if you're going to do it, boy, do it quickly. Before he comes back. He's almost used me up, but he has you now—it'll be your blood in the fountains next—"

THE FOUNTAINS OF MIRLACCA

Jazen opened his mouth to answer, and then shut it again. Blood in the fountains. Of course. The fountains of Mirlacca ran with human blood every day at noon—and in the rooms of the Baron Lasvennat they ran red at midnight too—backlash of the process of feeding a demon trapped within the physical confines of a mataal.

For generations the Lasvennat had been close to the imperial throne. Never in the forefront, but always hovering nearby, advising, guiding. Ruling, almost, from behind the curtains.

Using magic. Using one of the Yaan Maat.

The door to the little room opened, and Lasvennat stood there, framed and silhouetted by the light. Behind him Jazen could see Cadan, the boy Lasvennat had offered them so long ago.

"How dreadfully sweet," the lord said in his quiet, beautifully modulated voice. "Such a picture of pure, selfless devotion. I *am* touched."

Vettazen sat up a little under her own power. Lasvennat smiled.

"Oh, excellent," he went on. "I should have thought of it myself. You *would* last longer if you drank the spellwater, wouldn't you?"

Jazen glanced at the ewer. Spellwater? Lasvennat had used this in whatever process required Vettazen's lifeblood? He reached out and knocked the pitcher over, letting the contents flow out on the mosaic floor, soaking the hem of Vettazen's split skirt.

"Ill bred, but not entirely unexpected," the lord said, entering the room. "Cadan, fill it again."

The boy came forward to pick the pitcher up. His face was completely, and carefully, expressionless. He was wearing Jazen's knife.

Jazen snatched at it. Cadan fell back. Jazen actually had his hand on the hilt and the knife half out of its sheath when he was pulled away, as if he were no more than a child, by something he could not see. If he merely stood, arms outstretched, he could feel no restraints. If he tried to move, lower his arms, step forward, he could not. He was held, three steps from Vettazen's side, as securely as a parent might hold a child who had not yet learned the trick of walking. He could talk—he could curse, with all the language he had ever learned from Belzec at the forge—but he could not move.

Cadan stood up, brushed himself off, seated the blade back in its sheath, took the pitcher, and left the room without another glance.

Bewildered, Jazen continued to struggle. Whatever it was that held him tightened in subtle fashion. Lasvennat stood, head tilted to one side, one fingertip resting on the mole on his cheek, observing.

"The records say the more you attempt to escape, the tighter the bonds become," he remarked. "I am pleased to see this verified by direct observation. Don't you agree, Mistress Vettazen? Although your observation has been more direct than my own, of course."

Vettazen said nothing. Jazen, falling silent, glanced in her direction. She was still sitting up, her eyes still open; her mouth was pursed tight, as if there were words she would say if she might. Her face reflected helpless anger, and weakness.

"You have heard the sad news of His Highness's latest illness, I trust," Lasvennat went on, addressing Jazen. "It is a terrible thing to have the fate of an empire rest on the narrow shoulders of a sickly child. We have a responsibility to protect him. To keep him well."

"To extend your influence over him," Vettazen spat, her voice cracking. "You probably caused his illness to begin with."

"I?" Lasvennat appeared mildly surprised. "Surely not. It's a family trait, more's the pity. The Emperor, his grandfather, is afflicted as well, though, of course, he hides it better." Stepping over to the table, he pulled the box toward him.

"The only family trait I see is that your family has been working magic on theirs for centuries." Vettazen was beginning to sag again.

Lasvennat paused in the act of opening the casket. "Now, what an interesting theory that is, mistress. I confess it had never occurred to me before. I wonder if there might be something to it." His voice made the words a cultured, deliberate lie.

"Test it," Vettazen whispered. "Stop what you're doing and see what happens."

Lasvennat laughed, a light, practiced laugh. Cadan returned, placed the brimming ewer on the table, and stepped back, carefully straightening a pair of linen cloths hung over his left arm. He spared only a quick look in Jazen's direction. The boy looked, for an instant, frightened; Jazen couldn't blame him. Then Cadan looked at his master and an expression of quiet peace descended over his features, and Jazen shuddered.

"Oh no, mistress, I think not," Lasvennat was saying. "For one thing, that would mean not feeding my terrible friend, and that would make him angry. That's an experiment I choose not to perform, thank you." He paused. "I shall ask you to remain silent now. This is, as I'm sure you appreciate, a delicate process."

Turning his attention to the casket, he raised his hands over it, holding them palm to palm and the width of the box apart, beginning an unvoiced chant that gradually took on strength. He exhibited no uncertainty, no searching for words. As he spoke, the air between his hands began to blur, as if thickening.

Jazen opened his mouth, only to see Vettazen, on the floor beside him, shake her head, raising a hand to her lips with as much of her failing energy as she had left.

The domed lid of the casket began to rise under its own power. Jazen could see something moving in the darkness inside. Lasvennat continued his chant. Beside him, Cadan shifted his weight from one foot to another.

Lasvennat's hands drifted down to the partially open lid, lifted it. He reached inside and took out something small and flat, resting it almost reverently on the open palms of his hands.

It was a mataal, and like the mataal in Vettazen's study, it glowed. Unlike that one, however, this shone so brightly Jazen averted his eyes, unable to bear the sight of the lightning that crackled across its surface, twisting and snapping its way up Lasvennat's arms, his shoulders, up around his head and down his torso.

Lasvennat turned, the mataal still in his hands, his face exalted, reflecting the light, and stepped toward Jazen and Vettazen. The light rose up in a rope from the flat ivory and took a form like that of the imps in the forgefire, only the figure continued to grow, to mature, until the image was very like that of the man holding out his hands.

They did not see—none of them saw what Jazen saw—the image of a man no taller than Lasvennat, made of light, made of power. Still leashed to the mataal by a thick umbilicus of light but reaching for them—reaching for Vettazen as Lasvennat came closer, Cadan following close behind. It was clothed in light, in veils and fogs of sun and stars and fire, and it was too bright to look at—and Jazen could not keep from staring at it. If it had been a human man, it would have been beautiful. It was leashed to the mataal by a thick blue-white cord that twisted and writhed as if alive itself.

Lasvennat was nearly close enough to touch now—the figure of light more than close enough, beginning to bend over Vettazen, who sat looking up at the lord and the thing in his hands, but could not see the glowing shadow-figure at all. Her expression was despairing, afraid of the pain she knew was coming, but she was watching a man, not a demon. Lasvennat knelt before her, with a nobleman's grace, and the demon moved with him.

It reached out one radiant, taloned hand and brushed at the seeping wound on Vettazen's arm, and the gash split wide and gushed red. She cried out, surprised, shocked, and tried to pull away from the source of the sudden anguish. Jazen struggled too, shouting, trying to kick at the thing; and the demon straightened, turned, looked at him full on with luminous eyes.

Demonspawn . . .

They were eyes made of light and of hell's own fires, made of silver and smoke, fire and fog, wide and fathomless, utterly alien to everything Jazen had ever known. The thing's mouth opened wide, as if it were laughing, and he could see its fangs, down into its throat to the black flames within. A wild terror seized him; all the strength in his body drained out of him, and he could not, for the first few seconds, move.

Next to this thing looking at him, the imps of the forgefire were friendly, mischievous little fellows, the sparrows of the netherworld. This was some other thing. It looked at him with empty, hungry eyes, and raised one hand, still dripping with Vettazen's blood, and it shocked him out of his paralysis. Jazen screamed, again and again, fighting to get loose from the grip of the demon's eyes, to defend himself, to destroy the thing that stood before him. He couldn't break free.

Behind him, Cadan jerked, as if suddenly awakened, looked at the demon and *saw* it. He screamed too, dropping the cloths he carried and looking side to side as if seeking a path to escape. Lasvennat looked with confusion from Jazen to his squire, unable still to understand the source of their terror.

The demon, yawning with laugher, discarded Jazen and reached past Lasvennat for the boy. Both glowing hands reached out and stroked his face, holding the child's head almost as an obscene lover might, and leaned over him. The boy looked up into the face of the demon and he sobbed once, softly, and then slumped to the floor at the prisoners' feet, unconscious. The demon stretched out to take him. Jazen fought uselessly against his invisible bonds.

Lasvennat, still kneeling in front of the feebly struggling Vettazen, remained where he was, and Cadan remained inches out of reach of the demon, which was still tied to the mataal by the umbilical cord of light. Frustrated, it snarled and spun back on the man impeding it, striking him across the face. The touch seemed to tear away the noble's mental veil, and Lasvennat at last saw the thing his working had evoked.

He, too, cried out at the sudden apparition, and as he did so, the door burst open, the two bodyservants looking bewilderedly for the threat to their master. It was their ill luck to interrupt the thing as it reached for Lasvennat; the demon had reached the limits of its temper, and it spun and dived to the limits of its glowing leash, catching one of the servants by the arm and pulling it in.

The man had no more success in breaking away than Jazen. Pulled in by his own arm, he scrabbled for the blade he wore at his side, and slashed, desperately, cursing, screaming, at last weeping, at the glowing thing that held him, and finally at his own flesh in an effort to get away. The demon laughed and embraced him, folding its arms about him, and the man's cries were stifled as the Yaan Maat tucked his head into its shoulder, crooning.

The demon swelled and grew brighter, and the man's body jerked once, twice. Behind them, Lasvennat, still holding the mataal, tried to drop it and run away, somewhere, anywhere away from what he had called forth, but there was no room to get past the demon and its prey. The demon opened its arms and let what they contained fall to the floor, next to the still body of Cadan. It stretched, leaning its head back so far that its hair fell like a waterfall, and laughed again. The body of the servant was nothing but a crumbling husk. The cord holding the demon to the mataal twisted again. It was thinner now.

The other servant had fled long since, gibbering.

The Yaan Maat, strengthened by the blood and the life of the servant, pivoted gracefully back to the nobleman scrabbling on the inlaid mosaic floor at its feet.

"The mataal," Vettazen whispered.

The *mataal*?

Dalzen, Mikal claimed, had exorcised a demon once. Firaloy had burned a mataal in a cursefire, to free Meleas' sister. Vettazen had cast a demon out. Did she think that he, Jazen, could do what Dalzen and Firaloy had tried to do? Those were demons that had already possessed human beings, whose essence was no longer bound into the fragile mataal. And he was only an apprentice, and not a well-schooled one at that. He had only really performed one spell in his life.

Lasvennat mewled on the floor.

Vettazen, half-sitting, half-lying beside him, was looking up at Jazen with a shadow of the glare she had given him as he lay on the cot in the infirmary. She was staring at the only one of them left on his feet, while the demon who had already sipped her blood reached for her, slavering.

To devour her. And then Lasvennat. And Cadan. And then there would be only one left, and that one would be, not devoured as the others were, but possessed. And he was bound by—

He was bound by nothing. He had been bound by nothing but his own fear for quite some time. He could use magic—

Except that he had no magic, except the knife spell, and

THE FOUNTAINS OF MIRLACCA 197

Vettazen had warned him already about using magic around a live mataal. He couldn't imagine what it might do in the actual presence of a demon. But he had to do something, find something he could use—the demon had taken Lasvennat, now, by the hand, was lifting him up in a sublime caricature of noble courtesy—

His knife. The knife with the drops of his own blood and sweat, the knife that was a part of him, into the substance of which he had smashed the spirits of fire, defeating them, killing them—it was *his knife,* and he *needed* it, *called* it. The surge he had felt in the forging, in the seeking spell, flooded back upon him, and the Yaan Maat straightened, looked upon him with the eyes of hell.

A power he never knew he had lashed forth, across the demon, yanking the iyiza blade from beneath Cadan's limp body, out of the boy's belt, spinning the weapon to him so hard that the hilt slapped into a palm unprepared for it, a hand that dropped it.

And the demon, slashed by magic, screamed, and suddenly yet more power gushed out of the mataal, through the twisting cord and into the thing floating before it. Lasvennat threw the mataal away at last, and the demon turned, shrieking, reaching for him.

The water in the pitcher began to bubble upward, pulsing, some of the liquid falling back into the vessel to jet upward again, some of it soaking the top of the table. The demon touched Lasvennat, without delicacy this time, clawing at him. A great gaping hole appeared in his tunic, a deep, wide red hole. Lasvennat screamed. The demon, whimpering, leaned forward as if to bury its head in the man's wound, and Jazen understood suddenly that the slash of the iyiza knife had actually hurt the thing, that it was seeking blood and life and power to face him. The water pulsing from the ewer began to darken as the demon fed.

Jazen snatched up his knife and turned frantically to Vettazen, who had slumped back against the wall and was watching the demon suck life from Lasvennat as if she would take notes. The thing took up the mataal and held it to the gushing blood, stroked its victim's chest, pulling life from him, sucking loudly as the blood flowed too slowly out of the shrieking man. Lasvennat clawed uselessly at the carved disk.

The water wasn't water any more, and it arced high to the ceiling, splashing again and again as if drawing from some larger source than the pitcher had ever held. Looking at it Jazen screamed, "No!" and tried to think of it as water, only water, ordinary, everyday—

The demon turned somewhat away from the dying noble man and looked at Jazen again, laughing. Its substance was restored now, the cord that held it to the mataal narrowed. It was nearly strong enough to be independent of the mataal, to possess a human being. It reached for him as if to *take* him.

Jazen struck out wildly, once, twice, cutting across the incorporeal arm. He could feel no resistance, but the demon yowled in rage. The thinning cord brightened and pulsed, and Lasvennat collapsed, blood bubbling from his mouth. The pieces of demon's arm hanging in the air grew together again, becoming whole, and the demon itself pushed Lasvennat out of the way and reached wide to take Jazen, to contain him—to possess him—

Jazen struck out again and again with the knife, slashing back and forth. The demon followed him as he moved away across the room, away from Vettazen, until he stumbled over Cadan, still sprawled on the floor, and he staggered almost into the Yaan Maat's embrace. He flailed frantically, and the blade of his knife sliced through the cord binding the demon to the mataal.

The demon screamed, an unearthly sound only Jazen and Cadan seemed able to hear. Its face twisted, and behind it Lasvennat's body gushed blood from the wound and from every orifice, rising from the ground. The substance in the ewer turned darker still, pouring upward. The demon reached for Jazen again, paused, tried to go back to Lasvennat. It was torn between the two of them, unable to decide. The cord of light withered. The mataal in Lasvennat's hands turned dark, cracked in two—

—and as Jazen watched, as Lasvennat died, the demon was torn in fact, great veils of its substance tearing off first in his direction, then in that of the dying man, more and more rending away and graying, dissipating as if it were no more than dust, shredding. The remains of the demon howled, and vanished.

Jazen could hear only his own, harsh breathing, and that of Vettazen, still huddled in the corner.

He got up slowly, his hand still on his knife. Nothing stood between himself and the courtier, nothing but the blood. Lasvennat was dead, his lips curled away from his teeth as if still grimacing in pain, his fingers in a deathgrip on the broken mataal.

Sticking the knife into his belt, Jazen stepped around the body, carefully, and went to Vettazen, going down on one knee to lift her head. At first he thought she, too, was dead, but then an eyelid twitched.

"Well, boy, what are you waiting for?" she breathed. Then her head fell back, and the only signs of life were the pulse in her throat and the pressure of the air from her lungs.

Jazen gathered her up, ignoring her sudden groan, and looked around the room. There was only Lasvennat now, and blood, and the boy in the corner. Nothing remained of the being of light and fire and hunger who had raged there. Nothing.

The demon was gone.

Gone too was any uncertainty in Jazen's soul that he, Jazen sr'Yat, Jazen the Bastard, was anything other than human, as human as the boy quivering in the corner, or the woman fighting for life in his arms. He was not spawned of a horror like that one. If there was a division in the world separating him from the rest, the division lay between him as a part of humankind, and the Yaan Maat, and the purpose of his life would be to prevent them from taking possession of him, or any other of his own kind, ever. He held Vettazen close and started home, to his own home, to his guild, to the place he belonged. To those who knew that the Yaan Maat still existed, and were also committed to eradicating the horror: to the Exorcists.

ALL-NEW, ORIGINAL NOVELS BASED ON THE POPULAR TV SERIES

QUANTUM LEAP

__TOO CLOSE FOR COMFORT   0-441-69323-7/$4.99
Sam Leaps into a 1990s men's encounter group, only to encounter Al on a mission that could alter the fate of the Quantum Leap project for all time.

__THE WALL   0-441-00015-0/$4.99
Sam Leaps into a child whose destiny is linked to the rise—and fall—of the Berlin Wall.

__PRELUDE   0-441-00076-2/$4.99
The untold story of how Dr. Sam Beckett met Admiral Al Calavicci; and with the help of a machine called Ziggy, the Quantum Leap project was born.

__KNIGHTS OF THE MORNINGSTAR
0-441-00092-4/$4.99
When the blue light fades, Sam finds himself in full armor, facing a man with a broadsword—and another Leaper.

__SEARCH AND RESCUE   0-441-00122-X/$4.99
Sam Leaps into a doctor searching for a downed plane in British Columbia. But Al has also Leapt—into a passenger on the plane.

__PULITZER   1-57297-022-7/$5.99
When Sam Leaps into a psychiatrist in 1975, he must evaluate a POW just back from Vietnam—a Lieutenant John Doe with the face of Al Calavicci.

Based on the Universal Television series created by Donald P. Bellisario

---

Payable in U.S. funds. No cash orders accepted. Postage & handling: $1.75 for one book, 75¢ for each additional. Maximum postage $5.50. Prices, postage and handling charges may change without notice. Visa, Amex, MasterCard call 1-800-788-6262, ext. 1, refer to ad #530

Or, check above books	Bill my: ☐ Visa ☐ MasterCard ☐ Amex (expires)
and send this order form to: The Berkley Publishing Group 390 Murray Hill Pkwy., Dept. B East Rutherford, NJ 07073	Card#_____ Signature_____ ($15 minimum)
Please allow 6 weeks for delivery.	Or enclosed is my: ☐ check ☐ money order
Name_____	Book Total $_____
Address_____	Postage & Handling $_____
City_____	Applicable Sales Tax $_____ (NY, NJ, PA, CA, GST Can.)
State/ZIP_____	Total Amount Due $_____

World Fantasy Award–winning author
PATRICIA A. McKILLIP

"There are no better writers than Patricia A. McKillip."
—<u>New York Times</u> bestselling author Stephen R. Donaldson

Enter the dark and wondrous world of the Cygnet...
__THE SORCERESS AND THE CYGNET
0-441-77567-5/$4.99

"Inspired imagery and a perfectly paced plot mark this fantasy as one of the year's best."
—*Publishers Weekly*

__THE CYGNET AND THE FIREBIRD
0-441-00237-4/$5.99 *(coming in September)*

"Finishing a Patricia A. McKillip novel is like waking from a dream. There are the same lingering images, the same sense of having been otherwise..."
—*The New York Review of Science Fiction*

Available now—a powerful new hardcover novel
__THE BOOK OF ATRIX WOLFE 0-441-00211-0/$18.95

Horrified after unwittingly bringing destruction to his land, Atrix Wolfe fled to the seclusion of the mountains. Now the Queen of the Wood summons the mage to find her lost daughter and reunite the kingdom of Faery—a quest that could finally free Atrix Wolfe from his pain.

Payable in U.S. funds. No cash orders accepted. Postage & handling: $1.75 for one book, 75¢ for each additional. Maximum postage $5.50. Prices, postage and handling charges may change without notice. Visa, Amex, MasterCard call 1-800-788-6262, ext. 1, refer to ad # 556

Or, check above books and send this order form to: The Berkley Publishing Group 390 Murray Hill Pkwy., Dept. B East Rutherford, NJ 07073	Bill my: ☐ Visa ☐ MasterCard ☐ Amex (expires) Card#_____ ($15 minimum) Signature_____
Please allow 6 weeks for delivery.	Or enclosed is my: ☐ check ☐ money order
Name_____	Book Total $_____
Address_____	Postage & Handling $_____
City_____	Applicable Sales Tax $_____ (NY, NJ, PA, CA, GST Can.)
State/ZIP_____	Total Amount Due $_____

New York Times bestselling author

R. A. SALVATORE

__THE WOODS OUT BACK   0-441-90872-1/$4.99
"Fantasy...with literacy, intelligence, and a good deal of wry wit."–<u>Booklist</u>
A world of elves and dwarves, witches and dragons exists–in the woods behind Gary Leger's house. There Gary discovers he is the only one who can wear the armor of the land's lost hero and wield a magical spear. And if he doesn't, he can never go home again...

__DRAGON'S DAGGER   0-441-00078-9/$4.99
"Looking for a pot of gold? Read this book!"
–Margaret Weis, <u>New York Times</u> bestselling author
Gary Leger has finally returned to the land of Faerie, but finds that things have changed. The sacred armor and magical spear are missing, and evil forces threaten to destroy the countryside. Now Gary must traverse the enchanted world to battle the forces of darkness.

__DRAGONSLAYER'S RETURN 0-441-00228-5/$5.50
Gary longs to leave Earth behind and return to Faerie with his wife, and as war looms in Faerie, his friends wish he would come back too. With a brutal king and a powerful witch sowing the seeds of destruction, Faerie's heroic dragonslayer once again holds its fate in his hands. *(Coming in August)*

Payable in U.S. funds. No cash orders accepted. Postage & handling: $1.75 for one book, 75¢ for each additional. Maximum postage $5.50. Prices, postage and handling charges may change without notice. Visa, Amex, MasterCard call 1-800-788-6262, ext. 1, refer to ad # 496

Or, check above books and send this order form to:	Bill my: ☐ Visa ☐ MasterCard ☐ Amex (expires)
The Berkley Publishing Group 390 Murray Hill Pkwy., Dept. B East Rutherford, NJ 07073	Card#_____ Signature_____ ($15 minimum)
Please allow 6 weeks for delivery.	Or enclosed is my: ☐ check ☐ money order
Name_____	Book Total $_____
Address_____	Postage & Handling $_____
City_____	Applicable Sales Tax $_____ (NY, NJ, PA, CA, GST Can.)
State/ZIP_____	Total Amount Due $_____